THE
GOOD
MOTHER

An utterly gripping psychological thriller
packed with shocking twists

LIZZIE FRY

Joffe Books, London
www.joffebooks.com

First published in Great Britain in 2023

Cover art by Nick Castle

ISBN: 978-1-80405-722-3

PART ONE

*'Mother is the name for God in the lips
and hearts of little children.'*

William Makepeace Thackeray

CHAPTER ONE

'What have you done . . . *What have you done?*'

My voice is hoarse, a harsh whisper edged with a shriek. I don't need to repeat myself. I can see it with my own eyes, though my mind refuses to believe it. It has to be some mistake. There's no way such an ordinary Sunday evening could turn upside down.

This can't be happening.

But it is. I can't stop staring — my eyes are fixed on the bloody horror before me. Sound drops out, like we've been plunged underwater. I know I am speaking, but I can't hear my own words.

The fluorescent glare of the kitchen strip light seems to zoom in at me; there's dark edges to my vision. There's a dull ache in the back of my head. I feel nauseous, woozy with it. My blood crashes in my ears. I gag as the truth breaks through: *there is a kitchen blade buried deep in the left-hand side of his chest, right down to the handle.*

My husband's chest.

Dean blinks, confused. Eyes wide, he staggers backwards, both hands raised, fingers splayed in a supplicatory gesture. His own gaze is on the blade handle protruding from his flesh.

I know what he's about to do, even before he does it. He must know he shouldn't? Urgency slices through me. Sound pitches back in as my voice breaks through the muffling barrier of my shock.

'No no no no, Dean, don't!'

He pulls the blade out.

Instant regret.

Dean's eyes meet mine as his intellectual brain catches up with that primeval part of him that just wanted the knife out. Blood spurts in a terrible gory arc, splashing the yellowed kitchen wall, the black-and-white linoleum, the refrigerator. Me.

Dean rocks back on his heels, his eyes fluttering to the back of his head. I rush towards him, like I can catch all six foot, two hundred pounds of him.

I can't. He slumps to the kitchen floor, taking me with him. I knock against a chair, square in the ribs; it clatters to the floor with us. I don't register any pain, though an anomalous thought springs up: *that'll hurt tomorrow.*

'Oh God. Oh, no. No no no no.'

It feels unreal, like a movie unfolding around us. I try to catch the blood pumping from his chest. It wells up between my fingers. That absurd part of my brain that's proffering a running commentary on what's happening draws attention to the warmth of the blood, the sense of the life literally escaping Dean. A frustrated, frightened shriek escapes me as I try and think straight.

'*ShutupShutupShutupSHUTUP!*'

I search my panicked mind for first aid solutions. I should know this. What do I do? I finally dredge something up.

Put pressure on the wound.

A tea towel is trapped underneath the fallen chair. I snatch it, balling it up in my fist and pressing it against Dean's wound. He tries to scream but can't breathe. He gasps for air. I can hear the horrible rasping of a punctured lung. His skin is shroud pale, his pallor waxen. Dean claws at me, pulling my long hair like I can drag him back from the throes of death single-handed.

'Get my phone!' I scream.

Our son, Jack, just stands there. Blood is splashed across his *Star Wars* onesie. Head tilted, hands at his sides, his face eerily blank. Jack is as still as a statue as he stares at his father on the floor. My own brain on time delay, I take in just one movement from Jack: he rubs his thumbs against the pads of his fingers, a nervous tic of his since toddlerdom.

It must be the shock.

'Jack, sweetheart, get Mummy her phone.'

My son tears his vacant eyes away from his rapidly fading father, his gaze alighting on my face. That pounding in my skull that felt far away before rushes in at me and I have a vague recollection of hitting my head in the fight. As blue dots spring up in front of my eyes, I realise I am fighting unconsciousness.

There's a slowing down of that wet rasping coming from Dean. If we don't hurry, he will die right here on the dirty kitchen floor.

The corners of Jack's mouth tug into what looks like a smile. 'No.'

I force down another sob, extending a hand towards my boy before realising it's covered in Dean's blood. Jack doesn't move, his expression doesn't change. I realise he doesn't even look shocked.

'Please, Jack!'

The pleading in my voice does nothing. I am reminded of those times Jack had met my eye and stood his ground in toy stores over the years. All the parenting manuals tell you to pretend to leave them; that it'll make even the most defiant child back down and run after you. It never worked with Jack.

'He hurt you,' Jack says.

My vision gives a sudden lurch, bringing with it another surge of sour saliva to the back of my throat. I can feel blood streaming from my left nostril. It trickles down my lip, into my panting mouth. The coppery taste ignites a flashback, sending it spinning through my fractured mind.

Jack's right. Just moments earlier, Dean had grabbed me by the hair and smashed my forehead against the doorframe.

I am on a countdown myself. I will lose consciousness very soon.

I move my head, gritting my teeth against another burst of pain as I try to spot if Dean has brought his phone into the kitchen. I can't see it anywhere. I pat down his pockets, feeling a bump in the leg of his combats. Hope peaks as I pull his phone out, then crashes just as quickly as I press my fingers against the keypad.

The battery is dead.

That shriek I'd been supressing rips from me, 'Why does he never charge his damn phone!'

The handset falls from my hand. I try to fight it, but it's no good. I am powerless. I slump forwards, towards him. Even with my eyes closed, I can feel the life leaving Dean.

There is no way back.

It's a tale as old as time . . . Backed into a corner, between a rock and a hard place, the worm always turns eventually.

Sick of Dean's acts of intimidation and violence, I must have cracked. I picked up the knife from the floor and plunged it into his chest. As the red mist cleared, I will have panicked at the thought of leaving our son alone: his father dead, his mother in jail.

But it wasn't me.

I never stuck the knife between Dean's ribs. It wasn't me who forced the cold steel into his lung, nicking an artery along the way. I never even touched it.

It was our eight-year-old son.

Jack killed his father.

CHAPTER TWO

Ten Years Later

'Rats!' Maria exclaims.

My boss appears in the doorway holding a box of papers. Her long, curly auburn hair standing on end, her expression is wild with fury and disgust. For emphasis, she delves a hand into the box and scatters shredded paper like confetti. I grimace.

'Well, don't just sit there!' Maria shrieks. 'Call an exterminator!'

I know better than to dither. I grab the phone.

Maria leaves me to ring round all the exterminators I can find on Yell.com. It's not strictly my job as a junior archivist at the Atkinson Film Project, but that's by the by. If I protested every time she asked me to do something outside of my remit, I would be clashing with Maria every second of every day.

The project had originally been set up by a local feminist filmmaker and philanthropist, Dorothy Atkinson. In her colourful life, she managed to amass hundreds of boxes of film, stills, screenplays and antique filmmaking kit. It's my job to help sort and digitise the entire collection. When I'm not running Maria's errands, of course.

On the end of the line, a bored-sounding man quotes me a price for the rats. I suck in my breath over my teeth — it's steep.

'Thank you, I'll get back to you.'

'Yeah, whatever,' the bloke says.

I replace the receiver and dial another number. As I get put on hold — *again* — I let my gaze wander around my 'office'. It's little more than a glorified cubbyhole. There's a window, though it looks straight onto a brick wall. I'd chosen it because it was in slightly better shape than the others.

We're technically open to the public, but we don't get many visitors. As a young woman Dorothy had originally been most interested in female filmmaking pioneers such as Lois Weber, Alice Guy-Blaché, Germaine Dulac, Lotte Reiniger and Mabel Normand. As time went on, she collected all kinds of film-related curiosities. Dozens of typewriters, some of them purported to have been used by female screenwriters during the Golden era of Hollywood or at Ealing Studios during its comedy heyday. Box after box of unlabelled film cans. There's even signed photographs of dancers and performers, both male and female, some of them nude, all dedicated to her.

Dorothy must have been quite the woman in her day. Now it's our job to make sense of it all for her estate. I love it.

Five quotes received, I ring off and note them all down for Maria. All of them are in the same ballpark as that first bored-sounding exterminator's. Next, I ring one of the lawyers for the Atkinson estate. I present the quotes for their consideration but, as I expect, it's decided that it's not viable to spend so much. In his clipped accent, the lawyer advises me on the phone in no uncertain terms to take money from the petty cash put aside for emergencies. We would be putting down the traps ourselves.

I sigh, feeling like the condemned woman. I detest conflict and Maria won't be pleased; she's bound to bawl *me* out when I deliver the bad news. I decide to put off dealing with it until my mercurial boss crashes back in demanding to know outcomes. Decision made; I can feel the stress slipping from my shoulders.

It doesn't last. I'm about to get myself a coffee when my phone starts vibrating on my desk. My heart lurches in my chest when I see who it is. I snatch it up, almost dropping it in my haste.

'Mrs Rose, this is Sylvie Heath. I'm—'

'Yes, I know who you are.'

My tongue feels too big for my mouth. I hate having to talk to figures of authority; I always feel on the back foot somehow. Another hang-up Dean has left me with. I force a smile into my tone.

'How can I help, Mrs Heath?'

'It's Ms,' the other woman says. (*Of course she is.*) 'I was wondering if we could have a meeting about Jack today?'

Ms Heath's voice is studied-neutral: neither friendly, nor accusing. I don't want to go. I want to tell her where to stuff her do-gooding faux concern. She and I are not the same; I can hear the privilege of living a charmed life in her voice. When you've experienced a trauma like your husband bleeding out in your arms, it sets you apart. I am an outsider.

'Of course,' I find myself saying. 'What time works for you?'

'How about half four?'

I suck in a breath over my teeth. Maria won't be happy about me leaving early. She and her partner Louisa celebrate their twenty-fifth anniversary today. Maria's been planning for it all month. She's leaving early herself to get to an early dinner at the restaurant where they had their first date, then to some open-air performance art thing in a broken-down old church in Peckham.

It can't be helped. I'll have to tell Maria I will make up the time. I do way more than my fair share anyway — Maria's always off gallivanting somewhere.

I'm not complaining. Despite being the most chaotic individual I've ever met, there's nothing Maria doesn't know about archiving. I am lucky to learn the business from such a talented manager. If having to put up with a little mayhem is the price, so be it. As if party to this thought, I hear Maria bellowing from the other room through the wall.

'Shit a brick!'

The profanity is accompanied by a huge crash. I wince, though Ms Heath gives no indication she's heard either.

'Fine, I'll see you then.'

I hang up and amble in the direction of Maria's holler which comes from the records room across the hallway. It's a large room containing fifteen freestanding shelves, with yet more boxes of film cans, papers and other junk. Once upon a time, it had been a drawing room where prim and proper ladies received guests. Dorothy received them too, though there was nothing remotely ladylike about her parlour. There are still stick figures drawn in compromising positions on the bare plaster. I bet her 'tea parties' were fun.

'What's happened now?' I call out.

A few weeks earlier, Maria had accidentally knocked one of the freestanding shelves over, which in turn created a domino effect as it sent another six to the ground. All the rolls of footage between 16 May 1963 and 4 November 1997 had ended up on the floor and needed to be re-filed. It had taken us almost a week and set the project back weeks. I give up a silent prayer to the film gods that it's not as bad as last time.

'Help!'

I discover Maria has caught her long hair in a filing cabinet drawer mechanism. Tamping down the urge to laugh, I attempt to unwind it. Then I give up and hack through Maria's locks with the Stanley knife I always carry at work in my back pocket.

'Good thinking.'

Maria stands up straight, luxuriating in the ability to move her head. My pragmatic approach to problem-solving would not be prized by everyone, but Maria told me it's one of the reasons she hired me in the first place.

The bonhomie lasts all of five seconds when Maria asks me about the rat situation.

'He said the collection was "not worth it"?'

Maria does air quotes for emphasis, even though I'd been the one who told her the bad news. She paces up and down. If life were a cartoon, my boss would have a little storm cloud suspended above her head, complete with rain and neon yellow fork lightning.

'It's outrageous!'

I take a deep breath, trying to soothe myself against the noise. Preoccupied, Maria gives me no room to interject, or sympathise.

'Dorothy Atkinson was a *literal pioneer*. No — a genius!'

I'm not so sure. I love my job with all my heart, but I've seen little in the collection to dissuade my initial opinion Dorothy was more than a very horny old woman with a die-hard penchant for film. Only a couple of days ago I'd opened a dusty box to find something that looked suspiciously like a sex harness. Even after I'd pulled it from the box, I couldn't even begin to imagine how you would use it, or if I was holding it the right way up.

'We'll be overrun . . . The rats will probably get so big they'll attack us! How would the estate like it if we sue?'

As I hope, Maria appears to run out of steam once she's vocalised her anger. As one last demonstration, she sighs loudly, kicking out at yet more boxes with her boots.

'Right, well, I suppose I better get the traps then.'

I wince in anticipation as I deliver my next bit of news.

'I'm afraid I have to leave early, too.'

To my surprise, Maria just huffs an errant piece of hair out of her face.

'Fine. Whatever.'

She stalks off in the direction of the hallway. I hear her open the front door and leave. I wait approximately thirty seconds before the door opens again. I know she will have forgotten her big hippy bag. It's hanging on the newel post at the bottom of the stairs where she loops its long strap every morning. She does this every single time she tries to go anywhere. I hear her say the same thing every day as she comes back for it, too.

'For crying out loud!'

The door closes a second time behind her.

CHAPTER THREE

I barely make it to my appointment to see Ms Heath. I park outside on double yellows and find myself racing through the spooky, empty building. My shoes clack on the laminate as I run.

I've been here before, but it's the running that takes me back in time. I'd been working nine to five. Dean could have picked his son up after school, but that was too much trouble for him. Though he'd started life with a certain level of privilege, he'd taken to life on the fringes as a down-and-out. He loved the drama of being a paper gangster. Resentment against his parents cutting him off in disgust seemed to give him a kind of negative purpose in life.

Also, as Dean was fond of reminding me back then, Jack was 'my kid'. I was the one who'd apparently 'insisted' on having him. This meant Jack had to go to after-school club. I'd always been late, rushing from one thing to the next, trying to hold it all together as everything unravelled in my hands despite my best efforts. Meanwhile, Dean stayed at home texting his customers and taking enough ketamine to keep a shire horse in a coma.

I arrive to find Ms Heath and Jack sitting together in the classroom. My son's expression is impassive, his mood impossible to discern. My son is so thin, he's dwarfed by the large, round woman. Ms Heath is a woman in her fifties, with an all-encompassing bosom. She's decked out entirely in pillar-box red, with a shock of short, bright white hair crowning her head. She reminds me of a female Santa Claus. She indicates the chair opposite.

'Mrs Rose, how are you today?' She smiles at me; there's red lipstick on her teeth.

'Yes, yes, whatever.' I wave a hand at her, my irritation barely contained. 'What's all this about?'

Ms Heath's eyes bug in surprise. Too late, I realise I am supposed to reply in the positive. Throughout my childhood and teenage years Dad drilled into me the need to acknowledge and indulge people's pleasantries and platitudes, even if I felt it's a largely irrelevant practice. He did the same for everything he labelled my 'antisocial traits'. To my chagrin, he added stars and took them away on a chart on the fridge right up until I left home. When I returned, I had made him promise not to reinstate it.

I attempt to repair the damage and paint a smile on. 'Sorry. It's been a long day. Let's start again, shall we?'

I offer a hand to shake, which she does dutifully. Gawd, so many pointless little social norms to observe. Sometimes I wonder if I was born in the wrong country. I've read that people from other countries think the British have far too many of these expectations. Apparently in some cultures they don't even queue.

'I'm sorry to tell you this, Mrs Rose, but we have had multiple reports of Jack bullying other children.'

I gape at Ms Heath. '. . . Oh.'

I feel like I'm back in the headteacher's office, in trouble. I don't allow any of this to show on my face. I cannot show weakness. Prickles of resentment snake through me and Dean's words surface in my mind.

Everyone is waiting for us to screw up, he'd say, *and they're right to. You and me? We're nothing but trouble.*

I push this down. Dean was always going on about how we were kindred spirits, hell-bent on destruction; that I brought everything on myself; that I was as bad as him. As this thought intrudes, my father's kind eyes replace my dead husband's snarled, feral grin.

Put it in a box, hen, he tells me.

I envisage a jewellery box like the one Dad gave me when I was a little girl. It had been made of pink velveteen material, a twirling ballerina inside, her face slapped on with paint somewhere in China. I had loved that box so much! I never knew what happened to it, but back then when my parents argued I'd retreat to my room and open the lid, listening to the *Swan Lake* melody in discordant, slightly out-of-tune notes. It soothed me then, so it feels right to put all my bad feelings in that same box decades later, if only in my mind.

Ms Heath regards me and then my son with her big brown eyes. 'Jack, are you going to tell Mum what's been going on, or shall I?'

Jack shrugs, almost imperceptibly. He sits back in his chair, arms folded, legs spread wide, staring at a faraway spot on the wall over Ms Heath's head. It's a defensive position if ever I saw one.

My poor little prince.

His face has changed so much in the past year alone. It's more elongated than it used to be; there's a dusting of stubble around his lips and jawline. He's classically handsome, and what he lacks in height is made up for with his high cheekbones, jet black hair and blue eyes. He will be quite the heartbreaker someday.

'Yes, I'm afraid so.' Ms Heath blots her clammy hands on her voluminous skirt. 'Obviously, we have investigated these claims. We—'

'What are the claims?' I cut in.

Ms Heath purses her lips and picks up a piece of paper from her desk. She puts on a pair of glasses.

'Well, he has been taunting other students. Stealing their belongings and hiding them from them, whipping their chairs away from under them so they fall on the floor, that kind of thing.' She looks over her glasses. 'The most serious involves a boy who told us Jack stabbed him in the hand with a pair of compasses.'

Irritation courses through my veins. Bullying? Everything Ms Heath describes is tame and ordinary kid stuff. I remember seeing and being on the receiving end of far worse when I was at school. It's kids challenging boundaries. It's not cool to say it when 'toxic masculinity' is the woke phrase of the moment on TikTok and Twitter, but no one's told young lads what that phrase means. They're just doing what they've always done.

Except . . . that's not quite true, is it?

Not for Jack.

Before I can stop it, time slips away from me again. In my mind's eye, I see myself grabbing Jack by his skinny arms before the police arrived that terrible night.

We don't say anything, ever, I'd told him.

My son had stared up at me with wide eyes.

Am I bad, Mummy? he'd asked.

I'd blinked back tears and stroked his little round face.

No darling, you saved me.

My wobble over, certainty floods through me again. Jack is not a bad boy — he's already shown how he will stand up for me, his mother. Time for me to do the same. Indignant fury surges within me as I consider who could be behind this storm in a veritable teacup. A face comes to mind: the mum who wears tie-dye and is always handing out homemade treats when she drops her kids off at the school gates like a good Stepford wife.

'Look, there's a mother with a vendetta against Jack—'

Ms Heath jumps in. 'Yes, Mrs Finnegan told us about Jody's missing jumper.'

Vindication floods through me now. 'Then you know that she's been going out of her way to cause trouble for us. She—'

'Mrs Finnegan is not the only parent or student to file a complaint with us about Jack's behaviour, I'm afraid.' Ms

Heath glances at Jack. 'The school has been trying to work with Jack to find an appropriate solution for this situation.'

'Well, why is this the first time I'm hearing about all this?' I demand.

Ms Heath consults her bit of paper. She's prepared, I'll give her that.

'You were sent emails and messages via the school app on a number of occasions, Mrs Rose . . . Last week, on Thursday and Friday. The week before that, too.'

I bow my head, defeated. I've been so busy at work; I've been deleting emails unread. As for the school app, I installed it on my phone but could never get into it, so just left it deactivated in a graveyard folder.

'I see.' I find myself saying through clenched teeth. I don't trust myself to say more.

'We don't condone this kind of behaviour at Camden Academy,' Ms Heath declares, 'so Jack has been placed on internal exclusion for two weeks.'

Oh, no.

'Mrs Rose, do you know what internal exclusion means?'

I nod. I do know what it means: Jack will be removed from class but will still be expected to go into school. I suppose I ought to be grateful for small mercies.

'After the internal exclusion period, Jack will be able to return to class and his behaviour with his peers will be reviewed. I'm afraid that if there is no improvement, we will have to look at alternative provision for him.'

Every word feels like a rock on my head. Why the hell do these authority figures always talk in such hoity-toity, fancy ways? 'Alternative provision' for crying out loud (as Maria would say). He'll be sent to those places for naughty kids, 'pupil referral units'. In my dad's day, it was just called reform school.

But I've got the message, loud and clear: Jack will be out on his ear. This round beanbag of a teacher and all her cronies think I am a bad mother and Jack is a bad kid. I envisage locking all this in the jewellery box, allowing myself a quick fantasy of shoving a tiny Ms Heath, screaming in there in the dark as well.

'I understand.' I force the words out as I accept the paperwork from Ms Heath's outstretched stubby fingers. 'Jack, let's go.'

Jack trails after me, sullen and hunched, to the car. Walking back through the labyrinthine corridors feels like a metaphor for our journey back from the edges of existence Dean took us to. I'd dragged us back, inch by agonising inch, with only Dad to help me.

Now Dad is dead too, far too soon.

We lost so much time, thanks to Dean. Thirteen years my senior, Dean had been my older man, a real grown-up. I'd been enthralled to him. Yet as our relationship struggled on, I'd grown to hate him and his sense of entitlement. I realised far too late none of the things Dean wanted were me or Jack.

Given the extent of Dean's dodgy dealings, he was not unknown to the authorities. My story had not seemed like an outlandish lie. The police took in the sight of his body splayed on the kitchen floor, covered in congealing blood. They knew the calibre of the victim, so sought out evidence that confirmed their existing cognitive bias. They even missed Jack's *Star Wars* onesie, swishing around in the washing machine by itself in the middle of the night. In the law's defence, it was far more likely some dodgy lowlife rival had killed Dean for encroaching on his territory. The police were more likely to think I'd killed Dean than his own eight-year-old son.

Jack clambers into the car beside me into the passenger side. Exasperated, I look at him, waiting for him to break the silence. I decide to wait him out. When sixty seconds pass and nothing is forthcoming, I throw my hands up in the air.

'Well, what do you have to say for yourself?'

My son won't meet my eye. He shrugs again. A shocking image bursts through my mind: in it, I reach over the gear-stick, grab him by his neck. Then I slam his forehead against the dashboard. I shake my head, as if I can dispel the waking dream with literal movement.

Not real.

We've had a terrible start to the year. I'm frustrated and feeling out of control. We're both newly bereaved. Jack just lost his beloved grandfather, the only man who has ever shown him kindness. That's why he has been acting up at school. Damn it, why didn't I make this point to Ms Heath? I make a mental note to email her later.

'I can't have you playing up at school,' I begin. 'I—'

Jack interrupts me. 'They're just such idiots.'

'I can't believe *all* of them are.'

'You don't know, Mum!' Jack wails. 'It's torture, listening to them go on about stupid shit that doesn't matter!'

'Like what?'

'Stuff!' This is the most animated I've seen Jack since his grandfather passed. 'Their lives are so small, it's pathetic.'

His vehemence gives me pause. I recall feeling aggravated with my peers around the same age as Jack right into my early twenties, sure I was the 'only' one who could see real life for what it was. Had that been youthful arrogance? Or is Jack a chip off the ol' block?

I can't decide.

It doesn't matter anyway. Jack has less than a year left of school, his exams are around the corner. He's predicted good grades. I can't let his frustrations derail him now like I'd allowed myself to get lead astray by his father when I was at university all those years ago.

'I need you to do as you're told at school with this internal exclusion thing, okay?'

'I'm leaving school.'

Jack's voice is steady, defiant. To underline his point, he folds his arms, like it's all sorted. Panic floods through me. He can't leave school. He only has GCSEs. That might have been enough back when I was at school in the nineties, but Generation Z can barely qualify for a zero-hours cleaning contract with that now. I don't want him to struggle. I have worked too hard to make a better life for him after such a rough start.

'Oh no, you don't,' I say, 'there's no chance—'

He interrupts me again. 'I'm eighteen soon. I'll move out, get a flat.'

So he wants to play that game.

'And how will you do that?' I fix him with a humourless smile. 'You don't have any savings. You've never even had a Saturday job. You think I'm going to help you throw your life away? If you do, you have another thing coming.'

'I was thinking . . . Grandad's money?'

He says it so softly, I almost miss it. I sigh.

'The will is not settled yet. It takes ages. By the time it's done, your exams will probably be over, so you might as well do them.'

'It's a waste of time. I don't care about any of it. I—'

Now it's my time to interrupt. 'My house, my rules.'

'You always say that!' Jack scowls.

'Because it's bloody true!'

My voice softens, along with my attitude. I can see the tension in Jack's shoulders relax. He knows I can't stay mad at him for long.

'Look, Jack . . . I need you to go along with this internal exclusion thing. Keep your head down. Get on with things. Can you do that for me?'

'Okay.'

I extend an arm towards my boy, ruffling his hair. 'You're a good lad, really.'

Jack proffers a tight-lipped smile.

CHAPTER FOUR

Jack does all he can to avoid me the next morning, even walking himself to school. That's fine with me. Teenagers think the world revolves around them, huffing and puffing in that melodramatic way of theirs. Adults can't do right for doing wrong: ask them what their problem is, you're judgmental and interfering. Ignore their moods and you apparently don't care about them. *Ugh*. I consider sending him a text to wish him luck on his first day of internal exclusion but decide he will probably see it as a jibe.

At the Atkinson Project, I yawn as I lean over my desk to reach my computer. I press the ON switch on the ancient machine first as it takes forever to boot up. Rolling my shoulders, I move back out to go to the staffroom. I can hear Maria's heavy tread on the floor upstairs. She's laughing, like she's talking to herself. She must be on the phone.

The staffroom is in as bad shape as the rest of the building, dingy and packed full. I approach the state-of-the-art coffee machine that's buried under a stack of paperwork and a million coffee cups. They're dotted all over the sides, creating a trail towards the stained aluminium sink where there's yet more crockery, as well as dried-out takeaway and ready meal containers. Some of them have mould in.

None of them are mine. I have only one cup, one plate, one bowl and all of my food is labelled with my name in the communal fridge and cupboard. The rest of the disgusting detritus belongs to Maria. The coffee machine is mine, though. I spray it with antibac and wipe it down with a clean cloth. I keep both in my bottom desk drawer, to prevent Maria from using them on God knows what. The chance is small given she's allergic to cleaning, but you can't be too careful. Got to plan ahead, one of the few lessons I learned from Dean.

'Morning, beautiful.'

A man's voice in my ear makes me jump and nearly throw my coffee up in the air.

I swallow a screech as I whirl around, shocked at not finding myself alone. The chugging of the coffee machine, not to mention Maria's usual crashing around, must have masked someone coming in after me. My panic turns to laughter in an instant as I clock who it is.

'You nearly gave me a heart attack, Steve!'

In the doorway stands a tall, broad guy in a blue apron that reads *1939, Artisan Coffee*.

'Bad nerves.' Steve grins and pulls me towards him. 'I *did* knock.'

Our lips meet in a kiss. I press my body against his and am gratified when he does the same. We're still in the early months of our relationship, where we can't keep our hands off each other. We have limited options since Jack doesn't know about us. I never wanted to parade a succession of 'uncles' in front of him. Barring the odd Tinder date, I'd more or less sworn off men since Jack was small. Steve is my first real relationship since Dean.

'You free for lunch?'

I flash him a seductive smile. 'After a quickie, huh?'

Steve's flat's above his coffee shop, two or three streets away from the project. It wouldn't be the first time we'd had to resort to snatched moments in our working days. We'd only been going out a matter of weeks when my poor dad died.

I've got Jack, but we are both so busy: me setting up my career, Steve his business. He used to work in the City but had left the well-paid corporate rat race behind when he'd burned out at thirty-three. Back then, he'd worn a suit and his hair cropped close to his head. Now he looked like the archetypal hipster, complete with a beard and man bun. Not my usual type, but since *that* had included the likes of Dean, I'm happy to try something new.

'I just need to have a word.' Steve smiles, but it doesn't seem to reach his eyes. 'Come by just after one?'

Uh oh. Am I about to get dumped?

I tamp down my fears, feigning nonchalance. I turn towards the coffee machine, picking my cup back up.

'I'll see what I can do. We are very busy today.'

Steve smiles; he doesn't seem to notice my change in demeanour. He's distracted by the front door opening again.

'See you later!'

He's gone. As I sit down, I see a shadow make it into the hallway. Must be Louisa. She is much older than Maria and retired. She's a lovely, warm, rotund woman with short grey hair who loves crosswords and Chelsea football club. She spends most of her days baking or yelling at her television, urging game show contestants to *Deal or No Deal*. Sometimes she will drop by with cakes or other treats.

'Hey, Lou . . .'

I turn on my wheeled chair smiling, to find it's not Louisa standing behind me as I expect. I leap to my feet, self-conscious.

A young man in his mid-twenties stands in my office doorway. He's got the good looks of a model: high cheekbones, sunglasses even indoors. He's even taller than Steve. His angular face makes me think of a young Grace Jones, but he's all man.

He's dressed like something out of the 1980s too. The mum in me chides him instantly for not dressing warmly; it's January for Pete's sake. He's wearing a denim jacket, stonewashed skinny jeans on his narrow hips barely meet a neon yellow mesh top that grazes his belly button and looks amazing next to his dark skin. I've lived in trendy and diverse Camden most of my life, but I've never seen anyone quite like him. He looks like something out of one Maria's magazines and he absolutely knows it.

'Hi there. I'm Aaron.'

He flashes me a bright white smile, proffering a hand for me to shake. I take it. His palm feels smooth and soft.

'H-hi,' I stammer. 'I'm Natasha.'

Aaron takes his sunglasses off and drops them into the messenger bag slung across his chest. I just stand there, frozen like an idiot. I am horribly aware of the outfit I'd just thrown on that morning: a dark hoody, black jeans. No make-up. Such an ensemble against my sallow skin and dark hair must make me look like an Italian widow.

He flashes me a carefree grin, unconcerned. I guess Aaron must be used to having this kind of effect on people.

'Am I in the right place? Is this —' he fishes a piece of paper from the bag — 'the Atkinson Film Project?'

'That's right.' I gulp.

'Great!' Aaron indicates the mess. 'I wasn't sure. Didn't really look like I imagined, you know?'

I titter like a schoolgirl. 'We get that a lot.'

There's an awkward pause before I remember myself again. He must need something from the archives. Maybe someone from the estate sent him, or perhaps he is an interested student or civilian. From time to time randoms drop by. They're not allowed to take anything out of the collection, but they gather information for dissertations and personal projects. Dorothy had left instructions in her will this was allowed, much to the lawyers' chagrin. If they had their way, they'd box the whole thing up and sell it as blind boxes on eBay.

I fix my face into the most professional pose I can muster.

'So, Aaron. How can I help you?'

He gets straight to the point.

'I'm Aaron Gooding, the true crime podcaster?'

He says it like I am supposed to know who he is. I've never heard of him. I don't really listen to podcasts. I don't want to admit this though to Aaron and seem out of touch.

'I see,' I say, noncommittal.

He rolls his eyes, sensing my bluff right away. 'It's called *Crime Scribe*. It was listed as one of Buzzfeed's top true crime podcasts last year. I also made the *Guardian*?'

I leave the smile frozen on my face, neither confirming nor denying it. I'm painfully aware of how uncool I am, just standing in this bright young thing's presence. Aaron appears to need to prove his fame, because he whips his phone out and calls something up on his screen. He turns it towards me, inviting me to take it.

Sure enough, on the handset is a picture of Aaron. I note it's some lefty website, the kind that always had my dad ranting about the youth of today wanting everything on a plate. The young man looks serious and rugged and well-lit. The headline reads: *Is True Crime Copaganda?* Underneath, a subheading reads: *Aaron Gooding, 25, is challenging patriarchal and white supremacist norms in his award-winning podcast*, Crime Scribe.

So many buzzwords in one article makes my head spin. All it needs is some mention of 'wokism' or 'feminism' for a full bingo card. I swipe across the screen and sure enough, they're both on the next page. *Gawd*.

'Well done,' I say keeping my tone neutral and handing the phone back. 'How can I help you?'

Though he smiles back, there's a steely glint in Aaron's eye that intrigues me. It appears I have irritated him by not recognising him, or bigging him up. His ego emanates from him like a beacon as he pulls something from his pocket.

'I was doing some research into the Dennis Nilsen murders. Have you heard of *him*?'

I note the facetious jibe and purse my lips. 'Of course.'

Everyone in Camden's heard of Nilsen. He'd been one of Kentish Town's most infamous claims to fame. Dubbed the *Muswell Hill Murderer* by the press, Nilsen had killed at least twelve young men between 1978 and 1983.

Before cutting up the bodies in grisly fashion, Nilsen would spend time with his dead victims, bathing and dressing them like dolls. He was, in short, the kind of whack job usually seen in sensationalist movies and television shows about serial killers. It's always hard to believe such people can really exist.

'Well, did you know Dorothy Atkinson knew him?'

I'm blind-sided. I've been at the archives over a year, but never had an inkling Dorothy could have counted a serial killer in her circle of bohemian and alternative friends. A million questions erupt into being in my mind: had she known? Had she helped him? Could there be cans of film in here somewhere, of his victims' last moments?

No, surely not. Dorothy had some flamboyant tastes, but nothing we had unearthed so far suggested those included murder.

'Are you sure?'

Aaron presents me with what he'd pulled from his pocket, a badly blurred Polaroid. In it, Dennis Nilsen is unmistakable: the dark hair, the aquiline nose, the brow bar on his large spectacles.

Next to him, a much-younger Dorothy, laughing. She is in her late thirties or early forties and leaning into him, familiar, though it's hard to tell from just one picture what this could mean. They're somewhere with typically eighties décor, a riot of orange and mustard yellow. I realise it can't be the house we are standing in right now. She had only bought it in her sixties, plus every wall is white and graffitied with Dorothy's mad stickman porno.

'Where did you get this?'

Aaron flashes me a genuine grin at last. 'I never reveal my sources.'

Of course he doesn't.

'I was hoping I could have a look around, maybe cross-reference a few things.' Aaron sounds less cocky now. '*If* that's okay?'

I hesitate. I'm not supposed to take visitors into the archives. Maria is the one who decides who can and who can't peruse her beloved collection. But Maria is busy. I'm also certain Maria won't want to hear how her idol hung out with serial killers, even if it was just the once. She's likely to send Aaron away, with a flea in his ear, before she would even countenance it. I'm bursting with curiosity, though, so the decision isn't difficult.

'When my boss sees you, you're here doing a project for university on film noir. Okay?'

'Got it.' Aaron flashes me that boy band grin again.

'No filming or photographs,' I say. 'In fact, you can leave your phone and bag with me.'

Aaron nods, unlooping his bag from his neck and handing it to me straight away.

'Of course. I will abide by any condition you set.'

I've been a mum far too long, so I don't trust his automatic capitulation. I can see there's nothing bulky in his pockets; his jeans are that tight. I bid him to turn out his jacket pockets. With a sheepish grin, he pulls a second phone out.

'Got me.'

He hands it over and I slide it into his bag with the rest of his stuff. I shove it all in the cupboard under my desk, locking it in case I get called away and he's tempted to sneak back for any of his technology. I slip the key into my own pocket. There's no way he can hoodwink me.

'Wow, you really do think of everything.' Aaron chuckles, impressed.

'It's always the little things.' I grin at him. 'Follow me.'

I take him into the collection.

CHAPTER FIVE

All morning I keep changing my mind about going to see Steve. I can't concentrate on cataloguing, filing or digitising. The big hand and the little hand make their way around the huge reconstruction of the *Metropolis* clock hanging on the main office wall.

As I watch it, I chop and change. One moment, I am certain I am not going. I decide I will be dignified, accept my lot, move on. Perhaps I should just text Steve and tell him it had all been fun while it lasted, but I'd got the signal, loud and clear?

I should have known Steve wouldn't be in it for the long haul. I'm a single mother who's almost forty and in her very first proper job. Hardly a prize catch. I couldn't expect a go-getter like Steve who wants to establish his own coffee chain to think we have any kind of future. Yet the next moment, I see myself in my mind's eye begging Steve to think again, self-respect be damned. *Ugh*.

My eye strays to a collection of magazines on the counter, all Maria's. She has a fascination with celebrity gossip, which seems at odds with her nonconformist nature. On the front of one glossy, some film star I don't recognise smiles, promoting her latest project. Beside this, a caption for another article reads: *THE TRUTH ABOUT BEING ALONE (YOU WON'T LIKE IT)*. I shudder and push it away from me. It flops off the side, straight into the bin. *Result*.

I don't really know how to navigate romantic relationships. I'd been so young, barely in my twenties, when Dean and I had got together. I'd been in my second year at university studying English Literature and Film and Dean had been my professor. He'd been a specialist in television history. I'd heard around campus he was a married ladies' man with a penchant for female students. I hadn't let that dissuade me.

Like so many young women before me, I'd decided I would change him. Unlike my doomed predecessors, I'd actually succeeded. Dean ended his marriage and moved in with me. (By that point the university had found out about our illicit affair, not least my secret pregnancy with Jack. Since professor–student relationships were forbidden, he was sacked, but that's by the by. I'd taken the risk and got the reward).

The fact that 'reward' was Dean himself turned out to be a bitter irony. Practically overnight he transformed from a well-turned out, seemingly mild-mannered, soft-spoken man to a raging, sour individual who felt the world was against him. He felt he was better than the menial jobs he was forced to take after the university refused him a reference. He started day drinking and chain smoking, using up our limited money on his various indulgences.

Everything was my fault, of course. It seemed like Dean saw his fall from grace every time he looked at me. As my belly grew bigger, so did Dean's resentment. As time went on, I cut off my family at Dean's insistence. My father begged me to reconsider, but I let Dean sow the seeds of conflict between us. When Dad emailed me and told me I was still welcome home with the baby whenever I wanted, I blocked him online, sure I was not worthy of my poor father's love or help.

Yet if I'd never taken up with Dean, I wouldn't have Jack.

Our time under Dean's cruel thumb had been terrible, but Jack had been the one ray of sunshine that had kept me going. Dean could have provided for us; his work may not have been legal, but it brought the coins in. He kept us purposefully short, making me beg for our due. Most of it was spent on booze and gambling. Nappies, clothes, food, even time: all of it was doled out to me with a deep sigh, so I was left in no doubt we were nothing but a burden on him. His lack of regard for us was frightening.

God help me, I was glad when he died.

I still am.

As Dean's periods of unemployment had grown longer and longer, we'd found ourselves further and further out on the fringes of society. Jack grew from a colicky baby to a fractious toddler and then a solemn little guy; Dean's descent into crime became a freefall.

Our poky little flat was filled with boxes of contraband: booze, cigarettes and anything else he could grab a profit on. Before long, it was drugs. I had recurring nightmares that Jack would get into the cellophane packets and ingest something that would kill him or put him in a coma. Thankfully, that never happened, but home was not safe.

Things are different now. I might not have that much spare money, but Jack wants for nothing. He has everything he needs and some of what he wants. I don't starve him of resources, but I don't spoil him either.

Everything is as it should be.

The world might be certain single mothers are the devil incarnate and a drain on society, but I am the exception. I always have been. I've made sure people know it, too.

I've still not made my conscious mind up as the clock approaches one. Maria makes it for me; she is still in a foul mood. I can still hear her crashing around upstairs and swearing. I tell myself I'll just pop outside and escape her wrath for five minutes.

My treacherous feet take me straight to 1939, unbid.

The bell over the door tinkles. It's a retro place, decorated WW2 style. The counter is built like an Anderson air raid shelter; the pictures are lined with barbed wire; the menus are ration books. When Steve had described it to me, I'd thought it sounded quaint.

In reality it feels old fashioned, dark and rather depressing. Camden residents might feel the same way. I'm perturbed to see how quiet is, considering it's lunch time.

Steve's assistant, Zane, looks up from his green tea. He has the permanently bored look of most of Gen Z, along with a mohawk, nose ring and distinctive biomechanical sleeve tatts on both arms. He doesn't bother asking what I want. He points one to the side door that leads to the flat above, without a word.

I give him a perfunctory little wave and breeze past. As I climb the narrow stairs up to Steve's flat, my heart races a mile a minute. This can't be good.

Steve obviously wants privacy, so he must be planning to dump me.

Right.

Well, unlike women who read that stupid magazine, I can handle it. In fact, I will give him something to remember me by. Perhaps it will make him reconsider, or at least wish he'd not been so hasty?

I kick the door aside at the top of the stairs, making my presence felt like Jack does every time he arrives home. Steve sits on a stool at the counter poring over bills and receipts.

'Tasha, I . . .'

He looks up, his mouth a perfect 'o' of surprise. His eye strays to the clock; he'd lost track of time. I don't wait for him to say anything more.

Sitting down, he's almost the same height as me. I'm able to press my lips to his without having to stand on tiptoes like I normally would have to. My tongue snakes into his mouth, my hands finding my way under his shirt. He capitulates for a moment, allowing me to slip a hand through his button fly.

'Whoa, wait a minute.'

Don't say it.

Steve grabs me by the shoulders. 'What's got into you?'

Sullen, I step back, holding my hands up in mock surrender.

'Not you, apparently.'

Steve laughs, thinking I'm joking. His face falls when he realises I'm not. His eyes search my expression, his own inscrutable.

'What's this about . . . Tasha, this isn't like you. Are you okay?'

I try to smile back but can't manage it. I collapse on a nearby futon in the kitchen/living area of Steve's poky flat. Tears well up in my eyes. I lean forward, hiding my face with my hands rather than let him see.

'Just get on with it.' I whisper.

'Get on with what?'

Steve is beside me in just a couple of steps. He crouches down next to me, his hands on my knees.

'Splitting up with me!' I wail.

'Tasha, look at me.'

I sigh and take my hands away from my face.

'I'm not going to split up with you, silly.' Steve's voice is gentle. 'Why would you think that?'

Confusion and relief flood through me. Next, I'm mortified. He'd only said he wanted a word this morning. I'd jumped to conclusions.

What was I playing at?

Steve's right: this is not like me at all. I'm the pragmatic, straightforward type, yet here I am acting as tumultuous as Maria. But until this morning, I'd been clueless about how hard I'd fallen for Steve. The thought of being without him had been too much too bear. It made me behave like a hysterical teenage girl over the class crush.

'Because I'm an idiot,' I groan.

Steve chuckles. 'You are not. You're amazing.'

He falls onto the futon next to me. I rest my head on his shoulder, feeling contented for the first time in hours. I watch him stroke his hand up and down my thigh for a few moments. As my mind clears, I realise I still don't know

31

what he'd wanted when he dropped by at the archives this morning.

'So, what *did* you want a word about?'

'Okay, just hear me out.'

Steve tenses up. He sits forwards, his body facing mine. I mirror him, worried all over again. I can't imagine what he's about to say. He seems so earnest, so serious.

'We've been going out nearly six months and I think we're getting on really well, don't you?'

Mute, I nod.

'Well, I thought it would be really nice if I, uh, could meet Jack?'

I blink, working over in my mind what this means. It must show in my face, because Steve holds up both hands, his words gaining in speed.

'I know you wanted to keep your life and Jack's separate and I respected that. But, um, I don't think I can do that anymore, Tasha. Because . . . well, I think we could have a future together and obviously, that should include Jack. But I think me and him should get to know each other first . . .'

His words trail off, his expression as stricken as mine had been earlier.

'Or have I got this wrong?'

My answer: I grab his face in both hands and press my lips to his again. This time he yields, lying back on the futon so I'm on top of him. Our bodies pressed together, we run our hands over each other, lost in the moment.

He breaks away again, breathless. 'So that's a yes, I'm guessing?'

'Yes!' My gaze goes back to the clock. It's already approaching half past. 'I'd love to talk some more, but I have to be back at two.'

He smirks. 'You want to seal the deal?'

'You bet.'

We get lost in each other again.

CHAPTER SIX

Tuesday rolls in. Jack's first day in internal exclusion at school seems uneventful. I receive Ms Heath's report via email and acknowledge it instantly. While I'm at it, I remind her of Jack's grandfather's death and how Jack's had to see a counsellor about it. I won't give school any excuse to label me a 'hostile parent', but that doesn't mean I will let them condescend to me either.

At work, Maria reappears at the archives, now seemingly relaxed and carefree about the rats and the estate's lack of regard. I ask her how her anniversary dinner and show went; she tells me they never made it to either. I don't need her to explain, her loved-up expression gives it away. I'm pleased for her. Like most couples, Maria and Louisa have had their ups and downs, especially when it came to their foster kids Danny and Freya. It sounds like those two were right teara-ways as youngsters.

It's decided Steve will come to dinner at my place the upcoming Friday night. He'd wanted to take us out for a fancy meal, but I knew Jack wouldn't appreciate that. Like so many teens, he is suspicious of grown-ups flashing cash.

I float through the rest of the week, but I am realistic. As delighted as I am the two most special men in my life are about to meet at last, I know Jack well enough to guess his reaction. His grandfather was Jack's only male role model in the last decade, plus Dad only died three months ago. He may think I am trying to replace Dad or worry I won't have time for him anymore. The meeting will require careful handling. I realise Jack is likely to be monosyllabic, maybe even a little shirty with Steve. He will no doubt scoff his food and then retire to his room to play video games. Another reason for them both to meet at my place.

This way it will be as painless as possible, for all of us.

As part of that careful handling, I warn Steve about how the meeting is likely to go.

'It's okay.' Steve grins at me from my phone screen as we Facetime. 'It's been you and Jack a long time . . . And I was a teenage boy once myself, you know. They hate disruptions to the routine. Like dogs.'

I laugh, but Steve is closer to the truth than he realises. Barring his grandfather, Jack had always expressed distrust and hostility around older men. Jack goes out of his way to not speak to them, even teachers at school. It's not difficult to guess why.

After every violent outburst, Dean had always been as nice as pie. He'd sweep in with expensive gifts, all smiles and brittle hugs. He would expect us to rush towards him every time like he was a soldier returning from war. I would trot towards him, the obedient puppy, but Jack would hang back, scrutinising his father with narrow eyes. My heart would plunge into my boots because this would set Dean off all over again. I'd beg and plead with Jack to do what Daddy wanted, but Jack would roll his eyes at me like he couldn't believe I was so weak. He was right.

I *was* weak.

I know I am feeling out of sorts because this is a watershed moment. The first time a new potential partner meets your child is 'next level' stuff. Steve can't know anything about that terrible night. It would ruin everything. All three of us deserve this happiness.

Dean's death might have been years ago, but it feels like every detail has been imprinted on me, an indelible stain. There had been a tentative knock on the hotel door, the fifth day after Dean's death.

Our house was a crime scene, so we'd been unable to return. I'd been climbing the four walls of the dour Travelodge, wondering what the police could find in my blood-splashed kitchen that would prove things hadn't exactly gone the way I'd told them. As hours turned to days, I became convinced it was only a matter of time before they realised I'd lied, straight to their faces.

When I opened the hotel door, I'd been expecting to see the detective inspector in charge of Dean's case, his face grave and handcuffs waiting for me. Instead, a diminutive, moustachioed man in his late fifties waited in the hallway. His shoulders were hunched, hands shoved in the pockets of his dirty jeans. He was wearing a light jacket, completely impractical in such a chilly January. There was no hat on his bald head either. I knew the cold wouldn't bother him. He'd always run hot my whole life.

'Dad.'

I wondered how he'd found me. I hadn't so much as spoken to Dad on the phone since slamming the front door of the family home almost nine years' earlier, when Jack was still in my belly. I hadn't even asked Dad to the wedding.

Not that there was much of one. Dean had been adamant we couldn't run to a big do once he'd been fired. It had been me and the toddler Jack, Dean's nan and a couple of his mates at the local registry office. We'd gone to the pub afterwards for scampi and chips. I'd walked back to the house in my wedding dress, holding Jack's hand. Dean had stayed on to drink the bar dry, rolling back in at three in the morning.

'Tash. I heard what happened to yer fella?'

He couldn't bring himself to say the name. That was understandable. Dad had Dean's number, right from the very beginning. He had seen through the trappings of Dean's education, the big vocabulary, the designer knockoffs. Dad could sense the sharp edges of my husband — the kind of life I'd be destined for by his side.

Now we were free. At last.

Shame descended on me. I didn't want to have to lie to my own father. I'd told police that proper lowlifes had come to our home and attacked us. I'd claimed Dean must have owed them money. They'd hit my head against the doorframe and stabbed Dean with one of our own kitchen knives whilst our eight-year-old son slept through everything upstairs.

At the door of that Travelodge, Dad's expression softened. 'Why didn't you tell me things were so bad, love?'

A grateful sob burst from me. Dad moved over the threshold, wrapping his thin, boyish arms around me. I permitted the hug, savouring the musty smell of him. Dad released me from the hug, grabbing me by the shoulders.

'We'll get you both through this, you hear? Will seem like a bad dream soon enough.'

I nodded, averting my eyes.

I showed Dad through into the main part of the hotel room. Jack was seated on the end of the double bed watching television, far too close to the screen as usual. I'd given up chiding him about it. I'd let him zone out, do whatever he wanted since it happened. We both seemed to be moving through life in a daze; there and yet somehow not at the same time. It was completely normal after trauma, the police psychologist had advised. I had to take them at their word. There was no other choice.

Jack did not look up. I let my father drink in the sight of his grandson for the first time. Jack was always small, wiry, spring-loaded. I saw the ghost of a smile tug at Dad's lip as he made the same realisation. The family resemblance was so strong.

'Jack,' I prompted.

My son's attention fell on us at last. I could feel his blazing scrutiny from across the room as he eyeballed the strange man standing beside me. Anxiety rippled through him, making my heart sink. I realised he expected the worst. Men meant shouting, throwing things, pain. His own father's dark legacy. I'd been unable to protect him from it, so he had protected me instead.

My poor boy.

Dad edged forwards. 'All right, son. I'm Terry . . . Your grandad.'

Jack tilted his head, sizing Dad up. My father never raised a hand to anyone. Violence was just not in his DNA. This must have been clear to my son, because he stood up and proffered his hand, a charming yet bizarrely formal action for an eight-year-old.

'I'm Jack.'

Amused, my father shook his hand.

It was only later I wondered how my father had found us. When I asked him, he told me he had sweet-talked a police officer 'dad to dad'. That was Dad all over: he could get anyone to do anything without them even realising it. He knew the power of empathy and relating to others to get what he wanted. My brittle, black-and-white and impulsive ways were more in keeping with my mother's nature; she was more likely to resort to aggression and threats, so I did too. Dad did everything he could to knock this out of me without resorting to violence, hence the star chart. He knew how much I despised being treated like a child. Every night he would sit me down and go through his drills with me.

'But I don't care.' I would shrug.

'It's about social bonds,' he would say. 'Again: how was your day?'

'It was very good, thank you,' I would recite, parrot-like for him; the words felt false on my tongue. 'How was yours?'

'Good girl.' Dad grinned.

Back in my kitchen, I gravitate back to my Pinterest app. I want to plan a special menu for our dinner with Steve. I turn back towards the counter. Jack stares right at me, picking sugar pops out of the box and throwing them into his mouth like popcorn. I gave up asking him to stop doing it years ago. He casts an eye at my phone, his eyebrow arched in an unasked question.

I can't quite bring myself to jump in and tell him about Steve just yet.

'Got any plans this weekend?' I find myself saying, delaying the inevitable. 'Seeing friends or anything like that?'

As the words leave my lips, a sudden realisation comes with them. Jack has never brought friends to the house. He does go out, so I'd assumed he saw them at their houses, or hung around with them in parks or on the street in typical teen fashion. Coupled with Ms Heath's revelation about school and his resulting internal exclusion, now I wonder if he doesn't have any friends. No, he must do. Even loners and billy no-mates have confidantes, accomplices and moral support. It's very unusual for a child to have zero friends. I just haven't seen him with them, that's all. Jack is secretive, like so many teenagers.

Jack shrugs, belligerent. 'Might buy a new video game.'

I smile. 'You mean *I* might buy you a new video game.'

'Thanks, very good of you.' Jack grins as I fall into his trap.

I brace myself. 'Listen, I need to talk to you about something.'

Jack's expression is deadpan. 'Go on.'

I choose my next words with care. 'I thought I'd have my friend Steve over on Friday night. I thought we could all eat together?'

Jack regards me, chewing with his mouth open. 'You mean your *boy*friend Steve.'

Busted.

The absurd word *boyfriend* rattles around my brain. Steve is forty years old. He stopped being a boy a long time ago. I know I'm putting off my confirmation for Jack. I can't back down. Steve's tongue-in-cheek comment about teenagers being dogs boomerangs back to me. Well, they *do* say animals can smell fear. I brazen it out. I meet Jack's eye, defiant.

'That's right. We've been seeing each other for a while.'

'I know.'

Jack sniffs, putting his feet up on the chair opposite. I normally forbid this, but I am too curious to find out how he had deduced my new relationship. I eyeball him.

He snickers. 'I found a scrunchie that wasn't yours down the side of the sofa, so I figured you'd had someone here. I thought maybe you were seeing a woman, so I checked your phone history when you were in the loo. Then I saw his pic and realised he had a man bun. A hipster, Mum! Really? Lame.'

'He's not a hipster . . . !'

My words dwindle away as I realise not only had I thought the same thing, my kid's been snooping around my stuff. Fury surges through me, unchecked.

How dare he!

'This is my house, boyo. I'm allowed to have a life, too. Just remember that.'

Jack shrugs, flashing me a tight grin. 'Never said you weren't. But no need to include me in your little romantic meal for two, that's just weird.'

I sigh. Jack's a good boy, but like so many teenagers, careless with others' emotions, especially mine. I know it's because he's secure with me, certain I will always be there for him. At times like this, this thought offers cold comfort. It would be nice if Jack put my feelings first once in a while, instead of always taking the mickey. But again, that's just normal teenage stuff. I must rise above. I count to five, then respond.

'Steve wants to meet you.'

Jack stops throwing cereal into his gob.

'Why?'

'Because it's next level stuff,' I explain. 'It's no longer just a dalliance.'

'A what?'

'You know, not serious. A fling—'

'Okay, Mum!' Jack cut in, raising his eyes skywards. 'I get it. It's bad enough you're so much younger than the other parents and the lads at school say you're a MILF. I don't need to hear about you having sex as well!'

'I never said anything about sex . . .'

Bloody kids!

My cheeks flame. Jack mutters something about walking to school today instead. As he grabs his bag and trudges away from the table abandoning his beloved cereal box, his previous words register.

Kids at Jack's school think I'm a MILF?

In all my time as a young mother, I had felt frumpy, left behind, older than my years. All I could see were the stretch marks, the squishy belly, the dark rings under my eyes. I had no idea I still had the porcelain skin, high cheekbones, lustrous shiny hair. Now I am older (and rounder), I can see motherhood improved my figure, rather than diminished it: my larger breasts accentuated my tiny waist. I'd had the pixie-like Audrey Hepburn face on a voluptuous Marilyn Monroe body.

Not that Dean ever complimented me, of course. Once he had been fired from the university, he'd insisted I leave too, saying we couldn't afford me 'messing about' with a humanities degree. Even pointing out he'd managed to make a living for years 'messing about', he was adamant. He wanted me out of there and earning while he set up his dodgy empire.

I was certain Dean was the best I could do back then. I didn't believe I deserved any better and even if I had, I knew I was soiled goods. Dean told me often enough: he was the only one who would love me, or the baby in my belly. Other men might be interested, but none of them would stay; why would they want a woman with a kid that wasn't theirs? I couldn't resist it; I owed it to Jack to stay with his father. In the animal kingdom, male lions kill the cubs when they want to take over the pride.

By the time I was six months pregnant I was stuck behind the checkout of the local supermarket, scanning goods for hours before returning to our flat in a sinkhole estate that was one part concrete monstrosity and two parts Dante's nine circles of hell from *Inferno*. There I would help Dean package contraband until the early hours, before getting up the next day to do it all over again.

I had not expected to jump forwards nearly eighteen years and suddenly be a figure of admiration to my son's friends. Despite my irritation with Jack, this silly nugget of info lifts my spirits a little. With a smile in my voice, I call after him. 'Friday night, okay? Six o' clock. We are both expecting you there.'

'Whatever! God.'

The front door slams after him.

CHAPTER SEVEN

As Thursday fades away and becomes Friday, my own special dinner with Steve finally arrives. In the morning I awake full of nervous anticipation, though it's soon forgotten as a multitude of tasks at the Atkinson Project command my attention.

One of them is Aaron. He makes another appearance around midday, filled with questions about Nilsen and Dorothy. I steer him out of Maria's earshot, telling her the agreed lie, that he's doing a film noir project. Maria bats me away, her high of the previous few days is gone as she deals with the estate's lawyers on Zoom.

What a difference a day makes.

I am so busy rooting through the archives with Aaron, time gets away from me. He talks me through his fascination with crime and his future plans for his podcast as we pull more photographs from boxes, looking for more evidence of the link between Dorothy and the infamous serial killer.

Coming up blank, I blink and time seems to fast-forward. The shadows of shelves on the wooden floorboards lengthen as the sun dips behind the London skyline outside.

'Oh, shit,' I say looking at my phone. 'I have to get home.'

Aaron raises an eyebrow. 'I can lock up for you, if you like?'

'Hah, nice try. You have to leave.'

'Can I come back?'

I shrug. 'I can't stop you.'

Aaron grins, grabbing his messenger bag. 'Then it's a date.'

His words make me flustered. I'm with Steve. Aaron can't think I was flirting with him, could he? I'm far too old for him.

'Erm, not quite. I—'

He's gone. I sigh. He wasn't serious. I laugh at myself . . . I am an idiot, sometimes.

I race back home to get ready, my belly full of butterflies. I check the time on the clock yet again. It's still an hour before Steve arrives. Antsy and bored, I open the fridge just in case the food I'd prepared and marinated earlier has somehow disappeared.

No, still there. Obviously.

I'd decided to play it safe and go with Jack's favourite, chicken kebabs. I am serving them with his other favourite, saffron rice. I'd picked the best chunks of chicken, lining them up on the skewer with red cherry tomatoes and green peppers, the only fruit and vegetables I can get Jack to eat. It's so colourful and I know it will be delicious. I hate touching raw meat, so normally only make such fiddly dishes for Jack's birthday and other special occasions. I hope the significance will not be lost on my son.

Things were still difficult between us. Jack had been sullen at breakfast that morning, his body language rigid and resentful. I'd understood; he's not enjoying internal exclusion. I'd taken a deep breath and let it wash over me, as if I hadn't even noticed.

Then Jack had arrived at the archives that afternoon, wanting a lift home after school. He'd discovered me with Aaron, elbows deep in boxes in the main records room. His eyes had narrowed at the sight of my visitor, taking in his trendy look. Aaron smiled at him, amiable and distracted.

'I'm going to be at least another hour or so,' I'd said, my attention on the boxes of photos we'd unearthed. 'Why don't you go get that video game you wanted? My treat. Take my purse.'

'But I want to go home *now*,' Jack whined.

I rolled my eyes at him. 'It's only a fifteen-minute walk. I'll be in soon.'

'Fine!'

Jack swept out again. Seconds later, the front door slammed after him, just like it always did with Maria.

'Fiery one,' Aaron said, still shuffling through the photos in his hands.

'Typical teenager,' I countered.

A toilet flushes upstairs, bringing me back to the present. Jack is home. That's good. I had worried he might duck out all evening, just to make a point. I go to the hall mirror and inspect myself for flaws. I'm wearing my best dress, a wraparound designer thing I bought in the sale years ago. It makes my boobs look amazing. My hair is arranged in a messy bun, my make-up natural. Nothing here that could make Steve suddenly leg it.

Hopefully.

Unless Steve comes to his senses and realises he must be losing his mind. Why would someone like *him* go out with someone like *me*, for God's sake? I am soiled goods.

Deep breaths.

I give myself a pep talk in the mirror. I am letting Dean's old taunts rise to the surface again. It was never true what he used to say to me, but it's even less true now. I am accomplished, valued, worthy. I have built a life for myself and my son.

We are happy.

I turn away from the mirror and cast an eye around my spotless home. Steve has been here a few times, but this is different. He thinks we have a *future*. His flat above 1939 is far too small for all three of us, so I want him to come to my house and imagine himself here, with us. His coat on the hook in the hallway; his shoes on the rack; his pictures on the wall or mantelpiece.

Or would he want us to move somewhere new, a place we can all have a fresh start as a blended family? I'm surprised to discover this would be acceptable, too. Perhaps our time in my father's home is drawing to a close.

Jack's certainly is; he will leave home in the next few months, to go to university. He will want his own life. Maybe Steve and I will have our own baby. I smile as I imagine my son, all grown up, playing with his toddler sibling. I feel certain he would dote on a new brother or sister. Why wouldn't he?

We all deserve this.

I chuckle to myself. I have jumped way too far ahead. Steve wants to meet Jack, not move in. Perhaps that will be on the cards eventually, perhaps not. We will have to wait and see. That's the beauty — and agony! — of new relationships.

I pad upstairs towards the door to Jack's little box room, knocking first. The smell of fresh paint wafts out of his grandfather's room. I haven't finished yet, doing an hour or so after work every night. Jack's been mithering me about it. When I told him he would get his new room a lot quicker if he helped, suddenly he had to be somewhere else. Again, like any normal teenager.

No answer. I open the box room door. Jack lies spread-eagled on his bed, staring at the ceiling, eyes open. He is still in his school uniform. Like his grandfather, he's a slob: there's cups, plates and clothes scattered everywhere. I sigh.

'Steve will be here, soon.'

Jack mutters something indiscernible. I think it might be a swear word, but I decide to let it go. I need to pick my battles, tonight of all nights.

'Can you get out of your uniform, at least?'

Jack sits up and turns towards me. He swings his feet over the bed and to the floor in one robotic movement. He wants me to know what an imposition I am placing on him.

'Well, get out while I get changed then.'

I push down an angry retort.

'Thank you.'

Just then, the doorbell goes. The roiling in my stomach recedes. Relief and anticipation jolts through me. Before I can catch myself, I smile.

'He's here.'

Jack's face crumples in disgust as he takes in my joy, but I don't let him kill my buzz.

'Can't wait,' Jack declares, deadpan.

'Just . . . behave for once in your life, will you?'

I go down to answer the door.

CHAPTER EIGHT

Barring Steve's cheerful demeanour, the evening is every bit as excruciating as I'd envisaged. Jack won't even come out of his room until I call up the stairs multiple times. Eventually he trudges downstairs to the dining room, eyes on the floor, hands in his pockets. He gives Steve's hand a begrudging shake.

As I serve dinner, Jack announces he's not hungry. When I point out the meal is his favourite, he claims to have eaten earlier. I'm disappointed and more than a little angry. I had given him plenty of warning and specifically asked him to eat with us. I purse my lips in frustration, my jagged body language revealing my stress.

Steve's hand finds the small of my back. I know what the gesture means straight away: *don't worry about it*.

More deep breaths.

I place a plate of food in front of Jack in case he changes his mind. He doesn't. As we talk, he messes with the kebab skewer, pulling the chunks of meat, peppers and tomatoes off, one by one. I watch him draw a 'J' in the saffron rice with it. I feel like reaching across the table and slapping his face.

I don't.

The chat limps on. Steve makes every attempt to ask Jack about himself but is met with shrugs and one-word answers. Whilst I'd tried to prepare myself for this, the reality is more torturous than I'd expected. I realise what the odd, uncomfortable, rippling sensation through my muscles is: *embarrassment*. I've never felt this way about my own child before. I've always been proud of him before today.

My father had always said that parenting and punishment don't have to go hand in hand. A favourite saying of his had been: *When faced with love or severity, choose love*. No matter how poor my behaviour, he'd always tried to chivvy me out of it, rather than impose harsh penalties. Parenting blogs and magazines recommended something similar. The days of smacking kids or berating them are long gone. Thank God.

Remembering Dad's 'put it in a box' advice once more, I lock it up and I switch the subject to school and Jack's upcoming exams.

'Jack's very gifted at science,' I say with a smile, 'especially human anatomy. He wants to be a doctor.'

My ploy works in making Jack participate, but not in the way I hope. Jack lets out an audible sigh so hard it puffs up his fringe.

'No, *you* want me to be a doctor, Mum.'

Stung, I almost rebuke him. Jack has told me several times in the past year he's interested in medicine, now he's changing the goalposts? As ever, I push it down, anxious not to cause a scene in front of Steve. When Jack gets an idea in his head, true or not, he is prone to dig his heels in. There's no way he'd ever admit he was ever interested in medical training, at least not tonight. There's no point in pursuing the matter.

Steve smiles. 'So, what do *you* want to do, Jack?'

My son meets the question with a dark scowl. 'Why do you care?'

Steve absorbs this belligerent dodge. My fork clatters on my plate. Thoughts of my father fall away. My mother's own stern face invades my mind. Unlike my mild-mannered dad, she'd been a bit of dragon back in the day and like her, I've had a bellyful of this crap.

'Jack, look . . .'

Steve puts his hand on my mine, on the table. 'No, Tasha, it's fine. Jack has a point. It *is* a stupid stock question. In fact, I've been asking them all night, so I can see why he thinks I'm "lame".'

His well-timed *teen-speak* seems to land. Jack looks up from his cold plate, a quizzical expression on his face. I almost laugh. Young people always seem to think they invent everything: language, music, fashions. The idea adults might notice what they're doing, or — God forbid! — have actually experienced it first time around, never seems to occur to them. A smirk tugs at the corner of my boy's lip as he attempts to save face.

'Maybe it's *my* turn to ask a stock question?'

Alarm bells ring in the back of my psyche. I don't like where this is going, though I am not sure why. Jack is a bright boy, but he's only seventeen-going-on-eighteen. He might think he's a grown-up, but he doesn't have the skills to humiliate a real adult like Steve. My lover is candid and honest, so there's not much I don't know about him. Steve's been to university; travelled the world; worked in high pressure environments like the stock exchange. He has also known heartbreak.

Steve's last relationship broke down two years ago when his ex, Charlotte, got pregnant by accident. Despite the fact Steve had been thrilled, she'd decided she didn't want to continue with the pregnancy, or her relationship with him. It was that unexpected emotional catalyst that had caused him to burn out at work and ditch the rat race altogether.

As these thoughts occur, I feel a deep shame I have not told him even the official version of Dean's death yet. I resolve I will tonight, when Jack has inevitably excused himself from the table and stomped off back to his room.

Steve smiles. 'Shoot.'

'What are your intentions towards my mother?'

Relief flowers in my chest. Jack is only kicking out because he is worried about me. I can't blame him, after his father's domestic terrorism. We both carry the scars of the past at the forefronts of our minds. Where I saw hostility in my son's green eyes moments earlier, I now perceive what it really is: fear.

Oh, Jack.

Steve looks to me, then back to my son.

'I won't hurt your mum, Jack. I promise.'

'That wasn't what I asked.'

I lean forward again to say something, but Steve puts one hand on my shoulder and stops me. His gaze meets Jack's across the dinner table, the congealed leftovers of the meal.

I can feel Jack's scrutiny blazing at Steve, like it had at my father all those years ago when he'd come to fetch us from that hotel room. Back then he'd decided my father was benevolent; Dad proved it to him. I will Jack to allow Steve to do the same.

'Okay, my intentions . . .' Steve lets a nervous laugh loose in the air. 'Well, I have them. Is that a good start?'

Jack raises a single eyebrow: *not enough*.

Steve clears his throat. 'Okay, okay. Fine. Yes, I want this relationship to work out: marriage, a dog, white picket fence, maybe even another kid. All that stuff. I love your mother. I know it's not been long, but I think you *just know*, don't you?'

His eyes leave Jack's and meet mine as he says this. He looks so vulnerable, so hopeful, my heart just melts. I know exactly what he means.

I do *just know*.

I've never felt like this with anyone else. It is an alien feeling, completely new. Even so, I feel a certainty, a wholeness, that makes it seem impossible to be without him. I have found the man I want to make a life with, grow old with.

I squeeze his hand in mine. 'Yes, absolutely.'

We grin at each other.

I catch a movement in the periphery of my vision. Before I can turn back towards my son, Jack slams one palm down on the table. He lurches over the table across the space between him and Steve. He jabs one clenched fist towards Steve's face, hard and fast.

As it connects, I shriek in shock and anger, my brain translating what I'm seeing as a punch. I expect Steve's head to snap back, or even his chair to fall backwards, taking him with it. Alongside my perception of what's happening in the here and now, an echo of the past slices through me.

Me and Dean crashing together to the kitchen floor, taking the chair with us.

Stupefied, I stare at Steve, then at my son, whose shoulders are wracked with the effort of his own gasped breaths. He stares at Steve, disbelieving what he is seeing himself.

'No, Jack!'

Too late. Steve's head lolls down, a thin stream of blood streaming trailing on to his lap, the floor beneath him. The past and present smash together again. I can hear the wet sound of Dean's dying breaths in my ears again.

'What have you done!' I find myself shrieking again.

My mind reels. Unconscious? Must be a lucky punch. I have mental whiplash myself. I meet Jack's gaze and he stares at me, his face vacant. It's not shock, it's something else; I can't find the words for it. My poor brain searches for meaning, understanding.

I shut it all down again. This doesn't have to be a big deal. Jack got angry, scared, jealous. He's not the first teenager to strike out at a new potential stepfather and he won't be the last.

What now?

I must see what damage my son has done. I grab Steve's hair and lift his prone face, then wish I hadn't. His right eye is a mess, the orb burst like a balloon and the source of the blood. It leaks onto my hands, my fingers streaked with gore. Ocular fluid leaks down his cheek too, the inside of his socket red and bloody like raw meat.

That's not the worst of it. The wooden handle of one of the empty kebab skewers protrudes, buried deep in the centre of Steve's eye.

Jack did not punch Steve at all, he *stabbed* him.

The skewer must have gone deep into his brain. My shaking hand struggles to find a pulse in his neck. There is none. Steve lurches forwards into me, the weight of him almost pushing me off my own chair. I whimper with horror. Steve is dead.

Jack has killed again.

CHAPTER NINE

'. . . Mum?'

My son's voice brings me back. I don't know how long I've been sitting there, vacant and staring. My shocked gaze meets Jack's.

His brow is creased with reticence, his body language apologetic: shoulders slumped, head low. He looks like a teen who's just been caught doing something bad but ordinary, like I've just caught him sneaking in past curfew. He notices the blood on his hands and blots them on his shirt, like it's ketchup.

With a whimper I take in Steve's corpse, still leaning against me. I can feel something wet pooling on my shoulder. The greedy fabric of my dress soaks it up; my skin is tacky with it. The smell in the air is like that of a butcher shop, sickly sweet, mixed with the acrid stench of urine. I grab his head with two hands and push him away from me. Steve slumps to the dining-room floor with a soft *thunk*.

I don't need to check Steve's vitals. I know he is dead. He doesn't look like the pretend bodies on television, or from movies. No matter how good the make-up department is, they can never disguise the fact an actor is still alive. In contrast, Steve's flesh is grey, his lips blue. Yet it is more than that: it's the absence of life in him. Steve is gone. Only his meat shell is left behind.

How Dean had looked like, all those years ago.

This connection drives me to my feet. I race out of the room, through the hall and towards the front door. I can hear my blood crashing in my ears; feel the breaths caught in my throat.

I have to get away from my son.

There's something evil within him. It must be Dean's influence. This is his faulty DNA, his dark legacy, his demon seed. Nothing to do with me.

It can't be me.

'Mum!'

Jack's voice falls on my back as I run from him. The pained surprise in it arrests my progress, forcing me to stop as I make it to the front door. I lean against it, forehead pressed against the cool glass like a drunk. I don't want to turn around, see Jack's accusing and hurt eyes.

Oh God, how could he have done this . . . AGAIN?

'What do we do?' Jack says behind me.

'Just . . .'

My voice dies. What *do* we do?

I have no idea.

I turn on my heel and stagger towards the stairs instead. I can barely hold my own head up. I arrest my fall with my hands as I pitch forwards, scraping my knees on the bottom step.

It's the shock, I know. I'd felt like this last time, though mercifully the head injury Dean had given me at least meant I was unconscious first. It had also meant I'd had a plausible alibi for not calling it in to the police right away.

'What do we do?'

Jack's surprise becomes an anguished wail. He wants me to fix this, but I have nothing left for him. I can conjure no thoughts, no words into being.

I pull myself up by the banister and up the stairs to my bedroom. I slam the door after me, locking it with the hook and eye my father had put in years ago when I was a teenager myself. I haven't used it since I'd moved back home with Dad all those years ago. It's not sturdy enough. Panic surges through me and I grab my chest of drawers. It's heavy, made of oak. Straining, I push it in front of the door, barring it.

There . . . Jack can't get in now.

This thought shocks me from my reactivity. I fall into the chair at the end of my bed, hardly able to believe I am so frightened of my own child. Yet I am.

This morning, it had all been different . . . Or had it? Perhaps the truth has been here all along, yet I've refused to face it. I close my eyes, thoughts firing in my head like struck matches, one after the other.

True crime documentaries talk about the signs of a killer. One is childhood cruelty to animals. I had never seen my son treat a living creature badly, but now I think of it, I realise all our pets have met premature ends. The fish in the garden pond had vanished, overnight. My father mused a heron must be in the neighbourhood, adding it was odd it should eat all of the ten fish at once.

There had been two cats, Missy and Marbles, sisters we'd been given by an old neighbour. Marbles had abruptly run away when Jack was about ten, prompting my father to joke for years how we'd 'lost our Marbles'. Missy had been found, stiff as a board, out on the patio one morning. She'd not been particularly old, but then pets can die randomly.

Dad had a dog called Otto too, a big mongrel with a shaggy coat and three legs. He'd been a rescue and Dad's pride and joy, sleeping on his bed every night. A couple of years ago Otto had woken in the night, vomiting, shaking and howling. The vet had scrambled in response to my father's SOS, arriving at the house in the dark to put poor Otto down. My father had been beside himself, refusing to part with Otto's bowl, pet bed or lead.

Oh, God.

Had all of those been Jack, too?

No, Jack had loved Otto. And the cats. He'd always been petting them, like a normal child would. Yet my subconscious brings forth more details from true crime documentaries, against my will: killers-in-training leave the pets where they can be found, so they might experience the pain of the owners. Hadn't Jack been on hand to comfort me about Missy, or my Dad about Otto?

No, no. I can't think about any of that. Not now.

I fish in my pocket for my phone, but of course it's not there. I must have left it in the dining room, on the table. It doesn't matter.

I know I am going through the motions.

Even if Jack decided to keep his mouth shut on my behalf, an ambitious detective looking for promotion would not have to dig very deep in my file. What are the odds of me being the surviving victim of not one, but two random attacks in my home that left both men in my life dead? The police would call me an accessory and say I had obstructed justice over Dean's murder, as well. They would be right and I would go to prison too.

I won't be calling the police this time.

I can't.

What could I say to them? It's bad for both of us whatever way I serve it. Steve wasn't like Dean. He was a good guy; he'd never hurt anyone in his life. There could be no nasty gangster-types looking to make good on debts. Steve didn't live on the fringes, there wasn't anything remotely dodgy about him. The nearest Steve ever got to breaking the law was watching old *Justified* re-runs. He always enjoyed Boyd Crowder getting one over on US Marshall Raylan Givens.

I must do something, but I'm not sure what. The idea of covering up my son's crime is grotesque. Steve didn't deserve to go out like that; no one does. Jack deserves to face the long arm of the law, whether he's my flesh and blood or not.

As soon as this thought flits through my mind, I shut it down. If I tell the truth — or plead mercy for Jack for killing my boyfriend — I know the inevitable result. My son will throw me under the bus about Dean in return for my betrayal.

We will both end up in jail.

I blink and the clock has leapt forwards again. It is dark outside. Real life floods back in: the streetlamps have turned on; orange light dapples on my bedroom floor. I can hear the roar and see the flashing lights of aeroplanes in the night sky over London. There's laughter from the street as people cut through our street, making their way into Camden, to bars and clubs. I remember it's Friday night.

I feel something click inside me.

How quickly a brain re-knits its reality. I marvel at how I've already accepted I will be disposing of Steve's remains. I don't know how I will do it yet, but I will.

I need to do something about the mess downstairs; in my life. I can't just leave it. I can't just abandon my boy and let him go to jail.

I have to save him, this time.

CHAPTER TEN

Downstairs, Jack is in the living room. He's seated on the end of the coffee table nearest the television, far too close to the screen, zoned out like he would as a little boy.

It's some YouTube show. His gaze follows the two impossibly clean-cut American young guys on screen. They mix all kinds of gross combinations in a bowl and then dare each other to eat them. When one refuses, the other dumps it over his head in penalty.

I leave Jack to it. I scurry into the dining room, keeping my eyes averted from all the blood and Steve's corpse. I don't want to see the horror of his ruined eye, the dead flesh where once life flowed like electricity. I know that if I look upon his body again, I will be fixated by everything I've lost.

Like my father always recommended, I lock it down in that box in my mind. Steve and the imaginary ballerina can twirl around in there together for all eternity. It is all I can do as I struggle to pull my reeling thoughts together.

I need to concentrate.

The dining room has a bay window, looking directly on to the street. Relief surges through me as I take in the closed blinds. No one could have seen what happened from the road. Thank God.

I leave, peeking through the hall window next. I look at my watch: just after nine. The streetlamps illuminate hanging baskets and immaculate front lawns, shining off car roofs that cost almost as much as my house.

Ours is the shabbiest in the row. Dad bought it years ago, long before Camden was gentrified. These days the houses on my street are owned mostly by bankers, lawyers and other well-heeled professionals with more money in the bank than I can comprehend. Across the way I see a dog walker in a suit wander past, an elderly Alsatian loping after him. A group of young men in their early twenties amble past, their best shirts on, no coats, arms drawn to their sides to the beat the cold evening.

Life goes on. It always does.

My house is end of terrace. I'm not concerned about my immediate neighbour. Mr Chaudhry lives with his middle-aged architect daughter Rupinder, but she goes to the pub around the corner every night between seven and ten. She told me once she goes alone, just to preserve her sanity; she reads the paper and drinks shandy. Sometimes she just stares at the wall, she said.

I can understand why: Mr Chaudhry is a cantankerous old man, as well as very deaf. He won't wear a hearing aid. As usual, I can hear his television booming through the wall. It's the shopping channel. A bomb could have gone off in my dining room and he'd be none the wiser.

There are two student houses on our road. Buy-to-let millionaire landlords have rented them out to young people living it large on the Bank of Mum and Dad. They drive BMWs, wear designer clothes and smoke enough weed to make Bob Marley blush, sometimes right out in the street. Like proper old-school students, they let their recycling boxes overflow and they never put their wheely bins away.

My dad was always complaining about it. He said leaving the bins in the way of the pavement obstructed the route for disabled people and women with prams. He got into a shouting match with one group of girls from number 74 and was very put out when they yelled, 'Okay, Boomer!' at him every time they saw him after that. But those girls are always out on the town or stoned. They won't be lingering in the street.

Their other student compadres from the other shared house won't have seen anything, either. They're all boys and don't so much as open their curtains. Occasionally I see them emerge for university classes, blinking as their eyes adjust to the light, like trolls clawing their way up the embankment from under their bridge. Otherwise, they're locked in their house gaming, answering the door only for Deliveroo drivers.

My neighbours directly over the road are more of a concern. Celia and Jim Pengelly are in their late sixties. Jim had been a postman; Celia a teacher. They're the last of the old-timer Camden residents, like Dad had been.

They're also super nosy.

It's Jim more than Celia; he has an uncanny knack of knowing *stuff about stuff* when it comes to other people. It was him who knew number 55's husband had left her to 'find himself' in India; or that the eldest son from number 68 had killed himself. Everyone knew my dad had died suddenly too, without me telling anyone, which I put down to Jim. Maybe it's all the years he was a postman. Or maybe it's because Celia doesn't let Jim smoke in the house or even in the garden, which means he ends up doing it out on the pavement under the streetlamp.

I'm relieved a second time when I see Celia and Jim's car is missing from outside their house. There's only street parking here, like so many London suburbs. Just as I think this, I see the telltale headlights of their car, like I've conjured them into being.

I draw the curtains in the hall before they see me at the window. The last thing I need is Celia spotting me and trying to bring something round. She's done that before: casseroles; a book for Jack; a bottle of wine for me. She seems to think there's a connection between us, because we're not like all the other rich toffs on the road. It's been even worse since

Dad died; every time she looks at us, I can feel her pity radar go off.

I used to think her concern was sweet, but now?

She and Jim are a potential threat.

I turn on my heel and clatter back up to the airing cupboard on the landing. I pull down some old plastic sheets I'd last used when I redecorated the front room. Gathering them in my arms, I take them back down to the dining room and kneel on the floor, spreading them out on the laminate flooring.

Consumed with practicalities for the past few minutes, the knowledge of what's happened cuts through me again as my gaze falls on poor, dead Steve. As I feared, a deluge of feelings overwhelms me for a moment, making me gasp with pain and loss. Memories of our time together and things that never had the chance to happen shimmer in my mind.

Steve had given me so much hope for the future; he'd been my second chance. After Dean, I'd always felt I wasn't deserving of a real relationship; that marriage and happiness was something other people could have, but not me. It had been irrelevant, not even on my radar. Before Steve I'd muddled through life, but he'd made me see what was possible.

It's all been snatched away, by the one person I'd loved since I'd felt his tiny limbs move inside me.

Jack.

I lean forward like I've been punched in the belly, emitting a low, anguished howl. My pulse thumps in my temples and my vision wavers. My heart jumps around in my ribcage like a trapped bird.

Thoughts of running away clamour around my mind again. I must be insane to think I can get away with this? I'll be jumping at shadows for the rest of my life, unable to breathe.

I should ring the police, confess.

I've never been in trouble with the law before. I could tell them I freaked out. A good solicitor might be able to get me off. I probably live next to one. I could go out into the road and shout my problem into the air. Seconds later a bunch of them would crowd around me, competing for the case. Something like this is bound to be career-making.

Hell, maybe I could remortgage the house and get one good enough to get Jack off the hook, too? It's said that if you throw enough money at a case, you can buy justice.

Yet I know there's no way I can raise enough capital. I have credit cards for big purchases, but the limit on them wouldn't pay even a retainer on one of the capital's best solicitors. What I'd told Jack about my dad's estate not being sorted yet is true. Even if it was, my house is not in a good enough state to sell. No solicitor worth his or her salt would take us on for anything other than a guilty plea. Jack was unprovoked; his crime violent and bloody. He is guilty. He would be going away for a long time.

I can't let it happen.

I sit back on my heels, forcing my thoughts of mine and Steve's lost life together away. I must focus on the things that need doing.

Though my broken mind can't comprehend how much time has passed since Jack did what he did, I realise it must have been hours. There's now a congealed dark crimson pool on the laminate below the table, where Steve bled out from his eye. There's more smeared on the floor where he hit it as his body slumped from his chair. I don't have to touch it to know it will be gummy, penetrating the floor covering.

Before I tackle that, I need to move Steve.

Taking a deep breath, I spread the plastic sheet out on the floor, next to Steve. Fixing my gaze on the wall, I grab him by his shoulder and hip and push as hard as I can. He rolls with much less ease than I anticipate, but finally he is face down on the sheet. Relieved I no longer must look at his poor face, I wrap Steve in the plastic sheets, winding liberal spools of parcel tape around him. By the time I have finished, he looks like a plastic mummy.

When I am done, I regard the man-shaped bundle. I need to move him, but where? The shock means it's difficult to connect my thought processes. I am operating almost entirely on instinct. Despite having no destination in mind yet, I grab the big knot at Steve's head and yank.

Predictably, he does not shift; they don't call it 'dead weight' for nothing. After five or six minutes of huffing and puffing, I have only managed to pull a muscle in my shoulder. Steve hasn't moved at all.

'Jack!'

On the third yell, my boy skulks through. He blinks at me as he takes the odd scene in. I know I look a state, sweaty and half-crazed. I stand over the body, one foot on either side, my hair in disarray. I watch as Jack rubs his fingers across his thumbs in that idiosyncratic way of his, just like he did the night Dean died.

'What are you doing?' he says at last.

'What does it look like I'm doing!' I bark. 'Help me move him.'

Something akin to emotion flashes across Jack's face at last: relief?

I can't be sure. He must have been sitting in the front room, worrying about me turning him in. Weary frustration and hurt courses through me at this thought. How could my own son doubt me? I am a good mother, no matter what the likes of Ms Heath think.

'Where to?'

The solution leaps to my lips like it was my plan all along. 'The cellar.'

It's a little bunker room one storey down from ground floor level. All the houses on our road have them. They're dark, dingy and cold, their floors lined with red brick. Many of them have been converted into games rooms and dens, guest bedrooms or basement apartments.

Ours is full of junk: boxes of photo albums and keepsakes; fishing rods and equipment; an old chest freezer Dad used to keep his bait in when he went fishing up at the canal. Dad had never bothered renovating our cellar, despite my gentle chiding that it's prime real estate. We could have built outside steps up to the pavement; he could have let it out to a young professional starting out. He said he didn't like the idea of strangers hearing us crashing about upstairs. I'd been mad at the time, but I'm glad of his stubbornness now.

Even with Jack's help, moving Steve is an epic undertaking. We're only able to move him, bit by bit, panting with effort as we go. When we make it out into the hall, Jack opens the skinny door under the stairs, pulling the cord to the bare bulb. It illuminates the perilously steep, stone stairs down to the cellar.

My heart falls into my boots as I see how far down it is. Getting Steve down there will take all night. Jack must have read this on my face because he grabs my end of the sheet as well. He utters a roar and before I can stop him, hefts the body towards the stairs.

I wince as it slides down the steps and lands at the bottom with an ungainly *ka-dunk*. Shaken and horrified, I regard my son, my mouth opening and closing.

'Why did you do that?' I splutter.

'Just trying to help.'

He shrinks away from me in anticipation. He is right to: wild fury surfaces again, flooding through me as I grab my boy round the collar. I'm much too small and weak to hurt him; he could shake me off without any issues whatsoever. But Jack's eyes widen in fright at this uncustomary touch from me. He allows me to push him back against the hall wall.

'You fucking psycho!' I hiss, banging his head against the plaster.

'*You're* the fucking psycho!' Jack hollers, pushing me away.

I lurch backwards, gasping for breath.

Jack flinches, like he expects me to strike him; I realise my arm is in the air, ready to do it. Shocked, I catch sight of myself in the hall mirror.

What the hell am I doing?

Jack is right. My son might be a killer but I *am* the psycho, or at least doing a good impression of one. My eyes are wild with panic and anger. My face is flushed and red. My shoulders heave and there's sweat patches under the arms of my dress. I tamp my rage down, trying to still the adrenaline coursing through my veins.

I can't be around Jack right now.

'Put him in Grandad's bait freezer.'

'It's full of bait . . . ?' Jack protests.

'Well, take it out!' I cut in. 'It's not like he's going to be using it, is it?'

Jack opens his mouth to argue again but thinks better of it. He slinks off to the cellar. I stand there, staring at the space he's vacated, listening to my ragged gasps. It creates a litany in my head, as words repeat over and over: *this can't be happening*.

Yet it is. There is no escaping it.

Jack might have put the deadly events in motion this evening, but I picked them up and ran with them. I have covered up my boyfriend's murder. For real. I am now an official accessory. As this occurs, another thought swims to the surface.

Got to keep busy.

I march into the kitchen. In contrast to the rest of the street, it's at the back, along with the dining room. Dad had remodelled himself, plumbing everything in when my mother was still alive. I fetch the mop bucket and fill it full of hot water from the tap, adding a liberal dose of bleach and some bicarbonate of soda.

I drag it to the dining room and pour it on the blood-stain on the floor. It fizzes up straight away, prickling my nostrils. As I wait for the solution to break it down, I shake out a black plastic bin liner and shove the remaining food, the tablecloth, even the centrepiece into the bin. I transport all the empty plates and glasses to the dishwasher.

When I return I attack the big stain with gusto, but as I stand back, there's still a suspicious dark mark. I could scrub it all day and still be left with a stain that might as well broadcast *MAN MURDERED HERE* in flashing neon.

Now what?

The laminate will have to come up. Back in the kitchen, I open the 'useful drawer', the second one down from the cutlery. We shove all kinds of things in there, from Sellotape and Blu Tack, to takeaway chopsticks and the spirit level.

Sure enough, I find Dad's Stanley knife too. I'm relieved; I don't want to have to go down to the cellar to find his toolbox. Half an hour later and I've managed to pull up all the flooring in the dining room. I discover the blood has not made its way into the concrete beneath. The table is easy to lift; I chuck the chairs out in the hallway. I catch myself feeling momentarily grateful Jack didn't kill Steve in the living room, where there is a deep shag carpet.

I roll up the laminate, dragging it into the back garden, the dark stain facing inwards. I go back inside, grabbing all the cloths and sponges I used to clean up the blood. Growing up as the only child of an outdoorsy man, I was forced to accompany my father to his allotment in Camden during my childhood and sometimes my teen years too. He grew vegetables and flowers, but also loved to just sit out in nature, a tinny in hand and talking to the other gardeners. When I had cheeked him or come in late, he'd make me clean the shed and burn the garden waste, so I know how to light a decent bonfire.

I dump my macabre collection on the ground, covering it with a bunch of other detritus, just in case any of my neighbours look out their windows on to my garden. A couple of palettes; a couple of branches that have fallen from the long-dead apple tree; an old, mouldering box and the remnants of the fireworks Jack set alight in November and just abandoned. He never can be bothered to clean up after himself.

Like always, I have to do it.

I check for the direction of the wind and moments later, watch the small pile go up. The lino curls and burns quicker than I think it will, its plastic surface melting and emitting an acrid smoke. I don't want to attract undue attention; it's late. I don't bother waiting for it to be consumed in its entirety; as long as it's destroyed, that's all that matters.

Coughing, I pour another bucket of water on the blackened mess. I resolve to shovel it into black bin liners and take it all the dump later, once it's cooled down.

Have I forgotten anything?

Steve's car jumps into my consciousness.

I run through the hall and see his coat hanging on the peg. Are his keys in there? I pat it down, feeling the *clink* of metal in the left pocket. I pull out a Simpsons keyring, his car fob. Thank God. I wouldn't have wanted to have to unwrap Steve to take these from his jeans pocket.

I open the front door, pressing the fob as I go. I hear Jack appear at the top of stairs to the cellar. In the street, Steve's car *chirrups* as I press the fob button. I would have been able to identify it without spotting its flashing lights. It's an ordinary black Renault five or six years old, conspicuous next to the flash Porsches fresh off the forecourt.

'Mum, where are you going?'

I grab one of Jack's oversized hoodies from the coat pegs before I leave the house. I pull it on, putting the hood up. It's not the perfect disguise, but it will have to do.

'Clearing up your mess.'

'Mum, please . . . !'

I close the door on him.

CHAPTER ELEVEN

I'm halfway to 1939 before I realise my mistake. I can't just return Steve's car to the road outside his flat and place of work. A person or camera might see me, then I'll be sunk. Even if they don't see my face, it's clear I am a woman from my size. Steve was so tall, he towered over me. It would not take a genius to figure out who I could be, especially as Steve is bound to have told Zane, his assistant, he was going to mine last night.

The clock on the dash reads *3.41 AM*. It's now Saturday, a primetime day in the café world. It's also one of Steve's (only) busy times. Less than five hours from now, Steve is supposed to open 1939 for early morning joggers and yummy mummies going to yoga. When he fails to materialise, presumably Zane will go upstairs and check for him at his flat. He will obviously find it empty, so logic dictates he will check for his car. If he finds it, he might guess something is up?

It's a small risk, but one I cannot afford to take.

Unable to think of a solution for what to do with the car just yet, I drive around Camden for twenty minutes in the burgeoning light as morning breaks. I end up abandoning the vehicle two or three streets away from the Atkinson Film

Project, on a vacant lot off another well-to-do street. A board says the site is being developed for yet more luxury flats and a cinema underneath, but it's faded and dated 2019. When so many wealthy London residents get out of town for the weekend, I feel confident the car will stay under the radar for now. I can think about what to do with it later.

Muscles aching and stiff, I walk back to my house. Jack has not waited up for me, so I fall into bed. I manage to sleep for a few fitful hours, then drag myself up again and under the shower. I turn the dial as high as I can stand, trying to get the steam to blast away my guilt and anxiety.

My heart breakdances in my chest. I can feel my pulse working in my temples; my jaw clenches so tight it's painful. I massage my skull as best I can, but it's no good. Tears spring up for the first time and pour down my cheeks, indistinguishable from the shower's flow. After a good ten minutes of this, I turn the water off and stare at the tiles for another uneven length of time before dragging myself out to dry off and dress.

I check in on Jack as I make my way back downstairs. My son is still asleep, tangled up in his bedsheets, his sleeping expression seemingly untroubled and angelic. Could it be that killing is second nature to him, now?

No. It can't be.

This is all just a horrible mistake.

He didn't mean it.

I trudge back to the kitchen. I feel like a giant hand is pressing down on me from above, pushing me into the mud and making me move in slow motion. I attempt to eat something, but chewing and swallowing seem beyond me.

I sit in the bay window of the kitchen, staring out at the back garden and the blackened ruins of the laminate flooring. I know I should shovel it all in bags right now, but **my bones scream with tiredness.**

My phone vibrates with a text message about ten. It simply reads *YO WHERE STEVE*? I don't have the number stored, but I know immediately it's Zane. He's the only person I've ever spoken to who uses the term 'yo' unironically, plus it's too much of a coincidence. Steve must have left my number with him just in case; it's exactly the kind of thing a straight-up guy like him would do.

This forces me to consider where Steve's own phone could be. I still need to dispose of it, along with his jacket.

Hi Zane, I tap back, trying to remember exactly when I drove his car away from mine. *He not at the café? He left mine about two or three this morning.*

NO. NEVERMIND.

I try not to let Zane's brevity freak me out. I remind myself he's always been a young man of few words. He can't be suspicious of me. Why would he be? Strapping men of forty years old like Steve don't usually get spirited away in the night when they go to their girlfriend's houses. Zane will be telling himself that Steve has gone for a run and lost track of time; or that he had an emergency and forgotten to tell him.

Y'know, *normal* stuff.

The problem of what to do with Steve's body weighs heavy. I grab my phone to Google, before stopping. I know from TV cop dramas the police take devices and comb through search histories. There's ways to check this, even if you have deleted your browser history. I'm just an archives assistant. Should it come to it, I have no believable or plausible reason I can tell police for searching for ways to dispose of a body online . . . That's not the truth, anyway.

I grab a notebook and pen instead. Writing things down and keeping records has always soothed me. I've got volumes of diaries and journals upstairs dating back to when I was a little girl. It's one of the reasons I decided to go back to university after Dean's death and why I love being an archives assistant.

The pen poised over the page, no inspiration flows. I flip through my random memory banks for something of use. Two words that jump out of nowhere, possibly from another TV crime show: *BODY DUMP*??

I scrawl them on the white paper. That's right . . . I recall reading or watching something about a mafia crime family who chopped their victims into pieces, then paid off road workers to intern the remains into motorways and bridges. But I don't have the stomach to chop up Steve. Even if I did, I don't have the capital or contacts to conceal bits of him in various construction sites.

More snippets of information jump into my head as my pen digs into the page. There was a serial killer who used to dissolve bodies in acid . . . But I would have to buy a big bathtub or vat to put the body in; then huge quantities of said acid. My job pays peanuts and because my dad's estate is not settled yet, my finances are not great. This means I would have to use a credit card to manage it, which in turn would be a big fat red flag with authorities.

Another dead end. Literally.

I stab the pen into the notebook, breaking it. Ink smears across the page, which infuriates me. I utter a shriek and then grasp the book in both hands, tearing the whole thing almost in two. I throw it straight at the sink, where it lands in the stagnant water and submerges like a capsized ship.

Swearing to myself, I rescue it from the water, holding it between my finger and thumb. It's turned to mulch, covered in dish soap and scum, utterly ruined. I shove it all in the bin.

My fury spurs me into action. I grab my own car keys this time. There is one place I can go where I can come up with some answers, I am sure of it. It's completely analogue, because it exists in meat space, AKA real life.

Leaving no trace.

CHAPTER TWELVE

Too late, I catch sight of Aaron as I draw up outside the Atkinson Film Project. Shading his eyes from the sun, he's waiting outside the grandiose building with a slightly puzzled expression on his face, like he can't believe it's closed, even on a Saturday. As he spots me, he points at me, face split into a wide grin. He waves like an excited child as I turn off the engine and clamber out of the car. I groan.

Damn it.

'Natalie!' Aaron calls.

I can't be bothered to correct him. I don't return his smile as I fish in my pocket for the archive front door keys.

'We're closed, Aaron.'

'You said I could come back?'

'Yes.' I grit my teeth. 'But it's Saturday.'

'Is it?'

He seems genuinely surprised to hear it's the weekend. He's wearing bright orange trainers and is head-to-toe in neon paint-spattered stonewashed denim. His cap is set at a jaunty angle, sideways. On anyone else, such an ensemble would look ridiculous, yet somehow he looks like he just walked out of a Benetton catalogue dated 1993, in a *good* way.

I roll my eyes when he doesn't move. 'Come back Monday?'

'Come on, we're both here now.'

He flutters his impossibly long lashes at me. I'm so weary and stressed, I almost bawl him out. Then I realise I am looking at a gift. Spending time with Aaron today will mean an alibi outside the family. He can confirm I'm not with Steve today, when people start looking for him. Maybe I can get Jack to come down too, show his face. I remind myself too Aaron is a true crime podcaster, probably here to look for more information about Dennis Nilsen. I can pick this young man's brains for solutions on what to do about the problem of Steve's body during ordinary, relevant conversation. I would be crazy to turn him away.

I flash Aaron an indulgent smile and open the door for him.

'Oh . . . Go on, then.'

To my chagrin, Aaron seems to sense something in my abrupt change of mind. He tilts his head, assessing me. Too late, I realise I should have stuck by my original thought. Aaron thinks of himself as an investigative journalist. I must be full-on fruit loop crazy to invite him into my life right now. I've made a huge mistake.

'Everything okay?' he says.

That dark fury threatens to bubble up again. I want to scream it. *No I am not bloody all right! My son just murdered my boyfriend and I need you as an alibi for when the shit hits the fan!*

In contrast to my internal fury, I fix Aaron with a raised eyebrow and shrug. I cross the threshold, blocking his way in. I could win an Oscar with my performance.

'Fine, don't come in then.'

This bluff seems to distract Aaron from his hunch. His eyes widen.

'No . . . no! I want to come in.' Aaron gives me that boy band grin again, 'You're really helping me out. Sorry.'

I step aside, allowing him into the building. 'I know. Coffee?'

Leaving Aaron digging through boxes (once I've relieved him of his phone again), I skulk off to my office and fire off a quick text to Jack, telling him to come down to the project as soon as possible.

His reply arrives almost instantly: *Why?* x

Jack always signs his texts with a kiss. I've always thought it sweet; there can't be many teen boys who do so. But last night makes me wonder if everything I have taken for granted about my son has been a lie. Now I wonder if he is just mimicking the kisses I leave at the end of texts; perhaps he feels nothing for me at all? Maybe I have been nothing but a provider, a handy person to have in his corner. Nothing more, nothing less.

I shove these unwelcome thoughts back down and lock them away.

Because you need to show your face out and about after last night.
I don't get it? x

Just get down here, I type back. Then, because I feel guilty: xxx

I take two coffees into the archives. Aaron has taken off his denim jacket; underneath is yet another tight T-shirt. He bends over, rummaging through a bin of paper, his designer briefs peeking out over his belt.

The bin is full of shreds, balled-up papers and torn-up strips. I fight the urge to chuckle, despite myself. Dorothy was such a hoarder; she threw nothing away.

'That's just paper waste.'

Aaron just grunts and continues. I leave his coffee by the big metal bin for him, which he lets go cold as he physically gets into the bin. About thirty minutes after that, he surfaces, face triumphant. In his hand, a shred of paper with a large, looped signature. As I accept it from him, I know what name it will be.

'Dennis Nilsen,' I say, agog.

'The very same.'

As I wait, I Google 'Dennis Nilsen, signature' and am taken to a variety of news articles, websites and eBay listings. It would seem there's quite a few articles pertaining to the killer online, all better quality and more complete than the paper shred I hold in my hand.

I scan the rest of the paper piece, but there's nothing else legible. I turn it over, but there's different writing on the other side. I recognise the chicken scratch scrawl immediately as Dorothy's. It reads 'fruit', 'onions', 'coffee' before getting cut off by the shredder again. Whatever Dennis Nilsen had seen fit to write to our founder about, she hadn't thought it important enough to keep; she'd written a shopping list on the back of it. Interesting.

'What does this prove?'

Aaron surfaces from the shreds again. His brow furrows, as if he'd forgotten I'm there. There's sweat on his top lip.

'Honestly? Not much yet. We already know Dorothy and Dennis knew each other, from the photo.' He throws his arms up in the air, sending spirals of paper in all directions. 'Two of Camden's most infamous residents . . . him, the serial killer. Her, the eccentric spinster film pioneer. If I could just find something that definitively links the two of them somehow, that would be great for my podcast.'

'Maybe they were in on it together?' I muse as he dives back in. His enthusiasm is contagious. More than that, I welcome the distraction from the horror of last night.

'Wouldn't be unheard of,' Aaron's voice echoes inside the big metal bin. 'Killer couples are a thing. Ian Brady and Myra Hindley; Fred and Rosemary West; Bonnie and Clyde . . . Aha!'

He popped up again like a gerbil, presenting me with another shred. It reads 'Darling Dorothy' in Nilsen's distinctive, looped hand. He grins at me, eyes sparkling.

'Doesn't exactly sound like a business relationship, does it?'

I don't allow myself to get carried away, this time. '*If* it's from the same letter.'

Aaron dives back in.

Jack breezes into the archives over an hour later. I introduce the two boys properly this time. Aaron is warm and friendly, proffering a hand to shake.

Jake stares at Aaron's hand like he's not sure what to do, then something appears to click inside him and he grins back, taking it. It's a momentary lapse, but one that seems illuminating, not to mention shockingly obvious to me.

It could be the shock of last night, or maybe I am finally understanding Jack was always on the edge of existence. Maybe Jack has never been quite connected to everyone else, and just pretending he was? I'd been angry that people hadn't given my son the benefit of the doubt, but perhaps I'd given it to him too much? Do all killers' parents feel the same way? Maybe.

It's not like there's a support group.

Our afternoon is productive. Grateful for the distraction, I ask Aaron question after question as we work, especially about what Nilsen did with the bodies. The podcaster is only too happy to answer. It would seem serial killers and their practices is not just his special interest, but the obsession that takes over his every waking moment.

'Nilsen did the same as Joachim Kroll.'

I don't know who Joachim Kroll is. 'Oh?'

Aaron looks at me as if I am stupid, or mad, or both.

'The German plumber? He killed at least fourteen people, including kids, between 1955 and 1976. Kroll would flush parts of his dismembered victims down the toilet: small bones, flesh, organs. When the system backed up in his building, the people called in to fix it discovered it was clogged with human guts.'

I grimace. 'And Nilsen did similar?'

'Yup. Got caught the same way, too. Plumber came in, found suspicious bones. Nilsen tried to say they were from a chicken, but it was all over.'

Well, at least I know what *not* to do, though I'd already decided I couldn't chop poor Steve up. The acid tang of nausea floods through me at just the thought of it. Bright spots loom in at me momentarily. I avert my eyes from Jack. Neither of the boys seem to be aware of my growing discomfort.

'That wasn't the only way Nilsen disposed of bodies, though.' Aaron unwraps yet another ball of paper, checks both sides, then discards it. 'He also put bodies on the bonfire.'

I wrinkle my nose in distaste. How the hell had Nilsen got away with burning bodies in a built-up area like Muswell Hill? Even allowing for fewer people in the neighbourhood forty years ago, the stench must have carried for miles.

'Nilsen also hid bodies under floorboards.'

I absorb this titbit without comment. Again, that must have been smelly? Or perhaps Nilsen dried the bodies out somehow first, liked cured meat . . . I suppress a shudder.

The more I learned from Aaron about serial killers over the decades, the more I appreciate the supposed 'golden era' — where terrible things apparently *didn't* happen like they do today — never existed. That is cold comfort for someone like me whose son has killed two people before the age of eighteen though.

Absorbing Aaron's prattle, I thought over our options. Steve would be better off left in the freezer long term, though I don't like that idea. Absurdly, the idea of his poor corpse being in such a cold place disturbs me almost as much as him being killed in front of me by my teenage son.

I'd always thought with the flippancy of the living and healthy, when you're dead, you're dead. I've never been a spiritual person, so I'm surprised how much I want — no, *need* — Steve to be able to rest in peace. Being squished into a chest freezer in our basement seems like the absolute antithesis of that.

Aaron spends a similarly productive afternoon with us; I am grateful for the distraction. He discovers three more pieces of what he believes is a whole letter from Dennis Nilsen to Dorothy Atkinson. I have to admit that Aaron's suspicions seem accurate. It *does* seem like it could be a love letter.

Darling Dorothy . . . How I wish . . . those red lips . . .
Without you, there is no me. Dennis

'I thought Nilsen was gay?' I muse as I pin the shreds to a board.

'Love takes many forms, not just sexual desire.'

Aaron raises his eyebrows as his gaze meets mine. Across the room, Jack gives us both a blank stare over his phone screen. He'd collapsed there, bored and scrolling, after just half an hour of helping us sort through the tattered paper.

The podcaster plunges back into the big bin, still talking.

'Besides, it wouldn't be the first time a bad guy's homosexuality and deviancy were conflated to suit the dominant narrative, would it? We're all more than who we have sex with, even serial killers.'

I roll my eyes skywards but concede. Aaron might sound like a film studies degree textbook, but he has a point. Everything I know about Nilsen has been filtered first through sensationalist tabloid headlines, local gossip and murder myth-making via true crime documentary and podcasts. The latter is Aaron's domain too though, so he has no business being quite so lofty, but I let it go.

Darkness pushes its fingers through the big drawing room window. Orange streetlamps switch on outside, reminding us we should all go home. Aaron seems disappointed at having to leave the alleged love letter at the archives but agrees to it. Without my cooperation, his personal project would go kaput, after all.

Unfortunately for Aaron, too much of the letter is still missing to be truly damning for Dorothy. I'm not certain all the pieces we've found are even from the same one, but I don't want to take the wind out of Aaron's sails. He breezes out of the archives with a big smile on his face and a promise to come back on Monday, 'in the AM'.

'Well, he's annoying,' Jack declares as the door shuts after Aaron.

Biting back a tirade, I'm shocked by the ferocious rage still coursing through me as I regard my only child. I never would have countenanced feeling this way about him.

I want to tell Jack that Aaron is a *normal* bloke, with *normal* interests and pursuits. Sure, Aaron is not an orthodox kind of guy. It's clear from his dress and manner he does whatever he wants. It's also obvious those interests and pursuits are not exactly traditional either . . . That said, researching crime and having your own podcast about serial killers beats actually *being* one, hands down.

But I say none of this. Even so, my anger and resentment must be radiating off me like heat because Jack shrinks away from me, as he realises he's said something wrong.

'Let's go home,' I hiss, stalking out ahead of him.

Jack scurries after me.

CHAPTER THIRTEEN

After making Aaron our (unwitting) alibi on Saturday, we spent the whole of Sunday scrubbing the house from top to bottom. I made Jack hand over the clothes and trainers he'd been wearing on Friday night, which I burned with mine out in the garden. He'd cried when he saw his Air Jordans go up in smoke, the most emotion I'd seen him express in the wake of Steve's death.

Watching the flames, I'd zoned out. Steve and Dean's faces shimmered in the heart of the conflagration; my father's too. I wondered what he would think of me, hiding his grandson's heinous nature for a second time. Jack moved closer, his hand finding mine.

'Thanks, Mum.'

I'd almost flipped out, wrenched my hand away. His touch repulsed me. Then shame flooded through me next. What kind of mother was I, rejecting my only child in his hour of need? I'd forced myself to smile and face him, pushing brightness into my tone.

'What are mums for, hey?'

Jack had retired to his room to play video games. I'd sat in front of the TV evening news, the sound down but watching lurid headlines pass by: *HOMELESS MEN*

ATTACKED IN LONDON. The world's going to hell in a handcart, as my Dad would've said.

I felt so helpless: surely it's just a matter of time before someone realises Steve is missing and that I was the last to see him alive? In my mind's eye I can see blue lights flashing; lurid tabloid headlines; me, forced to watch Jack being led away, my own hands cuffed behind my back.

No . . . No. Never.

No one was taking my precious boy away.

I turned the TV off and put my phone down. I'd pulled a notebook from my bag, a pen. Both had been a Christmas gift from Maria; she'd had my name embossed on both. I'd been saving them for a special occasion, but then this surely counted as one.

Oh God, Maria.

What would she think of all this? She's the closest — perhaps only — real friend I have. She'd been such an exceptional mentor, encouraging me and ensuring I have all I need to do my job well. I can't bear the thought of disappointing her. As she appears in my thoughts, I can see her, nodding over my performance targets.

'Such attention to detail,' she'd said, 'you think of everything.'

'It's nothing,' I'd said, squirming in my seat. I wasn't used to compliments, even years after Dean's toxic influence.

'Credit where it's due,' Maria had instructed me, 'you've shown you're prepared to make the hard decisions. I like it.'

A sense of peace swells through me. Maria had been right. I have what it takes to ensure Jack can move on from this terrible mistake. I will take on the burden, so he might live the life he was meant to. I jot down list after list, trying to imagine all the worst-case scenarios that could happen next in a bid to avoid them.

Jack could tell someone.

(No, I would make sure he wouldn't.)

I could tell someone.

(As if!)

Someone could have seen us.

(I was certain no one had.)

There could be evidence.

(I'd burned it all.)

Someone might know Steve was coming here the night he died.

(Circumstantial.)

I'd thought of everything.

(Hadn't I?)

On Monday morning, I drag Jack from his pit and chivvy him through breakfast. He doesn't want to go to school. I can't blame him. The thought of having to go to work when everything has changed forever, (not to mention the fact Steve is still in the freezer in the basement), seems ludicrous. Jack glowers across the table at me as we eat in silence.

I pretend not to notice, scrolling instead through my calendar app. I note Jack has an appointment with his bereavement counsellor this afternoon after school. With a shamed twinge, I realise I have not thought of my father once this past weekend. There hasn't been time. The problem of what to do about Steve has occupied my every waking moment for the past forty-eight hours.

'You've got Cheryl today.'

'I know.' My son growls.

Cheryl is a tall, willowy woman in her late forties with the high cheekbones of a model. Dressed in designer clothes and expensive scent wafting after her, she reminds me of Cate Blanchett. Fear skitters down my spine at this unfortunate timing.

Might Jack confess to Cheryl? If he did, what would she do about it? I'm aware there's such a thing as patient confidentiality, but I'm pretty sure the therapists' ethics code does not cover murder. Jack seems to guess my thought patterns in that spooky way of his.

'I'm not stupid, you know.'

I feign confusion, though I know I am not fooling him.

'I won't say anything.'

Hurt, Jack shakes his head at me and rises from the table. Turning his back on me, he takes his bowl to the sink. He does not wait for a lift. He grabs his coat and his bag and sweeps out of the kitchen.

Real life rushes back in like the tide, buffeting me along like a piece of driftwood. In a daze I travel to work, wandering into the archives like an aimless ghost.

Maria runs around, inefficient and chaotic as ever, stuffing nooks and crannies where she thinks rats could be living. I let her get on with it. Her stream of invectives against the estate, the lawyers and all vermin in the universe washes over me. I hear none of it.

Monday drags on, every minute seeming like an hour. A part of my brain seems to float above me, giving me a running commentary on everything I do. It needles at me, reminding me Steve is dead and Jack killed him, a never-ending loop.

The knowledge wells up like a malevolent geyser, about to blow. I don't dare open my mouth in case it all comes rushing out in all its horrible, gory detail. Just like Dean's domestic abuse all those years ago, I lock it away just like my father taught me.

'What do we say, when we're angry or scared?' he would counsel.

'Nothing,' I would reply, dutiful as ever.

'Good girl.' Dad would grin at me.

I had to tell by his eyes; his lips were always hidden by that bushy moustache of his. Like so many of his generation, he saw no benefit to letting emotions splurge everywhere. My mother had been a mercurial woman, prone to ill temper and stress; she'd never been satisfied with her lot and made sure Dad knew it every chance she got. Faced with continuous accusations, mockery and fury, it was no wonder Dad thought yelling or even talking stuff through solved nothing. He'd been a man of action who fixed problems with logic. When there was nothing to be done, he was of the opinion it was best to let it go.

Dad had never had such a big problem land on his lap, though. I might have created all kinds of issues for him, especially in my teen years after Mum had died, but they were *normal*. I took up smoking for one summer. I dyed my hair and painted my room black. I came in late, gave him cheek. I drank too much and ended up in A&E. Even taking up with a loser like Dean, dropping out of university first time around and having a kid instead was the usual kind of thing families up and down the country go through.

Your son killing your boyfriend . . . not so much.

At the Atkinson Film Project, I stare at the mosquito in amber on Maria's desk, a replica of the one from *Jurassic Park*. I feel trapped between two plains of consciousness, waiting for something to happen.

I am relieved when Aaron turns up at the archives mid-morning. He chatters on in that self-involved way of his, searching for more paper shreds in that big bin. That lunchtime Maria slams out of the archives twice, as is customary, returning for her bag that second time.

Still in a daze, I leave the archives after her, turning on to the street beyond. I wander past a number of takeaways and overflowing bins; a crocodile of school children holding hands; then two big fellas in puffer jackets in the middle of a drug deal.

I avert my eyes from all of it.

I find myself outside 1939. It's open, though it might as well not be. There's not a single person sitting down at any of the tables, even though it's lunchtime. Zane stands outside, leaning against the wall. A cigarette dangles from his lips like he thinks he is River Phoenix, though he's far too young to know who that was.

As I wander towards the café, he gives me a cursory nod. I flash him a smile I don't feel, but it makes something shift inside me. I power from nought to sixty, going from vacant to seemingly cheery and carefree.

'Hi, Zane. Steve up in the flat?'

The words have the effect I want. Zane's brow furrows as his own mental cogs start to whirr. 'I figured he was with you?'

'No, I told you in my text. He left mine in the early hours of Saturday.' I force myself to look concerned. 'Wait . . . are you telling me you haven't seen him for two days?'

I wince on the inside: my words sound wooden, manufactured.

I must be a better actress than I think because Zane looks worried. There is no need for me to say it's not like Steve to go AWOL. I don't know Zane, but he feels a kinship with Steve, that much is obvious. More guilt rankles through me. I'd given zero thought to the impact this could have on Zane. I'd assumed he was just an employee, but maybe they were friends too.

Oh, God.

I hold out my hand for his keys. 'Maybe he's ill, let me check in the flat.'

Zane throws his cigarette away. I understand he wants to check with me. He takes me up the steep stairs to Steve's cramped flat. He knocks on the door, then lets us both in.

The curtains still closed, it's dark in the poky little bachelor pad. The only light comes from a slit-like skylight. Like the other men in my life, Steve had never been houseproud. In the little kitchenette, there's dishes still in the sink. In the living-room area, his futon is still folded out, a tangle of sheets on top.

The door to the cupboard-like bathroom is open, the shower curtain pulled across. It's the only unseen space. Zane strides through and wrenches it back, like Steve might be playing hide 'n' seek. Empty.

'You checked it Saturday, right . . . Has anything changed?'

Zane's beady eyes flash around the small flat, trying to remember.

'I don't think so.'

'What about his car keys?'

Zane checks the hook on the wall near the microwave. 'Gone.'

'Maybe he went to see his sister,' I say, forcing authority into my tone. 'Let's check with her. Do you have her number?'

Zane shakes his head. He seems disinterested in the prospect of calling Steve's sister; we both know there's no way he would go anywhere without telling us. Even if it was an emergency, Steve is the type of guy to drop a text or call later within a few hours.

I take a deep, shaky breath. I don't want to have to ask Zane this, introduce this horrible thought to him.

I have to.

'How did Steve seem to you, on Friday?'

Zane blinks. 'He seemed fine. What about you?'

'Same as you. Fine.'

I pause long enough for the silence between us to stretch to breaking point. I know he understands the subtext of my question. I can see Zane wondering what he's missed. I can sense the growing disquiet coming off him in jagged waves.

I've already driven Steve's stashed car all the way from Camden to Beachy Head, parking it on a headland car park, the keys locked inside. I travelled back on the train from Eastbourne, paying cash and wearing one of Jack's hoodies to obscure my face in case of cameras. I've thought of everything, just like I always do.

'He's been pretty worried, lately,' he whispers at last, 'about the business . . . y'know. Not doing well.'

My stomach goes into free fall. There it is.

I arrest my guilt and banish it. Steve *has* to become a doomed statistic; another lost man who kept it all inside and broke down when society turned its back on him. I have no choice. Steve is gone now, there's nothing else I can do for him.

I must do this to save Jack.

I'd understood it would be difficult to tell this terrible lie, but I'd underestimated the effect Steve had on others. Unlike Dean, who'd slipped from others' consciousness in a blink, Steve's impact is much wider than I could have comprehended.

Self-reproach surges through me. I am destroying Zane to save Jack. But what else can I do? Steve's body can't be found and there's no other explanation I can think of that can account for his sudden disappearance.

Ten minutes later, I tell Zane I have to get back to work. Zane accompanies me back downstairs and asks me to call him the moment I hear from Steve; he promises to the same for me. Shame lodges in my throat, sharp like a fishbone. I nod and give him an awkward hug goodbye. I can feel Zane's skinny ribs pressed against me. I'm reminded again of how young he is. Not much older than Jack, perhaps a year or two. God.

When Steve's vehicle is inevitably found at such a notorious suicide spot, will news of his friend's death change Zane? Probably. I know from bitter experience with Dean how adverse life events as a young person can steer you off-course, into wild, crackling storms of mental pain and doubt. There are no right answers here though; only wrong ones.

It would be worse if Zane found out what really happened to Steve.

His friend and employer's last moments had been unexpected and violent, at the hands of a young boy filled with rage, hurt and confusion. Zane would never feel safe again. I must remember my deception protects him. I return to the archives, tears streaming down my cheeks. People on the street part around me like ants around an obstacle in their path.

I am alone, just like I've always been.

CHAPTER FOURTEEN

I watch through the front-room window as two officers, one male, one female, appear out of their vehicle. Though they are both in plain clothes and their car is unmarked, they exude officialdom. They are unmistakable.

Here we go.

It's Wednesday. Zane texted me that morning. I knew he wouldn't be able to call me; young people go out of their way to never speak on the phone. His message is typically brief. It is also in caps without punctuation, replete with an emoji of a crying face.

POLICE CAME IN THEY FOUND HIS CAR THEY WANT TO SEE YOU.

Not long after Zane's text, I'd received a call from a DI Tom Judd, asking to visit me at my home. I'd told Maria I had an emergency and she'd waved me off, eyes wide but no questions asked.

A strange sense of calm settles over me now as I regard the male officer move towards my front door. No, I'm not calm; I'm fatalistic. I realise what happens next will seal my fate. I have no choice but go with it.

As the doorbell rings, my brain resets. I must pull myself together, take stock. Thank God Jack is at school. I must get through this.

I *will* get through this.

In the hall mirror I look drawn and haggard, much older than my years. But I have been worried about my boyfriend, who went missing five days ago. Look too in control in a crisis and everyone points the finger, especially at women. We must look like shit in a crisis or everyone thinks we're involved. The news taught me that. Since I *am* involved, I must do whatever I can to keep the spotlight off me and Jack.

I wrench open the front door.

'Mrs Natasha Rose? I'm DI Judd.'

I just stand there, looking stressed and quiet as the male police officer flashes his warrant card, placing it in his jacket pocket in one smooth movement. He's a tall, thin man in his late forties with a stoop and a long neck. If he was an animal, he'd be a giraffe.

'This is my colleague, Sergeant Carina Martens.'

The woman steps forward now, presenting her card like it's a trophy. I sense she's been promoted recently. She's in her early thirties and tall too, athletic with it, but standing next to DI Judd she looks like a little girl.

'Can we come in, have a word?'

I take them through to the living room at the front of the house. Twenty minutes later and the news Steve's car has been found at Beachy Head has been broken to me. As both officers drone on about what this could mean, I sit back in one of the armchairs in the front room. I know they won't be expecting much from me; they will assume I am in shock.

It's the truth. The fact there's police in my house and a body in my basement seem surreal to me.

'Natasha, is there anyone you'd like us to call for you?'

The woman is speaking now. I let my gaze drift back to her.

'Sorry, sorry. I just can't believe . . . ?'

I shake my head as real emotion bubbles up within me. Hot tears prick at my eyelids, raw pain slices through me.

Oh, Steve.

'We understand,' Martens says, a little too quickly.

It's clear to me she doesn't understand at all. This is all theoretical to her, a job. She's never had to deal with harsh, shocking realities in her own personal life.

DI Judd is another matter: his sympathy jumps out of him. It feels authentic, like he might have lived something similar.

'Natasha, was Steve having . . . *problems* lately?' DI Judd leans his thin elbows on his knobbly knees. 'Financial worries, bereavements, other stresses?'

There it is: the opening where I cast doubt on Steve's state of mind. I still hate that I have to do this, though it's easier than with Zane. I suppose it's because Judd and Martens didn't know Steve.

'His business wasn't going well.' I suck in a ragged breath. 'He took out a really large loan, I know it was keeping him up at night. He kept talking about how he couldn't fail . . . how he couldn't lose everything.'

The betrayal burns, from the inside out. Steve had not been losing sleep, nor had he said anything of the sort to me. If anything, he'd been cautiously optimistic for the future. He'd accepted most new businesses do not make a profit in their first year. He had regaled me with possibilities of turning 1939's fates around: free refill deals; a well-stocked toy box to tempt parents and their babies in; cleaning out the back room for groups and societies to meet. He was not immune to the café's financial concerns, but he'd had plans and solutions to combat them.

Martens takes out her notebook. 'When was the last time you saw Steve?'

'Friday night, last week. He came over for dinner. He seemed fine. If I had just known . . .'

Martens makes a show of noting the date down. DI Judd's expression is soft, understanding.

'Unfortunately, this is very common when it comes to men and mental health.' He sighs. 'No one realises until . . . well. Something like this happens.'

'But you only found his car, right? That means he could still be out there.'

Judd and Martens' gaze meet. It's clear they've been expecting this denial, which is why I have made it. I always think of everything; I never leave anything to chance. I know full well that no one just accepts someone is dead right off the bat, even when there *is* a body. When there isn't, it should take much longer.

The human brain takes a while to catch up when it comes to grief.

I know this from prior experience, after Dad. Jack seemed fine after that first day for the first week or so, almost as if finding his grandfather dead in his armchair had been a minor disappointment. Then on the tenth day, it was like a firework of grief had lit him up. He'd gone on the rampage in the house, howling like an animal and smashing the television and the glass in the back door.

I let DI Judd take me through the facts again. He reminds me of the significance of finding the car at Beachy Head; of my own words when I'd said Steve was dependable and unlikely to just wander off. The conversation goes round in circles as I bat half-hearted confirmations and rejections around.

I want the officers out of my house, but I can't afford to be too cursory. It might make their highly trained ears prick up. After five or six minutes of this, I let the tears I have been suppressing break forth. They murmur platitudes and I go to fetch tissues from the downstairs bathroom, bringing the meeting to a natural close.

Leaving me with a collection of suicide support leaflets, I see them out. Martens strides ahead, opening the front door and disappearing out onto the step, muttering into her radio. I'm perturbed when Judd does not go straight after his partner, loitering on the living-room threshold.

He nods towards the dining room across the hall.

'What's happened there?'

My gaze follows his. My heart sinks as I realise he means the missing laminate flooring. I could kick myself. I'd cleared away the burned bonfire out on the lawn, but I'd forgotten to close the door off the hall. I squash down my anxiety before it trips me up.

'Oh, the landlord wants to redecorate.'

We own the house. I am shocked at how easily I pull the lie out of thin air.

DI Judd nods. 'You got a good one, then. Too many of 'em don't seem to want to protect their investments these days.'

I tilt my head. 'Yeah, we're lucky.'

Judd digs in his pocket and produces a business card with an embossed London Metropolitan police crest. 'Call me, any time. Any time at all.'

I smile through clenched teeth. 'Of course.'

I close the door as he finally leaves.

CHAPTER FIFTEEN

'Let me do it.'

I reach for the knot of Jack's tie. He almost jerks away from my touch, but then remembers himself. He allows me to pull it out and re-loop it for him, so it's no longer trailing one ludicrous long tail out from under his jacket.

I look up and our gaze meets. Jack's blue eyes seem watchful, his body language guarded. He reminds me of Dad's old dog Otto, slinking under furniture when he'd done something bad. As this thought blossoms, a tumult of sorrow, rage and guilt obliterate it. The simultaneous, competing emotions feel like a blade punching into my chest, bringing with it visions of Dean's eyes rolling back as he fell to the kitchen floor, which morphs into Steve's corpse slumping from the chair.

The acid tang of nausea surges up my gullet. I clamp a hand over my mouth and lean against the car bonnet, my eyes closed. I try and concentrate on my inhalation, bringing clean spring air into my lungs.

I can't make a scene. I just can't.

'Mum?' I feel a tug at my sleeve. 'Are you okay?'

'Fine,' I whisper.

We're outside St Peter's church in Arlesey, Bedfordshire. It's three and a half weeks after *what happened*. (I can't say

'Steve's murder' or even 'death'. The words bring sour saliva with them and involuntary gagging.)

I'd received a call from Rosie McGrath, who identified herself as Steve's older sister. With a voice choked by dignified pain, she'd told me she'd tracked me down via Facebook. She'd said that she'd heard all about me. To make me feel even worse, she'd been empathetic and interested, asking me how I was holding up; she'd even expressed sorrow we had not all met yet. I'd known Steve and his sister were close, but I could hear the familial resemblance in the cadence of her voice and the way she related to me. Steve had been caring and compassionate too.

'It's only right you should be there,' Rosie said.

How right she'd been, though not because I'd been her brother's girlfriend. I *should* look on his relatives and appreciate what has been stolen from them.

So, I decided, should Jack.

I'd anticipated epic pushback, but he'd capitulated right away. It's only travelling in the car this morning that suspicion flowers its dark petals. Maybe it's curiosity that is Jack's motivator for wanting to accompany me? Perhaps it's another red flag I've missed . . . Hadn't I read somewhere that cold-blooded killers *like* to see how their actions have impacted on those left behind? I could be giving Jack exactly what he wants. Too late now.

No, I'm being ridiculous again.

Jack is not a cold-blooded killer.

He's just a confused, hurt boy in pain.

Over the past three weeks, I've told myself this every time someone offers me their condolences. I've averted my eyes every time someone has tried to express their solidarity, touching my arm or asking me if there's anything I need.

Maria bought me a huge bouquet of lilies for my desk along with a card emblazoned with the words *Thinking of you* in silver. Unable to take them home because the thought made me feel sick when Steve had been murdered at my father's house, yet unable to throw them away because Maria was there too, I'd left them in my office where they attracted Aaron's attentions.

'What's happened?' he enquires, with the subtlety of a brick.

I sigh. 'My boyfriend died. He . . . killed himself.'

Conjuring those words into being feels like a betrayal every single time. Aaron at least has the decency to look like he's rebuking himself mentally for his own tactlessness.

'I'm so sorry.'

'Don't bloody ask me if there's anything you can do.'

The harsh words slip out before I can stop them. They don't seem to give Aaron any concerns. He gives me a wan smile, like he understands. Maybe he does.

Arlesey is a pretty, but conventional commuter village for London: overpriced chocolate-box cottages nestle amongst new builds that would be a third of the price further out. A long high street winds through it; an old converted Victorian asylum looms on the hill.

St Peter's is an archetypal village church near the railway station off the main road; a quaint, simple building with several stained glass windows. It's fronted by grass and tombstones.

We're late. I'd picked the quickest route via the M1, but a combination of congestion and then a jackknifed lorry had caused tailbacks for miles. We'd had to trundle forwards, inch by agonising inch, for over an hour. I'd almost given up and decided to take the next junction so I could turn back. But shame is a powerful motivator; though I'd wanted to flick the indicator and turn into a service station, I had kept going.

I pick up the pace, beckoning Jack after me. I open the little wooden gate and we race up the path, making into the large porch. I can hear a hymn sung in lacklustre tones. Why do people insist on singing when people die? I can't think of an activity I could want to do less.

Judging by the mumbled voices, Steve's family and friends feel the same. I recognise the dirge; I'd hastily agreed to it with our own vicar for my father's funeral. The words spring to my lips as Jack and I nod at an usher and take a spot at the back: *Lord of all hopefulness, Lord of all joy, whose trust, ever childlike, no cares could destroy.*

The absurdity of the verses stops me in my tracks. I'm vaguely aware of Jack pulling on my arm again, but I wrench it away. Frozen in the aisle between the wooden pews, I stare up at the altar. Sunlight streams through the stained glass, dappling the flagstones. There's a large easel, holding a big photo of Steve in lieu of the coffin. In it, he doesn't have his long hair, though he has the beard he had when I'd last seen him alive, in my dining room. He's not posing for the camera but he's turning around and smiling. I can see why it was picked. It sums him up so well, a beautiful picture of a beautiful man.

Oh, Steve. I wish you'd never met me.

A woman in her mid-forties turns from the front and spots me. She's made up her face, but her hair hangs in straggly strands around her face, like she gave up her preparations halfway through. She's thin, so the swell of her pregnant belly is even more pronounced. A silver-haired man in an expensive suit has an arm around her, supporting her like she might fall back onto the pew. He's much older; I know from Steve he is a very successful businessman.

Two impeccably groomed children, a girl and a boy, hang on to Rosie's dress, their eyes wide and faces pale. They're the only children there. I've not seen pictures, but know instinctively who they all are: Rosie, her husband John and her two children Mia and Jacob, Steve's niece and nephew. He'd told me all about them, too. They were his whole family since their parents had died.

The entire exchange takes less than three seconds, but it's too much. I turn on my heel and race straight back out of the church. A nanosecond later, Jack scuttles after me. When he gets in the car, he shouts at me, telling me he'd thought I was leaving him behind.

I don't reply.

CHAPTER SIXTEEN

About ten or fifteen minutes after my freakout, the congregation starts to emerge from the church. They do not seem to be in any hurry to go anywhere, so gather out on the grass. Were this a standard funeral, they would be walking towards a gravesite, praying and throwing earth.

But this is a memorial, with no body. It's clear the people gathered don't really know what to do next. They dither by the tombstones until Rosie and her family come out, then surge around her, all keen to pay their condolences.

I'm still in the car with Jack outside St Peter's. I'd wanted to start the engine and peel away from Arlesey and from Steve's family. But a combination of shame, humiliation and sheer bloody-mindedness makes me see through my plan.

I had come here to show my face, as Steve's grieving girlfriend. I can't allow Rosie's only sight of me to be running from her brother's memorial. As time goes on, she might start to question why I'd had such a strong reaction. I had, after all, only been going out with Steve for just six months. Could it be a guilty conscience? I realise it's a small risk, like with Zane and Steve's car, but it's one I can't afford to take. I have thought of the possibility, so I must see it through.

For Jack's sake.

Rosie does not shrink away from the small crowd, overwhelmed. She draws her shoulders back and makes her way around the group like a pro.

As I watch her, I try and remember what it is she does: a teacher, maybe? That would make sense. She exchanges words with each person, accepting sympathies and well wishes for the safe delivery of the baby.

People fall away, moving back to their cars as they're invited back to Rosie's for the wake. As Rosie makes it to a glamorous woman in a grey trouser suit and kitten heels, I do see Steve's sister falter. Though she smiles at the glamorous woman, the set of her mouth hardens.

'I just can't believe it.' The woman steps forward for a hug. 'It's just horrible. Poor Steve.'

Rosie leaves her hanging and doesn't move to embrace her. She rolls her eyes at her, the smile sliding from her lips.

'I guess *you're* here for forgiveness, Charlotte?'

She spits out the words in a low voice, but standing so close, I hear it all. I understand who the glamorous woman is: Steve's old girlfriend. The one who'd sent Steve into a tailspin, terminating her pregnancy and their relationship in one fell swoop two years ago. Charlotte had made Steve re-evaluate his life and his place in the world. Because of her, he'd left his lucrative work in the City and started 1939.

With a surge of relief, I realise who Rosie blames for Steve's pretend suicide: Charlotte.

Oh, Jesus.

Guilt and yet more shame replace my gratitude. Yet another life ruined by Jack's actions and my covering for him.

I have no time to process any of this. Rosie turns her back on Charlotte as she makes it to me. She proffers a hand and I take it. Her palm in mine feels cold, tissue-paper thin.

'I'm so sorry.' The repetition of the words makes me balk. They seem so pathetic and inadequate, especially coming from me. 'That was rude of me, rushing out like that . . .'

Rosie flashes me an automatic, jaded smile. I understand she doesn't have any recollection of what I am talking about. The ceremony must have been just a blur to her.

'Don't mention it.' Rosie seems to lock in on my face, like she's seeing me for the first time. 'Natasha, I'm so glad you could make it.'

I feel outside of my own body as we continue to talk. Over Rosie's shoulder another man in a generic dark suit in my peripheral vision, hands in his pockets. He has his back to me. He seems familiar, but before I can double-check, he disappears behind a large obelisk and statues of weeping angels.

'You're welcome to join us back at the house?'

Tuning back in as she makes her invite, I almost accept. I arrest the words on my tongue just in time.

'I'm so sorry, but I have to get back to work.'

This well-worn excuse seems to have no impact on Rosie. She forgets me as her attentions are diverted by her children when they rush over, throwing themselves against her legs. Her husband ambles over to her, placing a hand to the small of her back, nodding at me. I watch as they move towards their own car. Some other couples fall into step with them.

I take it as my own cue to get out of there.

Slumped in the front passenger seat, Jack scrolls through his phone, size tens up on the dashboard. I open my door and slide behind the wheel, tamping down the urge to push his feet off. Maybe my irritation jumps out of me because he sits up and puts them down of his own accord. We sit in silence, watching the other cars start up and follow John and Rosie.

'Rough,' Jack says at last.

An involuntary snort makes its way out my nose. 'Yes, it was.'

The silence between us seems to well up. I've spent the last three and half weeks inside myself, trying to deal with the horror of 'what's happened'. I can feel all the words I want to say stuck in my mouth, as viscous as chewing gum.

I know I mustn't say them. Jack is all the clichés: a box of dry tinder; a bomb waiting to go off. How this happened doesn't matter anymore; it must never happen again.

Otherwise, Steve died for nothing.

'Jack, put your phone down.'

I force a pleasant tone into my voice, but there's still an edge to it. I sound half-crazed. Jack makes no move to stop scrolling.

'Now, please.'

Under sufferance, Jack abandons his phone on his lap. I can still see movement from a video flickering on the screen. I watch the little people within, faces leering in at the camera, rather than look at my son direct.

'You mustn't do . . . *this* again.'

'Do what?'

I can't believe he's playing dumb with me.

'*You. Know. What.*'

I curl my fingernails into the palms of my hands. I feel the sting as they bite into my flesh. I concentrate on the pain; anything to keep myself from grabbing my son around the collar. Is this where he got his violent urges from . . . Me? Or am I just desperate, wild with fear and heartsick at the horror of all this?

Please God, let it be the last one.

'That depends on you.'

'How?'

'Whether you bring any more boyfriends home.'

Jack's voice is small, anxious, yet this ultimatum sends another wave of fear through me. I don't need to be a psychologist to realise Jack had been jealous of Steve; or to see what he's doing now, even if he is not consciously aware of it himself.

Jack wants his mother to himself.

He wants control over my movements, my relationships. It's a classic child's move, though Jack is almost fully grown.

'Are you fucking kidding me?' I hiss. 'I've literally helped you get away with murder! No, you can't just make childish demands and expect me to go along with it. You should be the one falling in with what I want, not the other way around!'

My son's gaze meets mine. There's no concern there, nor empathy. It sends an involuntary shiver down my spine.

'Fine,' Jack says, 'then I guess I will just have to call the police, give myself up.'

Before he can dial 999, a shriek escapes my lips.

'Don't!'

He turns towards me, his face still impassive. Surely he can't mean it? He must realise he would spend the next two or three decades in jail, as would I. Yet looking at his stony expression, I just can't tell if he's bluffing me or not. Like with Dean, I have no choice but go with it. I try to calm my shallow, gasped breaths.

'Fine,' I murmur, 'if that's what you want . . . You have my word.'

I'm met with silence. I open my eyes again to discover Jack staring at me, head cocked, his phone camera in my face. Before I can tell him no, he presses the button.

He turns his handset around and shows me my own gaunt face and haunted eyes. I look like hell. Trapped and feral with it.

'Then it's a deal,' Jack says.

PART TWO

'Motherhood is the strangest thing, it can be like being one's own Trojan horse.'

Rebecca West

CHAPTER SEVENTEEN

Life limps on. I hear nothing more from Steve's family to my immense relief. The thought of having to so much as accept a Facebook friend request from Rosie, never mind talk with her about her brother, makes me feel nauseous and anxious in equal measure.

I go through the motions of my life, going to work and back again. I bat away Maria's sympathies and concern, telling her I just need to keep busy. It's the truth. In the evenings, I drink. The recycling box fills up with empty bottles far too quickly. The familiar thudding pain and queasiness of hangover becomes my constant companion. Feeling physically as bad as I do mentally seems comforting, somehow. A kind of symmetry.

Another constant companion, whether I like it or not, appears to be Aaron. He makes an appearance at the Atkinson Film Project at least once a day. Though he is still looking for scraps of Nilsen's letter to Dorothy, he hasn't found anything new in weeks.

In addition to the previous five pieces, there are three more. Again, they all appear to be in Nilsen's distinctive cursive:

Eyes of a devil
Dark part of me
Signs were all there

My nostrils flare as the apt nature of these missives land on me. The paper fragments feel like a warning from beyond the grave, from Nilsen to me. An old adage surfaces in my brain: takes one to know one.

The lack of progress does not deter Aaron; some days he arrives just to chat to me. Once irritated by his wittering on or threatened by the fact he was a true crime podcaster, I am no longer concerned by Aaron's proximity. Steve's death explained, suicide is not cool or mysterious enough for his podcast.

There's also been no developments from the police. I'd called them a couple of times for appearance's sake, complaining 'no one was doing anything'. I was reminded by the sympathetic DI Judd on the last one there was nothing *to* do except hope Steve's body might come in with the tide. Satisfied my elaborate ruse was locked down, I'd ended the call and have not contacted them again.

'How are you doing? I mean really.'

Looking up from the paper shred bin, I catch Aaron looking at me with compassion in his eyes. For some reason this infuriates me. I don't want his pity. I've always been a lone wolf, self-sufficient.

I've had to be.

I had been a motherless girl even before Mum's untimely death before I was just ten; she'd not been much of a parent, preferring vodka and television to me. Dad had tried his best and worked hard to provide me with material things, but he hadn't been able to give me what I needed emotionally. When it came down to it, I had learned the only person I could truly depend on was me. Now this self-styled bright young thing thinks he can sympathise with me? I don't need him.

I don't need anybody.

As ever, I tamp all of these harsh feelings down. Society doesn't take kindly to angry women. Everything is our fault anyway, but the angry woman is always first in line for finger-pointing and blame. I've seen it, time and time again on social media. Female truth-tellers get shot down in flames when they share their stories; so much for the 'be kind' mantra. I learned a long time ago it's better to create a mask. Smiles and warmth are the armour you need to slip under everyone else's radar.

Dad taught me that.

'Oh . . . you know,' I say, noncommittal.

Aaron nods, like he *does* know. There's something in his expression that tells me he has his own tragedies in his past. This understanding makes me feel a little less furious with him, but I remind myself I can't allow myself a single moment of complacency. Regardless of how pleasant and empathetic Aaron might seem, that understanding will not stretch to turning a blind eye to murder. Killing breaks the social contract; all bets are off.

I cannot put Jack in danger by letting my guard down in *any* way.

Perhaps I am overthinking it, but it is better safe than sorry, especially when our lives appear to be getting back on track. At home, Jack appears to settle back into his own routine without issue. He's served his internal exclusion at school and has returned to regular classes. I receive an email from Ms Heath, telling me Jack seems to have turned over a new leaf.

His attitude seems vastly improved at home, too. He breezes around the house like a normal teen. He spends too long scrolling on his phone, raids the fridge and plays video games. He goes to school and his therapy appointments. He doesn't mention what happened to Steve. It's like a door has been closed on the event, just like the lid on the chest freezer downstairs.

One morning, I can't contain myself any longer. Considering his threat in the car after Steve's funeral, I must double-check.

'What do you talk about, with Cheryl?'

Jack doesn't even look at me. He continues to crush dry cereal under his spoon on the kitchen table.

'This and that.'

My mouth clenches tight at his dismissal, to stop me spitting out the diatribe that's welling in my chest. I grind my teeth so much these days, I have permanent jaw ache around my temples. I'm eating paracetamol like sweeties.

'I realise that. I mean, do you speak about Grandad, or friends, or school . . . ?'

'Or murder?' Jack's gaze lifts to me at last.

I purse my lips. *Fine, if that's the way he wants it.*

'Do you?'

'No. Of course not.'

I lean against the counter, despair lancing through me. Jack's therapy sessions must be a charade. Any progress Cheryl thinks he's making is an obvious lie.

Though Jack had been an anxious baby and a melancholy child thanks to his father's abuse, he'd changed when we came home to Dad's. He'd been allowed to flourish in an environment that was not a minefield of potential transgressions, real or imagined. Dad had his faults, but he'd never made us walk on eggshells around him. He'd loved us the best way he knew how, looking out for us and providing for us however he could.

When Dad died, Jack had descended. The chatty, devil-may-care boy I'd known thanks to the loving influence of his grandfather was replaced almost overnight. His dark fury at the unfairness of my dad's sudden, premature passing opened up something terrible inside him. Something that had always been there, waiting to burst into being. Maybe it was predestined, created by Dean's persistent and terrible domestic abuse of us both whilst we lived with him. Or perhaps Jack is just his father's son. The endless question: nature, or nurture.

From where I am sitting? It seems to be a perfect, violent storm of both.

CHAPTER EIGHTEEN

Winter falls away to spring. In the second week of an unseasonably warm March, a weird, sweet yet foul odour starts to emanate from the cellar. At first, I think it is my own twisted imagination, a physical manifestation of a guilty conscience. When Jack complains too, I realise what's happened.

The chest freezer is broken.

Standing at the bottom of the steps, I hold my sleeve to my nose. I am grateful the chest freezer's lid seal is intact. Though enough of the smell has called me down to the basement, Steve's body is at least wrapped and packed tight inside. I curse as I see there's small puddles of water across the floor in places. The rest has worked its way through the cracks in the red brick floor. There's no flood now, which means the freezer has been broken for days. There hasn't been a power cut, which must mean it's the actual unit.

Damn it to hell.

'Here's the problem,' Jack says.

I peer around the freezer with him. Around the plug area, there's some exposed wires at the back and the remains of a very fried mouse. It's a fuzzy mess of fur and mould. A vision of Maria screaming about rats at the archive wipes through my mind. As Jack moves to grab the chest freezer's handle, I realise what he's about to do.

'Don't open it yet, for God's sake!'

Jack holds up both hands in surrender. The last thing we need is the worst of the smell to dissipate throughout the house. We will have to leave it until the last possible moment.

Panic skitters between my shoulder blades as I try and work out what to do in the meantime. Moving the chest freezer with Steve in it is the most obvious, but it's too heavy for me and Jack to get up the steep cellar steps by ourselves. Dad had it put down here by the men who delivered it. I would also need a small truck to move it; it will never fit in my car.

There's nothing else for it: the broken freezer must remain here. We will scour it out with bleach once we've taken the body out. Steve's corpse is the real problem.

We will have to put him somewhere else, but where?

I don't want to dump a badly decomposing body somewhere out in the world. It will only be a matter of time before it's discovered. The police will then guess correctly that Steve's car at Beachy Head is a ruse. It then won't be long before his last movements are traced back to my house.

I've kept me and Jack out of trouble this long by keeping Steve's body as close as possible. I don't want to change that now.

My eye is drawn back to the puddles on the uneven floor. I crouch down and grab one protruding brick with two hands. It comes away easily, crumbling under my touch. Joy and relief replace the sick panic in my chest as I comprehend what's underneath.

Earth.

A reprieve. We can dig down, place Steve's body underground, without having to leave the house. It feels like validation; as if fate or some kind of deity approves of my plan to save my son. *Yes, you are a good mother, Natasha.*

'Help me with this.'

I grab a crowbar from Dad's old toolbox to lever up the bricks. When Jack is not forthcoming, I glance up to find Jack sitting on the open-fronted steps. He watches my efforts, elbows resting on his knees, expression as blank as ever.

'Do you want to get caught?'

Finally: a reaction. Jack's eyes widen, like this possibility has only just occurred to him. Had he really thought I could make everything go away, just like that? Jack's faith in me being able to save him from the law might be misplaced, but it does show I still have value to him as his mother. My son catches up with me and what we must do.

We have to dig Steve a grave, then pour concrete on top of him, just like the victims of those Mafiosos everyone has read about.

Jack grabs a flat-nosed screwdriver and kneels next to me. After several hours, we've pulled up enough to accommodate Steve's long, lean body. My father had been a brick layer, like his father before him. Though I'd had zero interest in practical matters, Dad had insisted I learn them. He'd told me such matters were not just for blue collar workers; that any skill or trade can come in handy, at any time. How right he had been. Just like he'd taught me how to tend vegetables and build a decent bonfire, I know how to mix concrete.

Thank you, Dad.

After making a start myself, I leave Jack digging Steve's grave in the cellar with one of Dad's garden spades. He's disgusted it's all being left to him, though I don't have the strength to argue with him. He shouldn't have bloody killed Steve in the first place.

I drive out to a DIY store right on the other side of London, remembering to take cash with me to buy what I need for the floor. It's an independent place, lacking the technology of the big superstores. I avoid the sole camera at the door by walking through with my head dipped, a curtain of hair in front of my face.

I buy buckets, a board and a six-piece trowel set, as well as more tape and plastic sheeting in case we need to wrap

Steve up some more. Even though it means several trips, I don't allow anyone to help me take my purchases out to the car in case someone remembers doing so. As I slide back behind the wheel, I soothe my nerves by reminding myself I've thought of everything.

I am not only a good mother, but I am also a genius when it comes to practical matters. There are not many people who can cope with the river of shit that's been thrown at me in the past few months. Hell, my entire life.

So I nearly have a heart attack when I almost run my neighbour Jim over on the way back onto my street.

'Shit!'

Everything in the boot, as well as all Jack's junk on the backseat surges forward as I slam my foot on the brake. Jim just stands in the middle of the road. He stares at the bumper of my car, resting against his shin. I'd only just stopped. A few inches more and I'd have broken both his legs. At best.

Adrenaline surging through my veins, I park as best I can outside my home and clamber out of the vehicle. I feel wobbly with it. I lean against the bonnet, anger surging up behind my fear at what I'd almost just done.

'For Christ's sake, Jim, are you okay?'

The sound of his name finally grabs his attention. Jim is a little goblin of a man, even shorter than me, but he has a kind face. He looks to me and his face cracks in a nonsensical grin, motivated by relief and gratitude that I hadn't flattened him.

'Well, that was exciting,' Jim says.

I laugh, incredulous. 'What are you doing in the middle of the road?'

He holds up a plastic carrier bag. Another gift from Celia, then.

'Just a little something for the lad.'

I take the bag. 'Thank you so much. Bye!'

'Everything all right?'

Such an innocuous question; so inane. The British ask it of everyone, constantly. People must say it and answer it fifty times a day. The answer is always the affirmative. Even when you're not good.

Especially when you're not.

Yet somehow, when you're not, people know. It's a kind of magic. Yet Jim can't possibly guess what my real problem is. He thinks I am still grieving for my dad.

If only it was just that.

I force a smile. 'Fine, you?'

Jim rubs his cheek with his left hand; I can hear the bristles under his palm. Now he doesn't have to go to work, he doesn't shave every day. In his holey jumper and creased slacks, he looks like a benevolent tramp. Every newly retired man seems to go through this phase, until his wife either cracks and divorces him, or he pulls himself together for fear of being left on his own. Clearly Celia is not at the ultimatum stage yet.

Jim's beady eyes fall on the boot of my car. 'Let me help you with all that.'

'Oh no, I couldn't possibly . . . !'

Too late. Both Jim's hands are on my car boot door. He opens it and pulls it up with the surety and arrogant assurance of a man who's never really been told 'no' in his life. He whistles as he takes in the supplies.

'Doing some renovations, are you?'

I run with it. 'Something like that.'

'Let me know if I can do anything.'

He hefts the first bag of concrete mix out, taking it to my front door for me. As I grab the remaining items from the boot, I decide the path of least resistance might get him away from my house quicker.

'Thanks Jim, appreciated. I will.'

Jim flashes me a toothy grin and puts the concrete bag down on the step for me as I fiddle with my keys. For one horrible moment, I think he's going to try and come in with me. Then he tips an imaginary hat to me and retreats onto the street, lighting a cigarette as he goes.

I open the front door with shaking hands. I drag the heavy bag in and slam the front door behind me. I stand there for a few moments and lean my head against the wall, my body slumping from the near miss.

I listen out for the sound of the television: nothing. I abandon all my purchases in the hallway and stride back towards the cellar. I'd figured Jack would get bored and give up his gravedigging without my direct supervision.

I am pleasantly surprised by his industriousness. I find my boy shirtless and sweaty, approximately eight feet down in a big hole in the basement. As he feels my presence on the steps, my son glances up with a big smile, like he's a kid at the beach.

Grateful for any sense of normality or small connection between us, I smile back. Then the vile nature of the activity facing us slams back into my consciousness.

There's nothing normal about what we are about to do this afternoon.

This seems to dawn on Jack too, as his gaze wanders back to the chest freezer and what lies within.

'Let's get on with it.' I sigh.

CHAPTER NINETEEN

Moving Steve's body and cementing the floor over him, plus cleaning and disinfecting the house — again! — is as traumatic as I'd feared. The physical and mental toll is far in excess of my worst nightmares, but I tell myself it is no less than I deserve.

Once Jack had helped me get Steve into the makeshift grave in the cellar floor, I'd insisted Jack return to school. I didn't want to draw undue attention to us by having truant officers turn up at the house, especially after his recent internal exclusion. He'd gone without argument. I think he'd been relieved at getting out of the worst of it.

When I'd finally finished my gruesome duties, I'd crawled into bed. I was unable to stop shaking and crying, rocking back and forth like a patient in a mental asylum of old.

Over the next few days, Jack came to the door of my room in the morning and evenings. He said nothing, but left water, tea and toast. I once might have been touched at his consideration, but now it raised questions. Could he be mimicking what I'd done for him when he was ill? I didn't touch any of it, letting drinks go cold and food grow stale.

As I feel myself reconnecting, I grow restless. Oversleeping leaves me with a headache and a dry mouth, waking in the middle of the night. I go to the bathroom and drink from the tap. Then I drift through my home, blank-eyed and absent-minded, like a ghost in Wonder Woman pyjamas. As I wander past my son's room, I stop beside the open door. Jack's bed is empty.

Harsh, cold fear lances through me as my gaze falls on the tangled sheets. It's past two o' clock in the morning. I listen out for sounds, but the house is silent. I'd been on my way back from the bathroom, so I know he can't be in there. No lights are on downstairs.

My stomach lurches, a sick sensation spinning through me. I lean my head against the doorframe of Jack's empty room.

Where is he?

Why isn't he here?

I try and conjure up where Jack might have gone but come up with nothing. Everything has been a blur lately; it's like I am on autopilot. I've lost nearly twenty pounds since Steve's death. I've always been slim, so now I look positively gaunt; a walking skeleton with skin stretched over my bones. I've only been back at work a matter of days. I'd taken ten days' annual leave, telling Maria that Steve's 'suicide' had finally hit me.

In Jack's room, darkness peeks between the slats of stylish new blinds I'd put in for him. Barring his shared untidiness, every trace of Dad in the room is gone. Jack's dirty clothes are scattered on the floor. There's posters of bands I've never listened to on the newly-blue walls; books I've never read on the shelves, along with figurines from unfamiliar story worlds. Looking at all his stuff, I am confronted with the knowledge I don't know where my son retreats to inside his mind.

Zombie-like, I pick up Jack's clothes from the floor. My bones feel stiff, like they might creak in protest. I know it is somatic. My joints and limbs are supple and easy to move usually. It is the painful, screaming weight of unwelcome responsibility I am experiencing.

As I open the laundry basket to shove Jack's dirty clothes in, I gasp.

On the shirt in my hands: blood.

It's my dad's old Arsenal football shirt, one my mum had given him years ago. Now gore is splashed across the top of the chest area. My intuition tells me it will not be Jack's.

No, no no no . . . He promised me.

Before I can abandon it to the hamper, a barrage of memories rips through my mind's eye:

The eight-year-old Jack in his blood-splashed onesie, standing over his father's body in the kitchen and smiling.

My son at seventeen, leaning on the dinner table, hair askew and shoulders wracked with effort, his right hand covered in blood.

Then: a different Jack, much younger, perhaps four or five years old.

His head snaps sideways, as he's backhanded across the face.

He flings out his pudgy little hands in vain, but he does not manage to arrest his fall.

He disappears from view . . .

. . . Down the stairs.

I've always dodged the horror by trying not to think about the day Jack fell. He'd been badly behaved that day. He'd been throwing things and hitting, reacting to the toxic stress of his home life.

Fearing Dean's wrath, I'd done all I could to reason with Jack before my husband had come home. When that hadn't worked, I'd promised Jack sweets, ice cream, toys. Anything to try and keep my boy safe; to avoid Dean's temper that would explode next.

That hadn't worked either.

When Jack had bitten hard enough to draw blood, that backhand across the face was inescapable. It would have been bad enough on its own; an adult hitting a small child like that could cause a dislocated jaw.

We'd lived out in Epsom back then, the top flat in a maisonette that had stairs down to its own private hallway. Jack had been standing at the top of the stairs, on the landing.

Dean had promised me he would put a stairgate in, but he'd never bothered. The force of the blow had not just sent Jack tumbling down the stairs, propelling him off the first one. He'd lifted into space, turning in mid-air as he went. Landing at the bottom in a heap of arms and legs, he'd gone face first onto the ceramic hallway tiles. Jack broke his left wrist, dislocating his thumb and bashing his forehead and cheekbone against the floor, resulting in an ocular fracture.

Doctors said later that if he hadn't somehow made that turn, he'd have landed on the back of his skull and been killed. I'd thanked God or fate or whatever had spared him.

Social Services had come knocking, of course; no child can endure an injury of that magnitude and the parents escape investigation. I scrubbed the maisonette and put up photographs of us in glass frames (I'd not bothered after Dean had smashed my head against one, sending splinters of glass into the carpet).

I spent days combing the internet for advice on how to present as a normal, happy family. One blog suggested the smell of a cake baking in the oven is the 'epitome of domesticity'. I'd never made one before, so did half a dozen practice cakes before Social Services even came over. I was right to; the first three were hard and rubbery. If I'd dropped them on the floor they probably would have bounced.

Dean was charm personified, naturally. He'd always made sure we'd not gone to A&E for our other, much smaller injuries. Dean had also insisted on being present in every meeting, even answering for me when the social worker asked if I'd like to speak with him privately.

The day Jack had fallen, the social worker had done his best and rebuffed my husband, looking pointedly to me. But I'd known Dean would likely kill us both next time if I went against him and revealed the extent of his abuse.

I'd agreed it was a horrible, chance accident and promised to get a stairgate. I'd even shown them round the maisonette once we'd installed it, offering them cups of tea and acting as carefree as I could get away with when my child was in the ICU. The paperwork was eventually signed off and I was granted my reprieve from the authorities, though not from Dean. After Jack's accident, I worked hard to ensure Dean concentrated all his most violent efforts on me.

Anything to ensure my precious boy wasn't hurt again.

The assault of memories makes my head spin. Woozy with it all, I sit down on Jack's unmade bed. How could Jack wear his beloved, gentle grandfather's shirt to commit such an awful crime? A hoarse, incredulous bark of laughter erupts from me next.

How could he hurt people *at all*?

That's what I *should* be asking . . . I *should* be doing something about it, too.

I abandon the football shirt on Jack's bed and go downstairs. I falter in the hallway as I make a grab for my car keys on the hook.

Where the hell am I going?

Even if Jack is still in Camden, it's still a large borough. I grab my phone and press the button; Jack is number 1 on speed dial. It doesn't even ring; it goes straight to voicemail. My son's monotone voice kicks in, telling me to leave a message. I hiss in frustration, pocketing my phone again. I am left with no choice.

I must find my son and bring him home.

Now.

CHAPTER TWENTY

Driving around, I scan the dark shapes on the streets for my errant child. I start in the main high street first, scrutinising crowds around the lock as well as the tube station and the many pubs, clubs and takeaways. But I can't believe Jack would assault anyone in full view of crowds. He's too young-looking to make it into a bar, even with fake ID.

I turn the car away from the high street, towards the above-ground rail station. There's a small line of people waiting to go through the ticket barriers. As my gaze alights on the people there, I see a homeless man amble through, his cap out for money. A couple of clubbers give him coins, but a young man pushes him away, laughing. The homeless man lands with a bump on his rear, his coins rolling across the pavement.

As I watch the casual cruelty, the sight triggers a memory: me, watching the TV news the night Steve died. That ticker tape across the bottom of the screen reading: *HOMELESS MEN ATTACKED IN LONDON*.

Could Jack be the one attacking the homeless men?

Please, no . . . no.

YES.

Of course it is bloody Jack. I already know he's been up to all sorts while I was off work and recovering from having to move Steve's body from the freezer. I'd been so distraught at having to concrete over my lover's decomposed body in the cellar, I'd missed the signs.

Hell, I'd missed the signs, period: if the attacks on homeless men had been headline news the same weekend Steve died, then Jack must have been attacking them before he'd committed murder that fateful Friday night in my father's dining room. When had he started . . . after my dad had died? That seems likely, but then it's becoming increasingly clear I don't know my only child at all.

No, that can't be true.
He doesn't know what he's doing.
I can still save him.

I draw a blank trying to think where homeless people like to congregate, other than the rail station. I'd always tried to avoid thinking about such things. Not just because it's horrible to imagine people who are homeless in one of the richest countries in the world, but because it seemed too close to my own situation. Dean had held the threat of throwing me and Jack out on the street the whole time we'd been together. I'd had countless anxiety dreams of trudging the grey pavements in the wind and rain, the infant Jack in my arms. That dark vision returns to me now, transporting me back into my worst nightmares in a blink.

Stop it.

I take a hold of myself, banishing those horrible thoughts away, making room for more sensible ones. Searching anywhere sheltered seems like an obvious option; homeless people need to cut off wind chill and keep dry. Alleyways, all types of bridges, awnings and doorways all fit the bill. I give an inward groan as all these search options occur to me: there must be tens, if not hundreds, of all of them in the Camden area. In the absence of a better plan, I keep driving, hoping to spot a disturbance that will draw me to Jack.

The farce continues. White headlights and the red glow of taillights wash over my car as another car sails past me. I do yet more circuits of Camden suburbs. I don't see any movement anywhere; not even late-night dog walkers or drunks ambling on their way home. Frustration pools in my belly.

Where the hell is Jack?

As I turn on to another back street, a skinny and malnourished fox, its coat dotted with mange, rushes out in front of my vehicle. I spot the glint of my own headlights in its eyes first; it looks demonic.

I stamp on the brake, only just stopping in time.

Something is unleashed in me. I scream, balling up my fists and pummelling the steering wheel. A cacophony of noise rings through my ears, obliterating my thoughts with the force of a klaxon blast.

Finally, silence.

I blink and come to. My car is still in the middle of the road, not that it matters. There's no other traffic. Most of the windows of the houses are dark. The street is empty, save for a crisp packet dancing in the breeze. The fox is long gone. I turn the wheel and make a three-point turn out of there, back the way I came.

I'm wasting my time.

I haven't thought this through. What had I expected to do, drag my son off the street (and maybe even an unfortunate victim) by his ear like an old-fashioned fishwife? A bitter chuckle escapes my lips.

There's nothing I can do.

I lost the reins on Jack a long time ago, I just didn't know it. I've been kidding myself I am a parent. The reality is, it doesn't matter what I say or do. Hell, I know from the parenting memes on Facebook and teenagers' dances on TikTok that adults and kids are destined to never see eye to eye . . . even when everything is as it should be.

It's only a matter of time before we are both caught.

As kids get older, people say it gets easier. I have found the opposite to be true. Teenagers have a kind of regression, just like small children and the 'Terrible Twos' they warn you about. They have all the will and none of the rationale. They want what they want and to hell with the consequences.

This is all very well when a toddler wants sweets before dinner. The worst a parent suffers is a screaming tantrum, perhaps a few bites or scratches.

Teens are far worse.

Even normal teenagers who *don't* murder people have all kinds of inventive ways to torture their parents. The internet is full of 'Am I the asshole?' threads where parents and adult children confess their darkest deeds against their loved ones, especially at family gatherings like Christmas, birthdays or Thanksgiving. There are SOS messages from parents at the end of their rope on Facebook; angry rants by teenagers on Instagram.

It's part of life.

I recall Maria telling me about her eldest Danny and how he'd not spoken to her or Louisa for three whole months when they'd had the temerity to not buy him the trainers he wanted. Ungrateful little snot.

But she had said that was a walk in the park in comparison to their daughter. Freya had snuck out of her bedroom window every chance she'd got between the ages of fourteen and sixteen. She'd go clubbing mostly, but once Freya made it all the way to Birmingham, hitchhiking via a succession of lorries and private cars.

She was only found out because a couple of police detectives in an unmarked vehicle picked her up off a slip road into a service station. Both fathers themselves, the officers had bawled Freya out and insisted she call home immediately. They'd then waited with her while Maria drove up the motorway to fetch her back.

Freya would not tell Maria why she was running away. Now aged twenty-three, Freya apparently sees it all as a big joke. Maria laughs too as she retells the story, but I can see in her eyes it has never been funny to her.

Jack lacks both self-restraint and the ability to plan. Just like Danny or Freya, the here and now is what's important to Jack. He doesn't appear to understand the need for caution, or if he does, he seems not to care. Unlike Maria's kids, what his heart wants goes way beyond a new pair of trainers, or whatever was in Birmingham.

His lack of self-regulation could end both of us. He will do whatever he wants. He is out of control. But what can I do? I have absolutely no idea.

I head for home, a mothering failure once again.

CHAPTER TWENTY-ONE

I hear the scrape of Jack's key in the front door just after half five in the morning. Sitting on the stairs waiting for him, I'd been rehearsing what I could say to him for hours. I'd decided I had to keep calm, no matter what. I don't know if Jack has spared me thus far because I am his mother, or because it's suited him.

That may change if I freak out or go on at him. He may decide keeping me alive might just be too much hassle, especially now I have demonstrated how easy it was to conceal Steve's body in the cellar.

I don't want to end up next to my boyfriend under concrete.

All of these fleeting concerns fly out of my head when I see the state of my son as he drags himself inside.

'Jack . . . Oh, God!'

My son blinks and staggers to a halt, swaying like a drunk. His eyes are wide, spaced out. I make it down the stairs, closing the front door after him. I give him a wide berth just in case. He has the feral look of a cornered animal.

'What's happened?'

Jack opens his mouth to speak, but no sound comes out. My question is redundant, I don't need him to explain.

My son chose his victim badly tonight.

Whomever it was had fought back. He is in shock. His head rolls on his neck as he tries to grasp comprehension, make sense of what's just happened to him. His reaction had been different when he killed his father, or Steve. The only time I have seen him like this is when he fell down the stairs.

He's covered in blood, but this time I know by instinct some of it is Jack's. There's a dark bruise forming across one of his cheekbones. His left eye is purple and swollen, he has a split lip. He cradles his left hand in his right.

'Let me see.'

I approach him, palms out, like I might a wolf or other dangerous creature with teeth. Jack tilts his head and just stares at me, not moving. Even so, he seems surprised when I make it to him, like I have materialised out of thin air. I gesture to him to give me his hand. He capitulates, as obedient as a child showing a skinned knee from the playground.

His thumb joint is swollen and misshapen. His thumb is jutting out at an odd angle, dislocated again. He's always had a weakness there since the day he fell down the stairs as a toddler. Jack has had his thumb popped back in place a couple of times in the past five years; both times he'd shut it in the car door.

I know I can't take him to the hospital this time. He is covered in blood. Even if he changed before we left, I can't do anything about his cuts and bruises. Whoever had inflicted them on him might have given a description of Jack to the police. Taking him to a doctor with any kind of injury sustained in a fight would be like pointing a red arrow right at my boy's face with the words: THIS IS THE GUY YOU'RE LOOKING FOR.

I decide in the spur of the moment.

'Sorry,' I say.

Jack's brow furrows with confusion, then his expression turns to one of furious horror as I grab his left hand. Before he can wrench it from my grasp, I pop his thumb back in.

I wince as he howls in pain and retches. He shoots his right hand out to the hallway wall as his knees give way beneath him. As he breathes through it, tears spring up in my eyes. I hate hurting him, even after everything he has done.

'You're okay, baby,' I find myself saying, 'you're okay.'

I remind myself Jack is dangerous; that he could kill me if he wanted to as easily as he killed his father and Steve. Yet my treacherous mind creates a never-ending showreel of Jack's life: smiling on his sixth birthday, blowing out the candles on the Spiderman cake I'd stayed up all night making. Hollering for me when he was ten and stuck up a tree at the local park. Shivering and ill when he was fourteen with a temperature, crying with the pain of the flu. Every time he'd wanted me, the number one in his life, seeking me out for comfort.

My precious boy.

I take Jack to the back of the house, into the kitchen. Pale and listless, he falls into a chair. I open the useful drawer and pull out a box of ibuprofen. I present him with a couple and some water. He raises an eyebrow at me. I shrug.

'It'll take the edge off, hopefully.'

He takes the tablets as I search through the kitchen fridge freezer for ice. As I've been drinking a lot of gin and tonic since Steve died, I have half a bag in there. I pour it all into a large Pyrex bowl and direct Jack to plunge his hand in. He clenches his teeth but does it, hissing in pain. I make him keep it in there until his teeth start chattering with cold.

'Good boy.'

I fetch the first aid kit from the downstairs bathroom cabinet under the sink. It's well stocked and has everything I need: tape and bandages. I do like to plan ahead for every eventuality. I don't have a specialised splint for Jack's thumb, but that's easily sorted. There's a box of ice lolly sticks in the useful drawer. My dad always collected them for his allotment's vegetable patch. I grab the cleanest looking one out of there, then run it under the tap for good measure. Ten minutes later, Jack's thumb is taped up and supported.

'Better?'

Jack gives me a thin-lipped, distant smile. His eyelids are beginning to droop. I stand up, guiding him out of his chair and towards the stairs, up onto the landing. I take him into the bathroom where he just stands, vacant, as I draw him a bath.

I undress him like I did when he was just a little boy. I whimper in horror at his injuries. Under his shirt, there are red welts and black shadows across his skinny chest and ribs. There's another long, dark purple bruise at a diagonal angle across his shoulder blades. As I unbutton his jeans and he steps out of them, I find more on the backs of his legs.

'Oh, Jack.'

I expect him to tell me to leave rather than let me see him naked. When he doesn't, I pull his boxers down. I help him into the bath, reminding him to keep his hand elevated and his bandages out of the water.

He just sits in the water, staring ahead. I grab a sponge and dab at the blood on his face and neck. There's something soothing about tending to him. It reminds me that whatever Jack might have done, I am still his mother. He hasn't spared me because I am useful to him. He really does still need me.

I won't let him down.

CHAPTER TWENTY-TWO

'Wow, you look like shit.'

I look up from the boxes I am hovering over. Aaron stands in the doorway, messenger bag slung across his chest. Today, he's wearing another tight T-shirt adorned by a pop art Warholesque portrait of Frida Kahlo, showing off his toned arms. He's had a haircut; his fringe now flips over to the left, the right-hand side is shaved. Designer stubble dots his jaw. I'm pretty sure he's wearing black mascara and a nude lipstick. As ever, he can carry it off.

I also notice one other thing about him today. Alarm floods through my system and my eyes widen as I take him in.

'You can talk . . . what the hell happened to you?'

Aaron flashes me a rueful smile. Grazes cluster the right side of his face, like he might be dragged along the ground or a wall. They are raw and painful-looking. There's swelling around his temple and cheek too.

There's no doubt about it: Aaron has been in a vicious fight.

'It looks worse than it is —' he puffs up his chest — 'other guy came off worse.'

Disconcerted, I understand by instinct Aaron did not start the fight, but he finished it. Just hours earlier, I'd been tending to Jack's injuries . . . Now Aaron appears like he's done a few rounds with Mike Tyson too, boasting about how he put the other guy down.

'Who did it?' I demand.

'Whatcha gonna do, finish the job for me?' Aaron smirks. 'I can handle myself. You have to, even round here. It's fine.'

'No, I mean, did you know him?'

I mentally cross my fingers. Jack would not give me any details of what had happened last night. I'd assumed he'd attacked a transient, but what if it had been Aaron? Jack had already said the podcaster was annoying. If he'd chanced upon him around Camden in the dark, he might have become clouded by bloodlust. He could have become unable to resist his base impulses, just like I'd feared.

Even worse, Aaron is not a stranger. He has met Jack a couple of times now, right here in the archives. Once when Jack had swept in here after school; the other time the day after he'd killed Steve. If it was Jack who'd beaten Aaron up last night, the podcaster must surely remember him? Anxiety spears me in the chest as I search his body language and face for clues.

'Nah, never seen him before.'

I halt the audible exhale of relief that has built up in my throat. I send up a silent thanks to fate or whatever deity is protecting us. Another reprieve. I sit down on a box, groaning like an old woman. Aaron's brow furrows.

'Everything okay?'

Nope, not even a little bit, I want to say. But I don't.

'I'm just tired.'

For once, it is the truth. I'd left Jack sleeping but dragged myself into work. I have used up all my holiday and can't afford any more time off. I'd still felt pretty wired this morning, but the comedown had hit around lunchtime. I'm struggling to keep my eyes open and moving in slowmo. I feel as if concrete has replaced the marrow in my bones, I am that weary. I turn the attention back to him.

'You telling the police?'

Aaron snorts, like I've just said something ludicrous.

He sits down on a box, wincing. 'Fuck it.'

He touches one hand to his ribs. I note his knuckles are scabbed over. I would never have placed a guy like Aaron as someone who can handle himself in a fight. But I of all people should know we never can tell what others are really like. We only have assumption and guesswork based on outward appearances and behaviour, both past and present.

'Missed you while you were away,' Aaron says.

I blink, unable to compute for a moment, then it clicks. I'm only just back at work after taking ten days off to bury Steve, which means I haven't seen Aaron for almost two weeks. I can't imagine why he's bothered. He is only friendly with me to gain access to the archives.

Isn't he?

'Thought I'd have a little staycation,' the lie trips off my tongue, 'catch up on some reading, some boxsets. That kind of thing.'

'You deserve some time off.' Aaron smiles at me.

I don't know how I am supposed to feel when he says this. Another true crime documentary springs to life in my mind's eye. On my mental screen a dour, very serious-looking psychologist talks about the 'emptiness' of psychopaths; how so many feel like there's a void or chasm inside them. Some even describe wanting to fill themselves up with sawdust or concrete. Others would demand special privileges or rights to make themselves feel better. When I'd watched the show, I'd laughed and said to Jack that everyone feels that way. Now I'm not so sure.

Perhaps he is the way he is . . . because of ME?

No. Of course not.

That's ridiculous.

Back with Aaron, I flash him a grin full beam. 'That's very kind. Did you find any more of Nilsen's letter?'

I already know his search has ground to a halt, but my deflection works. Aaron leans forward like we are co-conspirators.

'That other one made me wait until she was finished in there every day because I am, quote, "hogging the archives".' Aaron does sixty-six and ninety-nines, just like Maria does. 'I wanted to say, "Bitch, hogging from whom? I'm the only one apart from you here!"'

He finally runs out of steam and tells me he made more progress while I was away. He shows me the strips he thinks are from Nilsen like they're contraband. I fetch the clipboard from my desk where it's been concealed from Maria. We argue and arrange the strips on the clipboard until we believe they're in some semblance of order:

Darling Dorothy
How I wish
those red lips
the eyes of a devil
powerless against your charms
hands bloody
in too deep
Without you, there is no me.
Dennis

I have no idea if the strips are in the right order, but once again the irony of many of Nilsen's words beyond the grave are not lost on me. I am in too deep; my hands are bloody with sin: without me, there would be no Jack, even.

'You think that's all of it?' Aaron says.

I turn towards him and discover his face close to mine. I realise our heads are bent over the clipboard, our bodies touching. As his eyes drop from mine to my lips, I feel like he is going to kiss me. But that's ridiculous. I have nearly fifteen years on this young man; I'm a mum of nearly forty. My son is closer in age to Aaron.

'Who knows?' I say, moving away from him.

The spell is broken. Aaron smirks, like he knows I know what he was thinking. Keen to avoid a post-mortem — the younger generation are so keen to dissect every single moment or emotion — I turn my back on him to put the clipboard away. Case closed.

As I look back to ask Aaron if he wants a coffee, the situation spins on its head again.

'Y'know, the fight last night got me thinking though . . . about these attacks in the borough?'

My whole body feels like it clenches up. I'd unwound far too soon.

'What attacks?' I'm amazed by how calm my voice sounds.

Aaron pulls something from his bag and chucks it at me: the *Camden New Journal*. It's today's. The headline reads: *LOCAL HOMELESS LIVE IN FEAR*.

Shit.

As I'd feared, Jack *had* been up to something while I interred Steve's body under the basement floor and then retired to my bed. I curse inwardly at my bad luck. Even though my son hadn't been the one to beat on Aaron, Jack is back in the podcaster's sights. Aaron is all about true crime. It stands to reason he would be interested in a local case.

'Oh yeah, I think I have seen something about this,' I lie.

My guilt must be radiating off me in waves. I chance a look at Aaron, but he's kicked back on the box, leaning on his elbows.

'Nationals don't seem interested . . . yet,' Aaron muses. 'My podcast might be able to break the story. Especially if that first guy in intensive care dies. Sorry, that sounds really bad, doesn't it?'

He must have noticed my grimace at his casualness.

'Just a bit.' I force jollity into my voice.

'I need something that will get my podcast to the next level. This could be it.'

NoNoNoNoNONONO.

I can't let Aaron investigate the local homeless attacks. It will lead him straight to Jack. I've listened to multiple episodes of Aaron's podcast. For all his talk of mistrusting authorities, I know he is a believer in natural justice; he thinks good should prevail. There is nothing just or good about Jack's violence, so I know Aaron will report his suspicions if he turns up anything incriminating. I can't allow police to even entertain the idea of Jack being the perpetrator. If they come to the house with a warrant, it will only be a matter of time before Steve's remains are discovered in the cellar.

Then we are both sunk.

I let none of this show on my face. 'Seems like a ball ache.'

It's the wrong thing to say; unnecessarily flippant. Aaron's forehead knits in curiosity. Before he can quiz me on what I mean, I jump ahead of him.

'I mean, you're nearly finished with the Nilsen letter,' I point out, 'that's surely enough to take your podcast to the next level? An iconic serial killer, links to a local woman like Dorothy, who possibly was even in cahoots with him?'

Though I'd never had any intention of allowing Aaron to take credit for the Nilsen letter, needs must. Maria would be furious with me and might even sack me if word got out, but I must weigh everything up. Between Jack and even my dream job at the archives, the choice is clear. There's no contest.

I choose Jack.

Every. Single. Time.

'Even if I find all the bits, authenticating it will cost a packet.' Aaron yawns, wincing again. 'Sometimes thousands. I looked it up online.'

'That's okay. The archives will pay.'

The moment the words are out of my mouth, I groan on the inside. There's no way the lawyers managing the Atkinson estate will agree to such a thing. They wouldn't even pay for an exterminator for the rats. The archives are nothing but a hindrance to them, an annoying sideshow in Dorothy's legacy. They've already sold off her many houses, vehicles, jewellery and art. They would have got rid of the archives a long time ago if her will had not expressly forbidden it.

Maria would obviously not agree to the archives paying for authentication of Nilsen's letter, either. Anything that called her beloved Dorothy into question would be met with extreme pushback. She still believed Aaron was a university student doing research for a film project, though only this morning she'd made it clear she hadn't quite bought the ruse. She'd stood over me in the office, a big smile on her unmade-up face.

'You know he's sweet on you.'

I'd glanced up from my computer, bleary and absent-minded after a night chasing after Jack. Maria must have mistaken my silence for distress after Steve's 'suicide' because her jolly expression crumpled into one of mortification.

'I am an idiot, sorry, Tasha. It's far too soon to say stuff like that, I feel horrible . . . !'

I'd waited for Maria to run out of words before replying, as is customary. 'It's fine, but who are you talking about?'

Maria's shoulders slumped in relief. 'The young lad, with the bag. Saying he has that project . . . yeah, right. Anyone can see it. He's starry-eyed around you.'

'Can't say I noticed.'

(Of course, if that near-miss kiss was for real she'd been right.)

Her smile had fallen from her lips again. 'No. Of course not.'

Maria patted me on the shoulder, like I was her grand-mother. Then she'd shuffled off, deep into the shelves and boxes before going for an ultra-long lunch. She's still gone, now.

My offer seems to have hooked Aaron, though.

'You think so?'

'Absolutely. The letter would be an amazing find for us . . . As long as we could get all the pieces.'

I remind myself all I need is Aaron gainfully employed and distracted. He will probably never find every shred of paper. I can probably keep my job and keep Aaron away from Jack. It's a win-win.

If by some miracle Aaron does complete the letter, I could just pay for the authentication costs myself and tell Aaron it was the estate. I have credit cards. Any price is worth paying to keep Jack's secret and to keep us both out of prison. As for Maria sacking me . . . well I'll cross that bridge if and when I come to it.

Aaron nods. 'Well, technically *I'm* doing all the finding.'

'Right. Well, I can still help you when Maria's not around. And obviously we can work something out with your podcast, too. It would be an exclusive?'

Unlike the homeless attacks story, I want to add but don't. I can't afford to draw him back to that. I wait, on tenterhooks, for his answer.

Aaron grins. 'Then what are we waiting for?'

CHAPTER TWENTY-THREE

I arrive home to find the house an abject nightmare. I can
see the front room in disarray to my left. Up ahead, at the
back of the house the kitchen is in a similar state. There's
dirty dishes in the sink and on the sideboard; the recycling
bin is overflowing; kitchen cupboard doors are open. Shoes
are scattered up and down the hallway, lying where they'd
been kicked off.

'Jack!' I holler up the stairs.

I drop my bag in the hall and move into the kitchen.
The house had been spotless when I'd left that morning; I
can't believe what Jack has done. By the look of it, he only
made himself some noodles: the grimy saucepan, the plastic
wrapper and foil packet of seasoning give him away. How
the hell has he managed to trash the place in so short a time?

I suppose I ought to be grateful this is the worst he's
behaved in recent weeks. Every evening we have sat together,
watching Netflix boxsets and eating off our laps. Since Jack
returned with the dislocated thumb, he's not left his bed in
the middle of the night. Everything appears to be back to
how it was B.S. (*Before Steve*). I dare to hope Jack could have
purged the violence from his system. Perhaps he won't go
looking for trouble again.

Fingers crossed.

'Ja—! Oh, there you are.' I jump as I find him behind me; he still makes me a little on edge. 'What the hell happened here?'

Jack shrugs. 'Just making dinner.'

'Well, bloody clean up after yourself!'

I move to go upstairs. As I turn, I hear him mutter something under his breath.

'You're so uptight.'

My edginess forgotten, I round on him, righteous motherly fury replacing any trepidation around my only child I'd felt seconds earlier.

'*What* did you say?'

Jack shrinks away from me, hands up in mock surrender.

'Fine, fine. I'll do it.'

'My house, my rules,' I hiss. 'Get it?'

'Yes!' Jack moves towards the sink and the dirty dishes.

Exhausted, I pull my clothes off and drag myself under the shower. I'd stayed late at the archives helping Aaron look for more paper shreds, just like I promised. Meanwhile, as I'd put up with Aaron's incessant chatter and been working hard to keep him distracted from the homeless attacks, Jack had been home creating a tornado of mess.

Bloody kids.

Turning off the water, I dry off and put on my favourite *Friends* pyjamas and fluffy pink slippers. Leaving my hair wet and straggly, I return to the kitchen to see how Jack is doing.

Even though I'd taken my time in the bathroom, he's made little progress. Like most teens, he moves in slow motion if the outcome of the task is not for him. At least that part of him is normal. That said, the sides are tidy; the dishes are clean and drying on the rack; the cupboard doors are closed. He is trying. I take pity on him and grab the recycling bin.

'You run the vacuum around and put the shoes away, okay?'

I grab the recycling bin and go out into the hallway, towards the front door. Jack scuttles after me. I can see his anxious expression in the hall mirror.

'Where are you going?'

I'm both touched he is worried and relieved he seems to still want me around. I indicate the bin in my arms, my pyjamas.

'Where do you think?' I smile. 'Look at me. I'm hardly going to be going on a date, am I?'

Jack scowls. 'You better not. You promised.'

I sigh, my good humour evaporated.

'I *know*.'

My son seems reassured. I don't add that I am still grieving for Steve. I don't want Jack triggered. I have worked so hard to restore everything to how it was.

I open the front door and take the recycling into the front garden to the bin store. Separating the plastic, cardboard and metal, I chunter to myself as I throw them into the different coloured boxes. Kids don't know they're bloody born.

A mother's work is never done.

The bin emptied, I stand in the cool night air for a moment. I can hear televisions, a muffled argument, a dog barking somewhere in the distance. A car glides down my street towards the junction at the bottom, illuminating my front garden and blinding me for a second as I look at its headlights.

As I blink, the lights reform around a male shape that seems to loom out of the darkness at me, almost making me shriek. I stagger backwards, out of his range.

'Sorry, sorry!'

It's Aaron. He's standing on the other side of my garden gate. Despite the chilly night air, he's bare-armed. He tokes from an e-cigarette, that messenger bag still slung diagonally across his chest. The unmistakable smell of cannabis oil wafts from him. I glance back towards the house.

'Aaron! What the hell are you doing here?'

I don't want Jack seeing him here. It could be enough to set off one of his murderous rages. I'd confirmed my promise to my son I wouldn't date anyone mere seconds ago. Though I am not interested in the podcaster, it's clear he fancies his chances with me.

'Nice PJs.' Aaron grins. 'You forgot this.'

Aaron presents me with my phone. I take it, puzzled. I'd shown Aaron out of the Atkinson Film Project. He can't have gone back for it; he doesn't have a key . . .

Wait a goddamn minute.

'You took this?' I accuse.

Aaron shrugs. 'You're welcome. See you tomorrow!'

He tips me an imaginary hat and swaggers off down the road. I watch him go, half-impressed by his chutzpah; the other half of me is incandescent.

What the hell was he even trying to achieve?

I open my phone and swipe through it, worried something incriminating I might have forgotten could be on it. To my relief there's nothing bar a bunch of work emails, some invoices, innocent photos of me and Jack, a few memes I'd collected from Facebook.

I groan. It's obvious. Aaron wanted to know where I lived, so was looking for my address . . . which he must now have, because I'd never given it to him and he was here tonight. How the hell had he got past my passcode lock?

Even as I ask myself this, I recall reading about phone apps that can run combinations until the code is identified. Unlike me, Aaron is tech-savvy like most of Gen Z. They live online, he is bound to have an app like that.

For crying out loud.

Letting myself back into my house, I'm grateful the kitchen is at the back of the house unlike most of the terrace. Dad had remodelled it himself years ago when I was still a teenager. That means Jack can't have heard my conversation or seen Aaron.

As the front door slams, he looks up from where he's making a cup of tea at the counter.

'Want one?'

My irritation melts. *What a considerate boy.*

I nod and join him in the kitchen. The (unsolicited and unwarranted) return of my phone makes something else occur to me.

'Did Steve's phone ever turn up?'

Despite turning the house upside down after wrapping up Steve's corpse in plastic, I'd been unable to find the handset. It hadn't been in his car either; I'd done a fingertip search of the vehicle before I'd abandoned it at Beachy Head.

Just in case.

Jack presents me with a mug. 'No, haven't seen it.'

I blow on my tea. Steve's phone must have been in his jeans pocket. I hadn't wanted to unwrap him to double-check for obvious reasons, especially after his body's state of decay when the chest freezer broke. If what I surmise is true, the handset will have run out of charge weeks ago and is now encased in concrete for good measure.

Or perhaps Steve never brought his phone to my place that fateful night? It's possible he left it plugged in by accident back at his flat above 1939. If that's the case, it will be long gone. I know Rosie's husband came down to Camden and emptied out the apartment and business. There's a big TO LET sign in the whitewashed window, the unit empty inside. I guess poor Zane will have moved on somewhere else by now. He'll be okay.

Now the rest of us need to move on.

'Night, son.'

I lean into kiss Jack good night on the cheek.

I miss, grazing his lips and laugh.

Oops.

He rolls his eyes at me.

'Night, Mum.'

CHAPTER TWENTY-FOUR

'Where are you going?'

Jack's demand is quiet, but it stops me in my tracks as he appears at my bedroom door. Fear ripples down my back as I continue brushing my hair. I feign nonchalance, trying to keep my tone light.

'Just some awards do.'

I'm telling the truth. I must go to the ceremony for work. It's an organisation I've never heard of; something to do with British culture and heritage. They want to give the archives a special commendation in memory of Dorothy Atkinson.

My gaze meets my son's in my dressing-table mirror.

'I told you no dates, didn't I?'

'I am not going on a date. I swear.'

I smile at him, but Jack's expression is stony. He doesn't believe me. He knows I usually share plans in advance. But I couldn't this time. In her usual scatterbrained way, Maria had announced only that morning we were both showing our faces that evening like it was a foregone conclusion. When I'd said it was the first I'd heard of the shindig, Maria had shrugged. She'd said I needed a good night out and few drinks inside me.

I couldn't argue with that.

'I don't even want to go,' I confess.

Again, it's the truth. I am tired after a busy week. With no time for shopping that day thanks to Maria, I've had to make do with a dress I bought a few years earlier for an acquaintance's wedding I'd ended up dodging last minute when I got mild food poisoning. The tags are still on.

'You going with a man?'

'With *Maria*.' I stand up from my dressing table, still fixing my earrings.

Jack scowls. 'I bet she fancies you.'

'She does not!'

I laugh but more unease skitters down my spine. I don't want Jack fixating on the idea Maria might make a pass at me. I like her and don't want Jack going after her.

'Gay people don't just fancy *everyone*. You of all people should know that.'

It's the right thing to say. Jack smiles, grudgingly impressed with my retort. He'd come out to me the week before his fifteenth birthday. I'd been a little surprised in the moment. Now I think back, I can see it. Anyway, it makes no difference to me.

Jack's seething resentment seems to deflate. Relief surges through me and I embrace him, luxuriating in the feel of his chin resting on my shoulder. I step back and kiss him on the cheek.

'I won't be late.'

'You better not be,' he mutters.

His demeanour doesn't concern me now. He was just worried. Teenagers are funny beasts: they want their independence but worry their parents will leave them. They're almost like toddlers; someone should send them all to Supernanny.

'You're my number-one boy . . . you know that, right?'

Jack shrugs, averting his eyes as ever. He shuffles back off in the direction of his bedroom. I smile indulgently, watching him go. Now I think of it, it's better he's gay.

I don't have to share him with another woman.

CHAPTER TWENTY-FIVE

'You find some seats if you can. I'll get the drinks in.'

Maria disappears into the throng around the bar. The building we're in is an exclusive club. Out front, there had even been a sliding peephole in the door. When we'd knocked, it had rattled back and a pair of impassive green eyes peered through.

When whoever was on the other side didn't say anything, I realised he was waiting for a password. Maria had pleaded with him to just let us in, but it was no-go. She ended up emptying her entire handbag into my hands in search of the invite. Thankfully she found it right at the bottom, shouting the password through the peephole in triumph.

It's dim inside the club. All around me are men in pressed tuxedos, women in expensive dresses. Waiting for Maria and alcohol, my eyes widen as I take in the clientele. Nearby is a middle-aged male actor better known for his outspoken, right-leaning opinions on Twitter. He sits in a booth, an adoring dolly bird either side of him. A female singer still famous for a number-one hit from the 1990s is seated at the bar, chatting with her girlfriends.

They're the only two celebrities I recognise, though I realise the others must be famous too. A couple of beautiful faces flashing back seem familiar; I realise I must have seen them online or maybe on billboards. Some of them are good-looking enough to be models.

'Natalie.' Aaron looms out of the darkness, a delighted smile on his face. 'I didn't know you were coming tonight?'

Like all the other men, he's wearing a dark suit, though his tie is neon pink. He swoops in and kisses my cheek like media luvvies are supposed to. Caught on the hop, fury floods through me before I have the chance to lock it away.

'Natasha. My name's *Natasha*,' I snap, correcting him at last.

Aaron chortles; my anger amuses him.

'Okay. Why didn't you say so before now?'

'I'm pretty sure I did,' I lie.

A little panicked, I look behind me; I can't see Maria in the crush by the bar. I will her to come back, rescue me. There's something about the way Aaron's been with me all this time, coming into the archives: flirtatious and familiar, letting his body touch mine when we clambered into the bins.

Maria's words from the other day echoed in my ears too: *He's sweet on you.* I don't want to spend too much time with the podcaster. I feel like my promise to Jack is being broken, against my will.

'You up for an award or something?' I struggle to find words, stay calm.

'No, I'm a member here.'

Of course he is. Someone cool and with-it like Aaron would never let an event like this pass him by. *Damn it!*

'So, what are you doing here?' Aaron leans against a tall bar table at elbow height.

I can't deny there is something appealing about being the object of desire in such a young guy, just like there'd been when Jack said his friends called me a MILF. But my ego is not important. Aaron's burgeoning interest is dangerous. For him, but maybe for me too. I can guess what Jack might do to both of us if he thinks I have betrayed him.

'The archives is getting a special mention or something.'

I say it with a dismissive wave, but Aaron's eyes widen. He's impressed.

'That's fantastic, you must be really proud?'

Thanks to Maria dropping the event on me, I've not had time to think about it. Even if I had, I have more pressing issues to deal with. A flush of guilt prickles my neck. I still miss Steve; going out and celebrating *anything* feels wrong.

But Steve is gone.

Life must move on.

Whether we like it or not.

I make small talk with Aaron for a few more frustrating minutes. When Maria has been gone nearly ten minutes, I start to look for another chance to exit. Men never like to stand between women and the lavatory, so I decide that's my best bet; then I can accidentally lose him on the way back.

'I have to go the ladies.'

Aaron nods. 'Hurry back, won't you.'

Not if I can help it.

I make it to the toilets without incident. In my head I'd decided I would escape via the bathroom window, but I hadn't reckoned with my inexperience of going out in the last two decades.

There's no window.

Despite the lack of natural light, the toilets are not hot like the bar; there must be an air conditioner in here. Unlike the pub and club lavatories of my misspent youth, the toilets are every bit as plush as the venue beyond. There's a marble countertop and mirror that runs the length of the back wall. The place smells of lavender and two women snort lines of coke while gossiping, right out in the open. They don't flinch as they see me looking around.

'You okay, love?' one says, pinching her nose between her thumb and finger like she's about to go diving. 'You need to ask for Angela?'

Something tells me this is code. The other one titters.

'It's for women on creepy dates. Go to the bar, ask for Angela. The barman will get you a cab.'

Perfect.

I affect a relieved stance. 'Thank you so much, you're lifesavers!'

'Men are the worst,' the first one says, her expression grave.

'Totally,' her friend agrees.

My mission in mind, I make it out of the toilets, my sights set on the bar. As I stride through the throng, someone grabs me around the waist, pulling me to him.

'Hey, where you off to?'

Damn it!

I grab the hands and try to extricate myself from them. I look up, expecting to see Aaron. I catch sight of a beard and freeze. For a moment I am locked in an embrace with the dead Steve, my face crushed against his rotten chest, the cloying smell of decay in my nostrils and the buzz of flies in my eardrums.

'Dance with me.'

The spell is broken. It's not Aaron, or Steve (*of course*). My unwanted suitor is a large, bearded guy in a crumpled suit with a ruddy complexion and acne scars on his temples and forehead. I know him from somewhere; he might be an actor. I can envisage him on my television screen, yelling at his underlings about catching perps. Some police procedural.

'Get off me!'

I renew my struggle, but this only causes the actor to lock his arms around my torso. His gaze is misty, a sloppy grin on his face. He's drunk as hell and amused by my protestations. He grinds against me in what he imagines is a sexy way. He succeeds only in pushing his semi against my stomach. *Yuk.*

What happens next is so fast I have barely enough time to take it in, even though it happens right in front of me. There's movement in the periphery of my vision; the feel of air as something moves at speed past my face.

A fist.

It connects with the actor's face, just below his left eye. He lets go of me at last and goes down. He hits the floor with a heavy thud that reverberates under my shoes even through the loud music in the club. The people dancing simply move to accommodate his fallen body; no one rushes over to see if he is okay. Stupefied, I whirl around and come face-to-face with my saviour.

Aaron.

'Fuck.' Aaron shakes his fist in pain. 'Always forget how much it hurts to punch someone. You okay?'

Vacant, I just nod.

He guides me towards a booth and slides in with me on the same side. He presents me with a glass of bourbon I didn't ask for. His own, probably. I don't like whisky but I gulp it down anyway, savouring the burn.

'You can handle yourself,' I acknowledge.

My assumption about Aaron's previous fight had been correct, then: he might not start such contretemps, but he will finish them if he has to.

Aaron shrugs. 'Got to. Men are the worst.'

His words bring to mind the women in the toilets just minutes' earlier. Only then I had been trying to escape *Aaron*. There's something a little ridiculous about a man using the same logic women have to, in order to keep themselves safe. Knights in shining armour like Aaron never realise they may still be part of the issue, however progressive they pride themselves on being.

I smirk at him. 'Like "rescuing" women, do you?'

'So cynical.' Aaron smiles. 'Maybe I am just doing what I think is right?'

'Isn't "right" a matter of interpretation?' I counter.

'Touché.' Aaron concedes.

Maria still hasn't returned from the bar. I take one last look around for her. Feeling suddenly weary, I make a decision.

'I have to go.'

Aaron pouts. 'Really? It's still early.'

'For you, maybe. I'm old, remember.'

'Not old . . . Vintage.'

'Same thing.'

'Hardly.'

I rise from the booth. I bend down, meaning to kiss him on the cheek goodbye. Not expecting it, Aaron moves so our lips touch. We both jerk our heads back, surprised.

'Sorry,' Aaron says. 'I didn't mean . . .'

He's silenced as I press my lips against his a second time, this time meaning to. I let him pull me back into the booth with him, so I'm almost sitting on his lap. As his tongue teases mine, the heat between us feels incredible. I forget all about Jack waiting at home. The rest of our surroundings and my inner critic melts away.

So what if the people around us are rich or famous? That doesn't make them better than me. I am with the best-looking guy in here, plus he's younger than me.

They should be the ones jealous.

Aaron breaks off the kiss. 'Wow. I've been wanting to do this since that first day I came into the archives.'

Pleasure blossoms through me, but it's quickly followed by an even stronger surge of shame. That first time Aaron had come into the Atkinson Project, Steve had still been alive. I'm still supposed to be grieving for him.

Too late, Jack's accusing scowl sears through my mind next. He's dangerous. He had specifically asked me *not* to date anyone . . . plus Aaron is literally a true crime podcaster! He could unmask us. I must be insane.

What the hell am I doing?

'This was a mistake.'

I try to turn away from him, run off. Aaron's arm snakes out and grabs my wrist, preventing me. When I turn around, there's another smile tugging at his lip. He's sympathetic this time like he expected my sudden change of heart.

'Is that what you really think, or what you believe you're *supposed* to think?' His eyes search my face. 'Why shouldn't you go out, have fun?'

'My boyfriend just died!' I hiss.

Aaron lets go of my wrist. He holds both hands up in surrender.

'You're right. Sorry.'

I just stand there. Despite my brain's best efforts to remind me about Jack, my body can't deny the sexual current between me and Aaron. I can feel a stirring within my core. He moves closer to me; I let him. One thing still confuses me.

'You can have anyone you want?' I mutter.

'I want you, though.'

'But why?' I take a deep breath. 'I'm not like you.'

'Exactly. I'm not a normal guy, Tasha. But you . . . you're dangerous. I could tell the moment I met you.'

His words feel white-hot with truth; they burn me. How can he know? By instinct alone, he's revealed me.

I like it.

I let him pull me back into a booth with him. I smirk, allowing myself to be carried along with him.

'If I'm so dangerous, shouldn't I be the one corrupting *you*?'

'Oh, you are,' Aaron says, 'I don't normally do women like you, I can tell you.'

I am distracted again. His mouth clamps on mine. I feel his hand resting on my hip. Need throbs through me. Aaron is more adept than Dean ever was. How can this be? He is so young. I feel myself melt around him as he takes charge. He's more aggressive than Steve ever was with me.

My dead boyfriend's face, his eye a bloody mess.

My own eyes open. I'm no longer in ecstasy, but a too-loud, badly lit bar in Soho. The shutters of my mind rattle down. I'm kissing a boy practically young enough to be my son.

I am turned off.

It's like Aaron's peeled back the respectable layers I have tried so hard to cloak myself with all these years. He might not know the exact details about Dean and Steve or Jack, but he can sense it, dark like a stain within me. Perhaps that's why I'd attracted Dean in the first place.

No. Everything has come from Dean. It all started from him, even Jack.

'Get off!'

Both my palms connect with Aaron's shoulders, pushing him away. He gapes at me, lust clouding his face. This drops from his face as I turn on my heel and run from the booth.

I race off, leaving him in my wake. Crashing through the double doors leading out of the club. I tense up as I run back through the hallway, my shoes clacking on the marble floor. The big bouncer sees me and opens the door obligingly, like he's used to people suddenly legging it. Maybe he is.

I falter as I make it into the cold darkness outside. I've left my coat checked in and forgotten my bag. My phone is in my bag, too. Typical. How the hell will I get home? I can't face going back inside, but I can't stay here. I hug myself, watching the hairs on my bare arms rise under the glow of the streetlamps.

I don't have to wait long. A minute or two later, the door opens again behind me and I hear Aaron exchange amiable 'goodnights' with the bouncer. He appears next to me, proffering my coat and bag.

Grateful, I take them. My teeth stop chattering as my arms make their way back into my coat sleeves.

'So . . . what's wrong?' Aaron shoves his hands in his pockets.

'I just *can't.*'

'You just think you can't. Give yourself permission.'

'Spare me the pop psychology, will you?' I snarl.

There's a pause. I can hear the hiss of traffic in the distance, the hubbub of voices from other bars and clubs. Aaron tilts his head at me, untroubled by my outburst. I stare back, defiant and vulnerable. I can't maintain my animosity. I feel hackles begin to lower. Aaron senses it too; he moves closer. I let him embrace me and rest his chin on top of my head as if I am just a kid.

'Whatever happened to you is in the past. I promise you are safe with me.'

I sigh, resting my face against his chest. I'm surprised to find grateful tears welling up. Finding another kind

150

man, so soon after what happened to poor Steve, feels like redemption.

But could it be an omen, too?

I *am* dangerous, just not the way Aaron thinks. Jack will become enraged and homicidal if he ever finds out. I'd promised him: no more boyfriends. Aaron might vow safety for me, but I can't promise him the same.

'Thanks, but I have to go.'

Aaron sighs but releases me.

'If you change your mind . . . ?'

I walk away from him.

'I won't. Night, Aaron.'

When I look back over my shoulder, he's gone.

CHAPTER TWENTY-SIX

I wake the next morning, in my red dress, shoes still on, star-fished on my bed. I groan as I roll over. It feels as if I have a hangover: my head bangs and my mouth is dry.

The light on my mobile is blinking; the notifications window tells me I have a bunch of messages from Maria.

Where are you??

I can't see you anywhere

I CAN'T BELIEVE YOU WENT HOME!!!

Before guilt kicks in, I cast my eye further down the thread. There's a selection of photos of Maria with a variety of famous faces. Charles Dance, looking very uneasy with Maria leaning into him with adoring eyes. Then Idris Elba, sticking out his tongue and holding up bunny ears behind Maria's head. Next, a female television presenter whose name I can't remember giving Maria a kiss on the lips. My boss had a good time without me.

I'm in the clear.

What will Louisa say about you and whatserface?? I type, adding a winky face.

The little bubbles pop up right away. Maria's reply comes in microseconds later.

Already shown her, she's well jel!!! So why did you leave?

I can't be bothered to get into it with her about Aaron.

Just had to get back for Jack, I thought he was ready for me to leave him for the evening, but he wasn't. Sorry I had to go without telling you x

No biggie, see you Monday!! xx

I'm about to put my phone back on the nightstand when the text icon flashes again. Expecting it to be Maria again with something she's forgotten to tell me, I open it.

So, can I take you on a date or not?

It's not from Maria, but Aaron. I am surprised and a little flattered by his directness. I am not used to such a lack of game play. Even Steve liked the thrill of the chase. He'd 'bumped into me' accidentally-on-purpose in the street in and around 1939 and the Atkinson Film Project for three agonising weeks before he'd asked me for a drink.

Our first date had been a much lower key and confusing affair than last night too. When Steve hadn't called or texted right away, I'd assumed he hadn't felt any spark between us. In my head I'd sworn off men forever and pretended it didn't matter to me. Then I cracked and ate a jumbo bag of Maltesers, drinking a bottle and a half of Pinot to myself. Steve must have been following old-fashioned 1990s dating advice though. Like clockwork on the third day he'd called me and asked me for a second date.

If only he'd stayed well clear.

I push this maudlin thought away. I glance at the clock on my phone screen: it's not even nine in the morning yet. I would have thought someone like Aaron would not be up for hours yet.

My finger hovers over my phone. I can't deny there's part of me that wants Aaron like he seems to want me. As an almost forty-year-old, the thought of any interested twenty-five-year-old — never mind one as good-looking as Aaron — feels intoxicating.

On the screen, those little bubbles start moving again.

Tasha? xx

I must end this madness right now, before someone else gets hurt.

Steve didn't deserve what happened to him, but I could not be expected to be psychic or read the future. In contrast, I cannot knowingly put Aaron in danger. I also don't know how Jack will react to me breaking my word. I daren't risk it. My gut instinct last night was the right one.

I don't think it's a good idea, I start to type . . . then stop.

If I tell Aaron I am not interested in him, he could be embarrassed enough to stop coming into the archives altogether. That would mean giving up on the Nilsen letter. Whilst that would be good for me with regards to Maria, Aaron might start investigating the homeless attacks instead. That would lead him straight to Jack.

Fuck.

Sorry, was just in shower — I marvel at how fast the lie comes to my fingertips — *why don't we talk about this on Monday? xxx*

A reply is almost instantaneous: *Why wait? I could come round today xx*

Aaron cannot come back to the house. That would be a disaster. Being Saturday, Jack is home. Bar the odd trip into town to buy second-hand video games, he's taken to lounging around the house at weekends, watching Netflix boxsets.

Jack will notice if I go out again, too. He has made it clear he is watching my every move. He might follow me and see me with Aaron, even if we meet somewhere neutral like a café. Jack won't believe me it's not what he thinks. I don't want to push my luck.

I'm away this weekend. See you first thing Monday? xx

To my relief, this appears to be good enough for Aaron. He sends me a selection of emojis, including some hearts, flowers and weirdly, an elephant. I send some back, smiling despite myself.

Once I am satisfied the three bubbles are no longer moving, I delete the thread. I need to get into the habit of hiding my tracks. I already know that Jack can get into my phone; that's how he found out about Steve, when he spotted his scrunchie downstairs. Even though I have changed the password and make sure he can't read anything over my shoulder, I can't risk it. Like Maria said, attention to detail is my forte. I think of everything.

I shower for real and dress, then meander into the kitchen with wet hair in a straggle down my back. I open the fridge to retrieve the egg box. I'm ravenous. A boiled egg and soldiers would fill the void in my stomach. There's something so comforting about nursery fare. I almost jump out of my skin and drop the egg box when a voice sounds behind me.

'You're up late.'

I sigh; there goes the last of the eggs. Now I'd have to have an omelette.

I shoot an irritated glance at Jack, who's seated at the table, delving in the cereal box as per. My gaze flies to the clock on the wall. Nine thirty.

'And you're up early,' I say, 'got plans or something?'

'Might do.' Jack regards me, his expression inscrutable as ever.

'Like what?'

I try to keep my voice breezy, but Jack does not fall for it. He shrugs.

'Oh you know, GBH, maybe a stabbing or two.' He rolls his eyes as he sees the alarm on my face. 'Relax, Mum. I've got a driving lesson.'

'With who?'

'That old Boomer over the road.' Jack yawns. 'You know, the one that looks like a tramp had a baby with Boris Johnson.'

'Jim?'

Confusion and hurt spears through me. Jim hadn't cleared this with me, or even mentioned it. Before everything had gone to shit with Steve, I'd been planning on teaching Jack to drive myself, like my father had taught me.

Keen to mark the occasion like the parent of a *normal* teenager, I'd planned ahead to Jack's eighteenth birthday, now just ten days away. I'd decided I would take him out to a nearby car park, introduce him to the clutch, pedals, gear stick and everything else he would need. I'd decided I would tell him he was a natural, just like Dad told me. (I wasn't of course, I was terrible and ran over every traffic cone Dad laid out, both on my birthday and for weeks afterwards. By the seventh or eighth lesson though, it had all clicked.)

Jim's stolen this from me. Bastard!

The dark vehemence of my inner voice shocks me. I blink, tamping it back down. I need to get a hold of myself. It's very kind of Jim to take an interest in my son. As this thought occurs, my brow furrows in suspicion.

'Whose idea was it, Jim's or yours?'

'I got sick of waiting for you to teach me.'

Pain hits me in the solar plexus as Jack takes this well-aimed jab at me. It's true; as soon as he'd turned seventeen, I'd told him I would teach him. Then I'd looked up how much the extra fee would be to put a teenage boy on my insurance and balked. I'd told him we'd need to wait until his grandfather's estate was sorted. Jack hadn't pushed, so I'd let it slide, planning on — and budgeting for — surprising Jack with lessons for his eighteenth.

Now it's all for nothing.

'So, *you* asked Jim?'

Jack shakes out the remaining cereal bits from the box. 'Yes.'

As he looks up, something on my face must clue him into my thinking. Disgust clouds his face as he answers me.

'Don't panic, Mum, I can control myself, you know.'

'Can you?'

It's a rhetorical question, but Jack answers anyway.

'Yes! God. This is not all an elaborate ruse to kill him.'

I reach across the table and grab him by the scruff of his hoody.

'You sure?' I hiss. 'We can't afford to draw any more attention!'

We end up eyeballing each other. Jack averts his gaze first, twisting away from me so I'm holding only air. He gets up from the kitchen chair, eyes wide, like I might race across the kitchen and strike him. I'm not having that. He's twice my size, for God's sake.

'Don't act hurt with me, boyo. It's not like you haven't got a track record.'

Jack's face darkens. 'I told you, I'm not *stupid*.'

With that, he grabs his hoody and makes to leave, without kissing me goodbye.

'Wait . . . wait!'

He stops where he is. I grab him and embrace him, but his arms stay by his sides.

'Give Mummy a kiss.'

With a resentful sigh, he offers up his own cheek. I'm not having that. I grab his face in my hands and kiss him under his eye. I feel him attempt to cringe away which brings me a flood of hurt and fury with it. I let go of him.

'Oh, that's nice. Here I am, breaking my back for you!'

'Yeah? I never asked you to,' Jack hisses at me.

'Maybe not,' I splutter, 'but where would you be without me?'

Jack averts his eyes and stares at the floor.

'Where would you be without me?' I fix him with my glare. 'Answer me, Jack!'

'Nowhere.' Jack sighs.

'Worse than that. You'd be screwed. There aren't many mums who'd do what I've done for you, you know. Some thanks would be nice!'

'Thanks,' he mumbles.

Forced gratitude is not satisfying. I feel weary with it all. I never asked for a homicidal son; there are no guidelines. I'm having to make it all up as I go along.

'Enjoy your driving lesson.'

Dismissed, Jack leaves.

I sigh as the front door slams, the metal clatter of the letterbox sounding too. It's quickly followed by despair. I have just been fighting smaller fires, but the true source of conflagration will never go out. So what if I keep Aaron away from Jack, or if I even manage to get my son to stop attacking homeless people?

As it stands, Jack is a liability.

I am paralysed by fear, waiting for him to lash out at someone else. Stranger or neighbour, it doesn't matter. Jack might be in denial about this, but I must face up to this cold, hard fact as his mother.

It is only a matter of time . . . Inevitable.

I abandon the broken eggs on the floor and sit down at the table, staring at the empty cereal box. It's all bright colours: red, blue, yellow, green. A cartoon character gives me the thumbs up, a big smile on its drawn face. Jack is far too old to be still eating this crap. It's no wonder he acts like a perpetual toddler in a tantrum and literally hits out, to devastating consequences.

I let him.

Jack is almost a grown man, filled with an adult's hormones, wants and needs, yet I've treated him like a child too long. I haven't expected him to take responsibility; instead I have made constant excuses for his behaviour. It hasn't ever mattered what he's done, I have justified it all. As Jack has pushed the perimeters of what is acceptable, I have extended my own to accommodate his increasingly twisted and warped behaviour.

But how can I stop him?

Maybe I should make a bloody star chart, like my father did for me all those years ago. I'd hated the humiliation of it, forced to accept and perform within guidelines he'd set. That said, it had worked, hadn't it?

No. I would never shame Jack like that.

My problems with Jack far outstrip any my father had with me, anyway. I'd been brittle, uppity, maybe a bit of a know-it-all. If I am truly honest with myself, I could be cruel too; I found it fun to poke at my classmates' weaknesses. I recall one other girl, a big, round, chubby thing whose name I've forgotten. I'd squish my nose into a pig's snout and oink every lunch hour as I passed her table in the cafeteria.

But there are worse things . . . besides, she lost all that extra weight in year ten. I did her a favour.

I grab the empty cereal box and drop it on the floor, crushing it underfoot. As I shove it in the recycling box amongst ripped envelopes, jars and wine bottles, I feel a strong resolve bloom in my gut.

Since Steve's death, I've been getting it all wrong. In my rush to appease Jack and try and ensure he never does something so awful again, I've thought I have no power.

I've let him walk all over me.

I won't be making that mistake anymore. It's true I must believe my boy is salvageable; that I can turn this situation around. It's also true genetics must surely have some bearing on how kids turn out. But I've let myself become consumed by the thought that Dean's demon seed and past abuse have made Jack this way. This means I've overlooked one important thing.

Nature might play its part, but so does nurture.

I have had my boy all to myself for half his life now. My impact has to equal Dean's. At the very least. I've been running scared too long.

I will take Jack in hand, even if it kills me.

My house, my rules.

CHAPTER TWENTY-SEVEN

Before I lose my impetus, I march out of the kitchen into the hallway. I open that skinny door under the stairs, pulling the cord to the bare bulb dangling from the concrete ceiling. The steep, stone stairs down to the cellar come into view under its harsh glare.

A musty smell wafts up from the subterranean room: damp mostly, but also something else. Decay? No, I must be imagining it. There's no way I can detect the smell of poor Steve's corpse rotting under the floor.

I put one foot on the steps and hesitate. I've never liked the basement; it's creepy. Since we interned my boyfriend down here, I want to go down here even less.

But needs must.

For Jack.

Careful, I pick my way down the steps one at a time like an elderly person or a child. I don't want to pitch straight down them headfirst, onto the hard floor below.

As I reach the bottom, I let my sights take in what's in there: the broken chest freezer; broken cables and half-empty tins of paint; Dad's old fishing gear; an old bike of Jack's that's missing a wheel; several spools of garden hose; box after box of random crap. It's a right state.

For my plan to work, it all needs to go.

Girding myself, I take trip after trip up those lethal stairs, dumping everything in the back of my car. There's an acrid stench to some of the boxes, like cat pee but different. I can't work out what it is until I find a box of papers and photo albums. I dither over them for all five seconds until I detect movement inside it.

A nest of baby rats.

Shrieking, I pick it up and move it at arm's length as fast as I can out of there, into the garden. I dump it on the grass and retreat just as fast. As I go, I hear the sound of cats from other houses jumping up onto our side of the fence. I lock the back door behind me. Safe in the kitchen again, I imagine the felines descending onto the box and peering into the box and their tiny, helpless prey inside.

Back in the now-empty basement, I feel like one of those baby rats. I freeze where I am, as if I can avoid the threat of my own thoughts and the plan that's forming in my mind. I stay close to the steps, like I am expecting a monster to appear in front of me. But I know that's not true. I'm going to put one in here.

Jack.

Sometimes being a mother means unpalatable choices that hurt you as well as the child. I've had to do horrible things to Jack since he was an infant. The day he was born, the doctor on her hospital rounds manipulated my boy's hips to make sure they were in their sockets, making him scream. Only after that was I permitted to take him home.

Days later, the health visitor was drawing blood from Jack's tiny ankle to check for disease and genetic conditions. Months after that came the vaccinations, which continued throughout his childhood and into adolescence.

Then there were all the other times: holding a cold, wet cloth to fevered brows despite screams and chattering teeth; picking gravel from wounds or tending to blisters and pus-filled wounds with stinging antiseptic. Every time Jack would yell, 'Don't, Mummy!', his mouth twisted and howling, his cheeks wet with tears.

I did it anyway. I had to.

It's what good mothers do.

Now I have to do something else I don't want to do.

For Jack's own good.

I pull my phone from my back pocket. As I expect, there's no signal down here. The house Wi-Fi still works though, so I open my YouTube app on a random video and turn the volume as high as it will go. Leaving it on the bottom step, I make my way back up the steps and back into the hallway, closing the door after it.

I can still hear the phone. It's faint, but it's there. I will have to soundproof the basement so no one can hear Jack down there. It's possible I could be overthinking it, but I know it never hurts to consider all possibilities.

Better safe than sorry, as they say.

My plan is a good one.

I already know there's been multiple precedents. It's suburban lore: who hasn't heard about junkies drying out in their relatives' attic spaces and basements? Or the stories about old people and the chronically ill falling and dehydrating to death, no neighbours bothering to check on them?

The evening news has filled us all in on how kidnap victims have lived under floors and roofs for years, even having babies and raising whole families with their captors. Unless they're caught red-handed somehow, no one ever knows, even in the middle of a residential area. Soundproofing makes sure the captive's wails, screams and hollers go unnoticed, before they settle into dejected compliance.

No one will be able to hear Jack, either.

I have a lot of work to do.

CHAPTER TWENTY-EIGHT

As promised, Aaron reappears at the Atkinson Project on Monday morning. I find him waiting on the doorstep, take-away coffees in hand as well a bag full of freshly-baked croissants. He's even brought enough for Maria.

'Someone's keen,' Maria says with an indiscreet wink to me.

'Sorry about her,' I say as she thanks Aaron for her coffee.

'It's fine,' Aaron says, that amused smirk on his lip again.

He trails after me into the project's office, while Maria retires upstairs to kick the ass of Dorothy's lawyers on Zoom. We'd received a load of papers before the weekend, all threatening to close down the project for various health and safety violations. The amount of legalese in them had been intimidating, but Maria had assured me it was all a bluff. I don't share her certainty but seeing her confidence had been encouraging.

As I make painful small talk with Aaron, I'm annoyed with myself for forgetting he was coming to see me. I had been busy planning my basement project all weekend. When Jack had returned from his driving lesson with Jim, he'd noticed the door to the basement was open. He'd found me down there, measuring and planning.

I'd managed to bat Jack's intrigued enquiries away, but later that evening he'd seen me on Amazon, looking for various supplies. Though I'd managed to close the window down before he saw anything too incriminating, he'd seen enough to clock my anticipation. With a triumphant grin, Jack guessed correctly it was all connected to a big birthday surprise for him. Even so, I just smiled, refusing to confirm or deny.

'So, have you given any further thought to what I texted you on Saturday?'

Back at the project, I blink as the wheel in my brain goes round and round. Oh, that's right: Aaron had suggested taking me on a date, blithely unaware that would put a target on his back courtesy of my son. At the same Jack is oblivious to my need to occupy Aaron, to ensure he doesn't start investigating anything that would lead the podcaster to my son's nefarious activities.

Talk about trapped.

'Tasha?'

This is it: crunch time.

In the moment, I decide I will have to risk Aaron investigating Camden's homeless attacks. Even if he does decide to do that, it's still only a 'maybe' that he discovers Jack was behind those. Meanwhile, if he and I go on a date, it's a 'definite' Jack would go after Aaron. He proved that with Steve.

'I've been thinking about it.' I choose my words. 'The age gap is a bit of a problem?'

'Not for me.'

I should have known someone like Aaron wouldn't be fazed by my being so much older. In fact, it's probably a plus.

'Besides, any man would do anything for you,' Aaron says.

His unexpected flattery feels like a lightning bolt. He's right: I do have a way with men. Call it 'feminine wiles', MILF factor or whatever you like: men do tend to get starry-eyed around me. Or maybe Dad's ability to get what he wanted out of other people had rubbed off on me after all.

His star chart had worked.

Now I think back, it's always been there; I'd just allowed Dean to beat me down with his never-ending taunts about me being frumpy, or fat. There's also a part of me that finds Aaron attractive, too. I struggle to rebuff him again.

'It's complicated. I have Jack.'

'You deserve your own life, too. Screw Jack if he doesn't realise that. He's an adult.'

I don't reply. Aaron's right, of course. But Jack is no ordinary child, almost-adult or not. I don't trust myself, so I pretend to be busy moving boxes. This doesn't stop the podcaster. Aaron trails after me into the archives.

'Tasha, you know I'm right. He'll be going to university soon . . . then what? If you don't let him go now, you're in for a world of pain when he really does leave.'

A pang dances through my chest; Aaron is more on point than he knows.

I'm not the only one with a secret. Jack's been acting cagey for weeks, snapping his laptop shut whenever I come in his room. At first I'd thought he might be watching porn, or at least looking at photos of his crush Will Smith, but curiosity had got the better of me.

Guilt had come next, but I also told myself I needed to make sure he wasn't doing anything stupid online that would drop us both in it. The last thing I needed was him making veiled comments on social media, or even just reckless Google searches.

Determined to discover what could be making him so guarded, I'd sent Jack out for a takeaway the previous night. I'd then snuck up to his room and opened his laptop. His browser window had sprung to life.

There it was: the Universities and Colleges Admissions Service site. He'd saved his password, so I had a good snoop around. He'd chosen universities in Scotland, Belfast, the Midlands and the north of England.

Not a single one had been within two hundred miles of London.

I'd ambushed my son with this knowledge when he'd appeared in the hall, whistling, Chinese food in a paper bag.

'I thought we agreed?' I hissed, holding the laptop up like an exhibit in a courtroom trial. 'Only universities in London, we said!'

'No, that's what *you* said, Mother.' Jack's expression had gone from cheerful and carefree to stormy in a microsecond. '*We* never agree anything. You tell me what to do and then expect me to jump to it.'

'That's not what this is about!' I couldn't believe my ears. 'This is *me* keeping *you* safe. You know full well you can't control your urges by yourself! I'm trying to help you. Do you want to get caught?'

If I wanted to make a connection with Jack, it didn't work. Instead he smirked, pulling his phone from his pocket.

'Tell you what, I'll just call the police. Won't make any difference to me, locked up by them or by you. Same diff.'

On instinct, I hit the phone out of his hand. It landed on the kitchen tiles, drawing a gasp of surprise and fury from Jack. Adrenaline courses through me, my fear morphing into delight in a microsecond.

Serves him right.

'You better not have smashed it!'

'I bloody pay for it anyway!' I hollered back. 'I pay for sodding everything! And I'll be damned if I pay for your sick urges with *my* life, rotting away in jail!'

I was angry again. My emotions felt like a shoal of fish, moving back and forth, together and against one another, all at once.

'You're mental,' Jack growled.

'Yeah? Maybe I am mental —' I jabbed him in the chest — 'and if I am, it's *you* who's done this to me!'

'You're the adult.' Jack's expression was maddeningly blank again. 'If anyone is to blame for the way I've turned out? It's *you.*'

Suddenly I'm bored. 'Oh, piss off out of my sight.'

'Fine.'

Jack thrust the bag of food at me and left.

I can't tell Aaron any of this, of course. In the archives, he reaches for my hair and tucks a strand behind my ear. Tender, like a lover.

'Look, I get it, he's your baby' — Aaron's voice is soft — 'but you know what they say . . . "If you love somebody, let them go".'

I let him pull me back towards him. He pushes me against the shelves, planting a kiss on my lips, his hand creeping beneath my blouse. Before I can surrender totally, I break off the kiss and take a deliberate step away from him, smooth my clothes.

'You sound like a Facebook meme, do you know that?'

Aaron grins. 'Erm, Instagram, thank you. Facebook is for old people.'

I'd been trying to break the mood, but our words sound like flirting. I try again.

'Old people like me?'

'Never.'

Damn it.

There's movement by the door. I look up, expecting to see Maria. My eyes widen as I see who it really is.

Jack.

I force myself not to jump back from Aaron; that really would look suspect. Jack wanders into the room, his brow furrowing as he detects the weird atmosphere. My son is in his uniform, though he appears to have lost his school bag and tie.

My brain rebels: it's far too early for him to be home from school. Panic skitters through me next.

How much did he see or hear from me and Aaron?

'Jack!' I say, my tone false and breezy. 'What are you doing back already?'

My boy stops and tilts his head. 'Free period. I forgot my biology textbook, so I came back for it.'

My relief is eclipsed with confusion. 'Okay. Did you leave it here?'

'No. I forgot my key as well.' He holds his hand out for mine.

Now I get it. Jack knows my keyring holds the only copy of the key to the basement. He wants to skulk back to the house, scope out the subterranean room. He's trying to figure out what I'm doing down there.

'No problem.'

I grab my keyring and pull off the front door key for him, leaving the rest of the keys in my possession.

'There you go.' I smile.

'Thanks.'

I see Jack's momentary disappointment, but he hides it again. Such is the power struggle between us. He nods at Aaron, who's watching him with beady eyes. My son doesn't seem perturbed by Aaron's scrutiny.

'All right?' Jack says, his voice gruff.

'All right,' Aaron echoes.

Unable to think of a way to get the rest of my keys, Jack retreats back out into the hallway. The front door slams after him.

'Well, he didn't seem overly bothered.' Aaron purses his lips. 'So what's really going on?'

I decide to play it safe and go with his expectations. Men like Aaron have certain beliefs about themselves and women; they like to be the hero, the rescuer. That's okay, I can pull that off and give him what he wants.

'I'm just finding it difficult adjusting, okay? Jack's my only child. I hate the thought of him leaving home. After the year we've had with my dad dying, then Steve . . . I guess I am just trying to ensure his last few weeks with me are as perfect as possible?'

I hang my head, like I am trying not to cry. It works. Aaron gathers me in his arms and embraces me.

'It will be okay,' he says.

I know it will.

CHAPTER TWENTY-NINE

It's time for the second part of my plan.

It's Friday night and the day before Jack's birthday on Saturday. I leave Jack with pizza money, telling him I have to pop out to buy a gift.

It's not a lie . . . not really.

I keep on the clothes I wore to work that day. I don't bother to get too dolled up; I don't want to raise Jack's suspicions. Besides, where I'm going just having a vagina makes you fresh meat. In contrast to the exclusive place that hosted the awards do, Blue Balls is every bit the skanky dive bar.

On the corner of another back street, it's surrounded by takeaways and overflowing red Biffa bins. A couple of sandwich boards advertise various daytime and happy hour deals, all spelled wrong with apostrophes in the wrong place. A large blue neon sign flickers with the bar's name. It might have been stylish, back in the eighties, but now it just looks sad.

As I approach, I see a rat skitter across my path, as large as a guinea pig. It gazes at me, used to human presence. I shudder at the sight of the vermin and hurry towards the double doors of the bar.

A middle-aged doorman stands outside. He's not in a suit, though he still has the earpiece that curls around his bullneck and into his zip-up hoody. He opens the door and a skimpily-clad woman in her mid-forties staggers out on perilous stilettos. She throws up in the gutter, accompanied by a blithe-looking friend in a bandeau top and matching skirt.

The friend watches her retch dispassionately, like this is a weekly occurrence. She clocks me and raises an over-plucked eyebrow in challenge: *what are you looking at?*

I know enough now about London's nightlife to avert my eyes. The doorman does not engage me in conversation. I breeze past all of them, as if they are invisible.

It's busy. A wave of heat of human bodies and accompanying body odour assaults me as soon as I cross the threshold. It's every bit as broken down inside as it looks on its exterior. The bar is rammed as tattooed staff buzz up and down, delivering shots and bottles to outstretched hands. Booths are filled with couples and friendship groups; the air is thick with laughter and profanity. Biker types with beer guts crowd round two or three pool tables, accompanied by bottle-blonde women with far too many years on the clock to be wearing so few clothes.

On instinct, my eyes search the crowd for Aaron, just in case. I can't imagine him going to a place like this, but stranger things have happened.

The memory of him pushing me against the shelves in the archives room floods back to me. I tell myself that if he's here tonight, it's a sign from the gods, or fate, or the universe, or whatever other force is fucking my life up and making me do this. If Aaron is here, I will abandon my plan. I will abort tonight's mission.

Of course, Aaron isn't here.

I'm almost disappointed. I take a seat alone at one of the few unoccupied tables. I know I won't have to wait long. I shred a beermat under my fingernails as I wait. Deep down, I know there's zero chance of a bright young thing like Aaron coming to a downmarket place like this. It's the guilt talking. I push it down.

I'm only doing what I must, to protect Jack.

About five minutes into my vigil, a huge man with a tray stops beside me, a pissed-off look on his face. On the tray, a cocktail. It's pink, with a maraschino cherry garnish and even has a bendy straw and an umbrella floating in it. It's the type of drink a man buys a woman when he thinks he's being slick, or funny, or both.

The barman presents it to me, at arm's length, as if it's contraband.

'This is for you —' he jerks a thumb at a man sitting at the bar — 'from that geezer.'

I glance over to the man at the bar. Not bad-looking, he's tall and broad across the shoulder, with a touch of beer belly. He's taken the time to shave his head Jason Statham-style to hide his bald patch. He's a few years older than me, though he still dresses like a teenager: skater jeans and chain, a trackie top zipped all the way to the top. When he raises his pint and grins at me, I see he's got a gold tooth and a handful of sovereign rings.

Perfect.

'Thank you.'

I take the drink and the barman trudges off, glad his stint as matchmaker is over. I have barely enough time to put the straw to my glossed lips before the man leaves his bar stool and joins me at my table.

'All right, darlin'? Not seen you in here before.'

I suppress a laugh at the cheesy pick-up line. 'That's because I have never been in here before. Hello, I'm Natasha.'

'I'm Boz.'

The man falls into the chair opposite me, kicking back like he's known me for years. Within ten minutes he's told me all about himself: how he's divorced, no kids, a business-man 'between projects'.

Even in the sweaty heat of the bar, I can smell the bullshit radiating off him. What he doesn't say tells me more. His bulging wallet, full of twenties. The broken skin around his knuckles; the nervous twitch and raw nostrils. He's a drug dealer or debt collector, with a coke habit that makes him reckless.

'You talk pretty posh. Slummin' it or something?' Boz grins.

That never-ending disconnect. I've never fitted in anywhere, a walking contradiction. Over-educated single mother, no trade; I've got cash flow issues and nothing of material value I've earned. Yet I've inherited bricks and mortar from working-class parents who made a mint when the market wasn't screwed over by sub-prime lending and austerity. I'm too chavvy for the yummy mummies, but too posh for the commoners.

I decide to embrace his perception of me.

'You could say that.'

Boz's gold tooth gleams in the dim light of the bar. 'Honest. I respect that. Can I be honest, too?'

Another explosion of gin and grenadine makes its way up the straw, into my mouth. I gulp it down; I'm going to need the Dutch courage. I nod at him: *go on, then.*

'Posh girls are great in bed, I reckon. They love a bit of rough.' He runs his tongue across his top lip as his eyes gobble me up. 'That why you're here?'

I flutter my eyelashes. 'Maybe.'

Boz gives a mighty chuckle. 'Then it's your lucky night, sweetheart, 'cos I can take care of you. Wanna go back to my place?'

I pretend to think it over. 'I have to work in the morning. It's better if we go back to mine.'

I take a last slurp of my pink cocktail and stand up. Boz blinks; he'd anticipated more resistance on my part. He rises too, grabbing my wrist.

'Wow, you really aren't kidding around.' He pulls my hand to cup the bulge in his jeans, giving me a leer. 'Well, nor am I. Last warning, love.'

I keep my poker-face smile. 'I can feel it. Good.'

Leaning forwards, I brush my lips against his. Even with my mouth closed, I can taste the stale beer and cigarettes on his breath. As I step back, he stares at me in wonder, like he can't believe his luck a bird like me has delivered herself on a plate to him like this. I've completely and utterly hooked him. Tonight's mission is almost complete.

It's now or never.

'There's just one thing I need you to do for me.'

'Name it,' says Boz.

CHAPTER THIRTY

Despite another late night, I'm up early the next day, preparing Jack's birthday breakfast. I make him kippers, his favourite. The strong waft of frying fish rouses him from sleep. He appears in the kitchen all smiles, completely oblivious to what's waiting for him in the basement.

'Happy birthday, Jack!'

Still in his pyjamas, my son allows me to give him a peck on his cheek as I place a plate in front of him. I watch him wolf down the kippers, pouring him a glass of orange juice.

I cradle my coffee cup in my hands as I watch my only child eat. I like kippers too, but don't put one on my own plate. My stomach churns like a boat on choppy seas. I can't seem to catch my breath as anxiety presses down on my chest.

Jack senses me looking at him and glances up, curious. I hide my unease with a typical 'Mum' comment.

'Eighteen, wow. I remember the day you were born, you—'

'"Took twenty-two hours to come out and almost killed me doing it",' Jack cuts in, butter on his lips as he finishes the tale for me. 'I've heard the story. Over and over again.'

Jack wipes his mouth with his sleeve and lets his cutlery clatter on to his empty plate.

'You don't need to worry about me knocking anybody up, Mum. Not my style.'

'That is one benefit of a gay son, yes.'

Jack's eyes widen. 'Wow, you actually said it. That's progress.'

I shake my head at him. I wish my issue *was* Jack getting someone pregnant: making life, rather than taking it away. But I don't want to go into that, it's his birthday after all.

Despite the story my son tells himself, I have never had any issue with Jack being gay. Whatever creates killers, there's one thing I do know: it's not homosexuality that makes my son a ticking time bomb. Aaron taught me that. What was it he'd said, back when I first met him, and we were looking for the Nilsen letter paper shreds?

We're all more than who we have sex with, even serial killers.

Picking up a small gift box with a large ribbon on top from the sideboard, I place it in front of Jack. He pulls the lid off without care, revealing the gift inside.

It's a big metal vintage key, battered from use. Jack recognises it right away with a grin. He's been trying to swipe this from me every day for the past week.

'The key to the basement?'

'That's right.'

Jack jumps up from his chair, running back out into the hall. A childlike giggle leaves him as he brandishes the key. Leaving my cup on the table, I follow quickly behind him. I can't afford to miss a single second of this.

'So, what have you done . . . Did you get a pool table down there?'

Jack fits the key in the basement door lock. He doesn't notice my sad eyes or pained expression as I choke out my reply. He's too excited.

'You'll just have to wait and see.'

My son clatters down the steps, into the dark room below.

'What the . . . ?'

As I make it into the subterranean room, I can feel the confusion radiating off him in waves. Jack stands in the cellar, his stance just like the night he killed Dean: hands down by his sides, rubbing his thumbs across his finger pads as he takes the details of the room in.

His head jerks from item to item, like he can't quite believe what he's seeing: the manacles and chains attached to the wall; the dentist's chair, replete with restraints. I'd realised people buying such things from a sex catalogue online does not arouse suspicion . . . Especially when it arrives in brown, plain packaging and the company names have 'vanilla' alternatives for your receipt. Handy.

Jack turns to me, his expression quizzical. As he clocks the tears shining in my eyes, that's when my son freezes. He understands at last why I've brought him down here; why I have created this room for him.

I inhale a shaky breath. I don't want any of this, but I have to contain the monster my child has become *and* make sure he doesn't leave for university hundreds of miles away.

'It's the only way.' I whisper.

CHAPTER THIRTY-ONE

I slam the basement door shut, locking it as I told Jack I would. Though I've soundproofed the basement with the help of a YouTube tutorial, I don't feel quite strong enough to test it yet.

What if I can still hear him, from up here?

I might lose my nerve, call it all to a halt. Better I leave for a couple of hours, let Jack get it all out of his system. Then I can return when I feel stronger.

My next actions are a blur. With what feels like the blink of an eye, I am behind the wheel of my car and driving. The familiar garish landmarks of Camden high street flash by as crowds of Saturday local shoppers and tourists attending the markets make my vehicle slow to a crawl. It's a lovely, clear morning.

How can the sun be shining when I've had to do what I've done?

I make it over the bridge and pick up speed, my body knowing where I am going before my brain catches on.

Aaron comes to the door of his shared house in just his boxers and a T-shirt. He blinks against the light. I've woken him up. Seeing me on his doorstep seems to revitalise him. The sleep falls from his face as he takes me in.

'Tasha.' Aaron grins.

I don't speak. I step across the threshold and press my lips to his. He feels warm and smells and tastes musty, but I don't care. Cold terror has taken hold of me at the thought of my son in the basement.

I must do something, *anything*, to forget.

'This is a surprise,' Aaron says. 'I thought this was a no-go, you said?'

'I say a lot of things,' I reply, 'now take me to bed.'

Without another word, Aaron takes my hand and I follow him up the stairs to his large attic bedroom. The only thing out of place is the tangle of sheets on the unmade bed.

Unlike every other male in my life, Aaron is tidy to a fault: there's zero clutter, alphabetised labels on his shelves. He's set up a small studio in one corner; there's a mixing desk, a number of lights, a reflector board, a number of backdrop cloths.

'Are you sure?'

'I told you, yes. Get on with it.'

Aaron shrugs: *fair enough.*

With a lazy smirk, he pushes me back onto the bed. Shedding his own clothes, he kneels over me. He seems to want to take his time, undoing my shirt buttons one by one.

Frustrated, I jump up from the bed, pulling all of my clothes off myself. He chuckles as he watches my speedy striptease. I eyeball him in defiance.

'I want you. Now.'

'How bad?'

'Bad.' I inhale deeply. 'I want you to hurt me.'

It's the wrong thing to say. Aaron tilts his head, uncertain. I can feel the moment getting away from me. I'd assumed he would be like most men I'd known over the years: eager for whatever he can get, however he can get it. I've never known men to care about enthusiastic consent, or even whether I'm enjoying myself, to be quite honest. The only one who'd ever checked was Steve. Even then, that had been lip service. Literally.

I flash Aaron a coquettish smile. 'Oh, you haven't done that sort of thing before?'

My well-aimed barb hits home. Aaron's ego rises just like his cock. It's all back on.

'Of course I have.' His irritation replaces any trepidation he might have had. 'But *you're* sure?'

I nod. Aaron gets off the bed and leans in toward me, brushing those gorgeous lips of his across mine. It's a different kiss to the one we shared at the club, or in the archives at the Atkinson Project: full of heat and animal promise.

Without warning, he grabs my hair, twisting it in his fist. 'Like this?'

I emit an involuntary yelp, but the pain sends an electric shock down my neck towards my groin. He throws me down on the bed like a caveman. He clamps his mouth on mine before nipping my neck, my breast, pinching my skin between his teeth.

'How about like this? Say it's what you want.'

'Yes . . . yes! It's what I want.'

Aaron grabs my throat with his other hand. My arms are free by my sides, but I can't move. My body stiffens in panic. Before I can protest, he slackens his grip in response.

'Sssssssh.' He plants another kiss on my lips.

I mutter a wordless encouragement. Aaron grabs for something on the nightstand: a box of condoms. I hear the rip of foil. Frustrated at waiting again, I kick out with one of my heels catching him on the shoulder.

He laughs. 'You'll pay for that.'

'I'm counting on it.'

Still kneeling, Aaron grabs my legs, pulling me across the bed towards him. He squeezes my neck a second time as he thrusts hard into me.

I arch my back, my eyes rolling back in my head. I can feel the pressure building as I try and draw breath into my lungs. Bright spots jump up in front of my eyes. A buzzing noise rips through my ears.

It feels like I am floating away.

Part of me welcomes it. In this fantasy I can just disappear, into nothingness. No one knows where I am. Jack is still locked in the basement at home. Problem solved. Forever.

What the hell am I doing?

Aaron releases my throat from his grip. Orgasm sweeps through me. It makes me bare my teeth as it flowers in my arms, my solar plexus and between my legs. A ferocious assault of memories accompanies it. Images sear through my brain and steal my breath like Aaron had moments before:

> *Dean staggering backwards in the old flat, pulling the knife from his chest.*
>
> *Steve's head snapping back under the jab of Jack's fist.*
>
> *Jack opening that gift box with the basement key in it.*
>
> *Boz grinning, that gold tooth shining as I open the cellar door.*
>
> *Jack rounding on me in the basement when he realises what I've done.*

In the attic room, Aaron grunts and rolls off me, getting rid of the condom in his wastepaper basket. He snickers in triumph as I lie back on the bed, gulping for air like a dying fish. The room spins as if I'm drunk.

'That what you had in mind?' Aaron says.

I attempt to get off the bed and stand up, but my legs are too shaky to hold me. I slump to my knees by the bed. My shoulders are wracked with exhilaration at what has just occurred. At the same time, my heart thuds with fear at what could have happened had he not let go. Tears course down my cheeks.

'Natasha, what's wrong?' Aaron joins me on the floor, his face creased with concern. 'Did you not like it?'

I open my mouth, but no sound comes out.

I liked it too much.

I scared myself.

I wish I could blink out of existence.

Sensing words are beyond me, Aaron picks me up and places me in the bed, joining me. He pulls the duvet up around our naked bodies like a cocoon. He pulls me close to him, my head resting on his chest as he tightens his arms around me.

I can feel the rhythmic beat of his heart, as steady as a metronome. It helps me focus my own shallow breaths and quiet the anxiety skittering around my ribcage.

'Better?'

'Better,' I sigh.

As Aaron rests his chin on my crown, I feel safe, for the first time in six months. Since Steve's death, since my dad's. I can feel myself drifting off, in Aaron's arms. But I can't allow myself this comfort.

I don't deserve it.

Jack is never going to stop killing. I know that now. It is in his blood; it's what powers him. I can kid myself that I can reason with him, negotiate with him, or try and keep others safe from him. I can't do that, but nor can I turn Jack over to the authorities.

I'm left with only one card to play.

The basement is for Jack, yes . . . But I was never going to lure him down there and keep him locked up like a pet.

Quite the opposite.

Like so many parents who are unable to dissuade their teenage offspring from risky behaviour, I've had to bring it into my home to keep an eye on things.

My treacherous mind had sought to remind me of my failure as a mother as I'd tried to release the guilt and self-reproach out of my body with Aaron. As the other memories had rolled through my mind's eye, there had been two last images my brain had lingered over:

> *Boz, terrified, naked and restrained in the dentist's chair, a ball gag in his mouth.*
>
> *Jack's predatory smile and his glinting steely eyes as he loomed over him.*

I've made my son a kill room in the basement.

I will pick his victims myself and deliver them to him.

My house, my rules.

PART THREE

'*How sharper than a serpent's tooth it is to have a thankless child*!'

William Shakespeare

CHAPTER THIRTY-TWO

'So, this is it. All over.'

Maria stands back, taking in the archives with tears in her eyes. We'd received a final letter that morning, informing us the building housing the archives is to be sold off. The collection will be split up, the good stuff sent to various museums. The rest will end up in landfill, discarded as trash.

Needless to say, my boss is devastated. I am more pragmatic. I've loved my time at the archives, but I've always known my time here was finite. We've managed to digitise, label and sort all the most important boxes in Dorothy's collection. The estate lawyers have always been hostile to the project. Being legal eggheads, they were bound to find a loophole allowing them to sell it off eventually. I'm just surprised it's taken them this long.

'Arseholes, I could kill them,' Maria says through gritted teeth.

A cynical smile tugs at my lip. People say this so readily. When it comes down to it, they don't have the guts.

Not like Jack.

If there's one thing my boy has, it's follow-through.

Don't get me wrong; his activities make my skin crawl. I wake in the night, heart racing, unable to believe what I am facilitating my only child to do.

I have no choice.

There was no way I could let the situation continue the way it was. It's like Steve's murder opened up some kind of gateway to hell in Jack. Violence is all he can think about nowadays. It's clear it is an addiction for him. If I had just sat back and allowed him to take it out on homeless people the way he was, it would not be long before it was traced back to him and by extension, me.

It's better this way.

It's Aaron who gave me the idea. I listened to all his podcasts on my phone about serial killers. One episode made me realise Jack is what Aaron calls a 'thrill seeker'. He craves the high violence gives him. Psychopaths of his type tend to have shorter careers, because they get caught as they find self-regulation too difficult *(duh)*.

Steve had happened behind closed doors. The only reason Jack never got caught for any of the homeless people was because he only been seen by witnesses at a distance. He'd attacked people with no personal connection to him. He also has no criminal record.

All of this has been blind luck.

The moment Jack gets arrested, his DNA taken, it's all over. I recall wondering how Dennis Nilsen had got away with his dark activities right in the middle of Muswell Hill. Deep down, I'd already known the answer, even then.

We have to tempt his victims to the house, like Steve.

The likes of Fred and Rosemary West made it work in their 'House of Horrors' down in Gloucester for decades, so it's not like it can't be done. Everyone turns their heads away from what goes on behind closed doors, especially those just an adjoining wall away. Domestic abuse and violence happen so often, it's normalised; people are surprised when others tell they had a happy childhood.

Our new arrangement has been hard-going and has required some considerable tweaking.

Jack's first potential victim had been a complete disaster. We'd spent days picking him, driving around London's back roads, inspecting ragged tents for homeless victims. We'd noticed a young blond man in his mid-twenties out near the embankment. Most of his teeth missing, he nearly always had a can of white cider in hand, even early in the morning. I told myself this meant he would be too buzzed to know what was going on. This would help get him in the car but also be a mercy once my son started his 'work' on him.

I'd waited in my vehicle nearby, the licence plates smeared with dirt. I'd been on edge, almost vomiting with the anticipation. I'd nearly had a heart attack when Jack had slammed against the passenger side window, nose bloody, shoulders heaving, cradling his hand again. Thankfully, it wasn't completely dislocated this time, just painful. Through laboured breaths Jack told me it had not gone well. He'd ended up pushing the boy off the bridge. I saw later in the paper Jack's botched victim was assumed to be a suicide, weirdly symmetrical after Steve.

Even though we'd never even got Jack's victim in the car, never mind back to the house and the dungeon below, the elation of that night kept Jack sated for a few days. I dared to hope that might be enough, at least for a couple of months.

Within forty-eight hours his homicidal urges needed seeing to again.

After another abortive hunting trip, then another, it became obvious Jack lacked the skills to net the men we needed. It did not escape me all the men Jack preferred were the tall, lean type like his father. As Aaron always mentioned on his podcasts, most serial killers have a 'type' after all.

Despair seared through me. I knew if Jack did not kill soon, he would simply go on the rampage. Then we'd both be sunk.

Then I had a flash of genius.

Jack had not been happy at first. He didn't like the idea of me 'whoring myself out' to random strangers in bars. When I assured him there would be none of that, just the 'promise of it' to get them back to the house, his ears pricked up.

Suddenly what we both needed seemed within reach.

So far it's worked, though I will admit to our new life being a bit of a struggle to get used to.

'What can you do?' I shrug.

Back in the archives, Maria rounds on me, eyes wide as what this means for me occurs to her. 'You're a single mother! Those bastards would have you out on the street!'

I don't believe she's really bothered about me, or the financial bind I might find myself in. I play along and proffer comforting words, like she expects me to.

'It's fine, Jack is eighteen now,' I remind her. 'Dad left me the house, no mortgage. We'll be okay. Worry about yourself and Louisa.'

Depressed and dejected, Maria tells me to take the rest of the day off.

I'm pleased. It's only eleven o' clock in the morning, but it's a sunny day and blue skies. I'd walked from home today, so decide to take up her offer. I give her a quick hug goodbye, then grab my bag and files, promising myself a posh coffee on the way home.

I am so busy enjoying the unseasonably warm weather, I don't realise where I am until I am standing right outside: 1939. I'd meant to go to the Costa on the high street, but my disloyal feet have brought me straight here.

Steve's old place is no longer vacant. It is one of those microbreweries now. On the window, a variety of flyers advertising a cider festival; a DJ playing that weekend; an LGBT night. I peek through the glass: inside it's decked out *Ye Olde Worlde* style: dark wood and stone, leather couches and flagstones. It even has the obligatory stupid name: The Sleepwalking Flamingo. It seems appropriate. Steve had been a hipster at heart and he loved a good craft ale.

I sigh, my breath frosting the glass. I try not to let my mind wander to thoughts of Steve or what he might think of me. I had been a different woman when I'd started going out with him. Dad was still alive. I was enjoying my job at the archives. Despite the trauma of Dean's death Jack was — *I thought* — a normal teenager.

Anything had seemed possible, back then.

'Got a light?'

'Sorry, I . . .' My automatic apology arrests in my throat as I turn, catching sight of who's behind me. '*Zane?*'

Steve's old assistant is almost unrecognisable; only his nose ring and biomechanical sleeve tatts tell me who he is. It's barely six months since Steve's death but the impact on Zane's body makes it seem longer. He'd always been impeccably turned out, but now his clothes are creased and dirty. His skin looks grey; his eyes puffed and red; nose raw. His mohawk is gone. His hair hangs in limp, straggly strands around his gaunt face.

Had it just been losing Steve that's done this to him? Or had it been the icing on the very shit cake of Zane's life?

Either way, I know I am to blame, not just Jack.

I'd been the one who'd involved Zane in the deception of Steve's disappearance. I had introduced Zane's brain to the thought of Steve, jumping from the edge of the cliffs, his body lost to the sea, eaten by fish.

What have I done?

I force down these errant thoughts before they run away with me. Plenty of people are faced with tragedy in their lives, but don't go to pieces. Zane must have been unravelling already. People on social media are always saying Gen Z are a bunch of snowflakes with no resilience. None of them were ever allowed to fail at school; they got medals for just turning up. Maybe he had a helicopter parent doing everything for him at home.

None of that is my doing. I'd seen to it Jack was never like that. Zane's mother should have done the same. Stupid woman, bad mother.

Zane seems like he is on time delay as he takes me in. He smiles as he recognises me.

'Natasha. All right?'

I smile at the young man and beckon him with me, trying not to balk as the smell of his body odour infects my nostrils. I assuage some of my shame by taking him with me to a nearby café, buying him a coffee and a hot meal. After twenty minutes of stilted conversation — neither of us can talk about Steve — I bid him my goodbyes and walk the rest of the way home.

As I make my way into the house, I feel lethargic, like the marrow of my bones has turned to concrete. Despite trying to make myself feel better, I know Zane is just an innocent; he should never have been caught up in this shit. Nor should have Steve. I'd signed his death warrant by taking up with him. It had been accidental, but it was still on me. We could have had the whole nine yards: house, dog, two point four kids. Normal, happy. Instead Steve is under the floor and I am in this daily nightmare, trying to keep Jack in line.

Now, all I can do is try and right that balance. If Jack is going to kill, no more good men should suffer.

Only bad ones.

CHAPTER THIRTY-THREE

'Are you avoiding me?'

Standing over yet another box of junk that needs disposing of, I stop as the familiar voice washes over me. Despite myself, Aaron's smooth tones create a warm feeling in my chest, bringing an involuntary smile to my lips.

I realise, too late, that I like him.

As this thought occurs, another image slices through my mind's eye: Aaron, strapped in Jack's dentist's chair, his fingernails missing. He's covered in his own blood, wounds all over his beautiful body. I'd promised Jack no more boyfriends, but for Aaron's own sake I must make sure he gets the message.

Fixing my expression to one of stony indifference, I turn towards him.

'Oh . . . hello.'

Aaron stands in the doorway of the archives, his arms crossed: a defensive pose if ever I saw one. He looks tired, like he's had trouble sleeping. There's bags under his eyes and his complexion is ashen. He seems to deflate at the carefree timbre of my voice.

'I guess that's a yes?'

I indicate the boxes all around me. 'I've been really busy with work.'

He scoffs at the age-old excuse. For some reason, I find myself doubling down. I hate the idea he thinks he means nothing to me, even though that would save him from my screwed-up life . . . not to mention Jack's homicidal urges.

'The archives is closing down.'

Aaron's eyes widen. 'What? Since when?'

'We heard a couple of days ago. We have to be out in a fortnight.'

'But you won't be able to get the rest of the collection sorted in just two weeks!'

I shrug. 'I know. We have to try and find anything of value and hope we find it, because otherwise it's all going in landfill.'

Aaron punches the wall. Despite his progressive nature, I already know he is not above such a macho display from the way he laid out that guy at the awards do. From our time in his attic room, I also know he has a few dark secrets of his own.

'So typical of lawyers,' he says. 'Do you want some help?'

Before I can reply in the negative, he lets his messenger bag drop to the floor. He rolls up his sleeves and grabs a box of his own.

'Anything in particular you're looking for?' he says, breathless.

I can tell I won't be getting rid of him anytime soon. I decide to go with it. I could do with the help. Maria is upstairs stuck on hold with the estate pleading for more time.

'Dorothy bought seven Oscars. We're missing one that was Alfred Hitchcock's as Best Director for *Rear Window*.'

'On it.'

He grins at me. I smile back as his positivity washes over me. Sometimes I feel as if I am only valued otherwise for my labour. I've had toiling for the estate and for Maria. Jack likes me for what I can give him, whether that's feeding his voracious appetite literally with a full fridge or delivering victims to his kill room.

It's different with Aaron.

Unlike everyone else in my life, he has no expectations of me and no agenda. It feels wonderful to be with someone pure. I push away the thought he might find out what I am really like. I tamp it down like I always do and concentrate on small talk instead. Though I want him gone, I am painfully aware it's because of Jack, not actually what I want. The awkwardness stretches between us like viscous chewing gum.

* * *

Hours into our search, Aaron yells. I turn from a box of yet more mouldering film reels to see him holding Hitchcock's Oscar aloft and punching the air.

Caught in the moment, I shriek as well, delighted to see it. I'd been searching for the damn thing since I joined the archives years earlier. I'd emptied, catalogued and digitised box after box, but it had eluded me. Still holding the statuette, Aaron throws his arms around me and we jump up and down in triumph.

What happens next is inevitable.

When he kisses me, I kiss him back. When he pushes me against the shelves, a shower of papers comes down as a box falls off the end of one unit. This doesn't stop us. We fall amongst the detritus, all hands and lips, elbows and knees.

Afterwards, Aaron sits up and retrieves his shirt. 'So, er . . . what's next?'

I roll over and grab my skirt, shucking it back on.

'There's some Golden Globes and BAFTAs in here too, maybe we could find them?'

'That's not what I meant.' Aaron fixes me in his gaze. 'I mean, what's next for *us*?'

I freeze as I finish redressing and buckling my shoes. I say nothing, my brain in spasm. I'd let myself get carried away in finding the Oscar; I've undone all my good work in ignoring Aaron, keeping him at a distance.

Since Jack would never allow me to break my promise of no more boyfriends, the only thing I can do is break Aaron's heart and send him on his way.

It's the only way to keep him safe from my son.

'Tasha?'

Aaron's voice is so tentative, so hopeful; I can't help but think of Steve. Unwanted flashes of that terrible first and last dinner with Jack rocket through my mind. Like always, I slam them back in that box, deep down in the dark part of me.

I proffer a tight-lipped smile. 'I've got Jack.'

Aaron rolls his eyes; he doesn't understand. Why would he?

But if Jack found out about us, he would kill Aaron and do it slow. If he were to discover I've been carrying on with Aaron, Jack won't care I only strung Aaron along at first to protect him from the podcaster's investigations.

'Yeah, I know. He's eighteen now, Tasha.'

Aaron doesn't deserve to wake up in my son's basement of horrors. I have seen the bodies after Jack is done with them before they're dispatched under the basement floor. Aaron shouldn't die, strapped and screaming in a dentist's chair, choking in his own blood. I can't let it happen.

I won't allow it.

'He's still got school.' My tone is not convincing.

'You know that's just an excuse.' Aaron's expression darkens. 'Why won't you let this happen?'

I dig deep, trying to work out what he wants me to say. Confusion swirls in my brain. I had no idea men had feelings. I'd always assumed they're not like women; that they don't think of the future.

Growing up, I'd seen my dad thrive alone and thought he might even secretly prefer it. I had always suspected his stories of my mum were heavily idealised. Before her illness consumed her, I only remembered a short-tempered, irascible woman who was never satisfied, always shouting.

Dean had always made it clear he blamed me for getting pregnant with Jack, that he was stuck with us, against his will. It was clear he didn't love us.

'I want us to be together,' Aaron declares. 'For real. I'm not playing.'

I sigh as these words are breathed into being. I'd thought Steve was the aberration. I'd figured the movies and books telling of happy ever afters were just crazy writers high on printer ink and wish fulfilment. I had decided, a long time ago, that men who made commitments must have been chivvied into it by women.

Yet here's Aaron saying these things to me now when I'd given him zero reason to. Men always want what they can't have.

Why the hell does he have to go and spoil it?

I spring up from my space on the floor, instinctively putting distance between us. I whirl round to see Aaron staring at me with sad eyes. I should have known it would come to this. He might be a man of the world, but he's still a lot younger, less cynical, and much softer than I am. I'm an idiot. I raise my hands in surrender.

'I can't, I just can't,' I attempt to explain, but I just dig my grave further. 'It's just . . .'

My words trail off. I have nothing. I can't tell him about Jack. I can't tell Aaron anything. There is no future for us.

This realisation makes the shutters come down in my brain. I visualise myself taking any feelings I have for Aaron and taping them up, secure. I open that velvet jewellery box and shove them in with the ballerina, along with countless other things that other people receive, but I am not allowed to have.

'Say something, for God's sake.' Aaron sighs. 'I'm telling you I think I could be falling in love with you, Tasha?'

My brain flails, useless. What the hell is love? If it's making room for someone in your heart, then I only have limited space.

Jack must be my number-one priority.

He is my child; he never asked to be born. He certainly never asked for a shitty father like Dean. I have spent years trying to make that up to him. I've done everything I can . . . and then some. I've gone further than any other parent would, but that's because I am a good mother. The best. But the authorities wouldn't see it that way.

I am in it up to my neck.

I can't pull Aaron down into the shit with me. He is not like Dean, Boz or the other men. He is a good person, like Steve. Though pain lances through me, I remember my promise to myself.

I will not take any more good people to their graves.

I say nothing. My silence speaks volumes to Aaron.

'So, it's like that, huh?'

'I'm sorry . . .'

My words seem wooden again. Aaron hears the falseness.

'*Don't*, Natasha.'

His harsh tone wakes up something cruel in me. I chuckle, though there's no humour in it. 'Christ, you're acting like a woman.'

'One of us has to,' Aaron retorts, eyes blazing.

'What the hell is wrong with just having a bit of fun?' I demand. 'Why do you have to go getting so emotional about it? It's sex. Get over it. You're pathetic.'

Elation floods through me as I watch his expression crumple. I don't know why I am so delighted to see him vulnerable like this. Why I feel the urge to smash him down like a child stamping on ants? I suppose I relish the power. Jack had taken it away, making me promise him I'd live like a nun. We've been locked in a power struggle ever since Steve; now I think of it, probably even before that. My dad's sudden death unleashed something in Jack that I've had trouble containing ever since. Now Aaron has unwittingly put me on the spot with his podcast, his interest in the homeless attacks as well and now his bloody feelings. Ugh.

When am I ever going to catch a damn break?

Jack is safe now, his activities confined to his dungeon. I can't do anything about my wayward son's trespasses against me, but I *can* remove the threat of Aaron.

'You're a bitch.'

'I know.' I shrug. 'I'll show you out.'

'No need, I know where the door is.'

'Oh, but I insist.'

Aaron grabs the rest of his stuff; his fly is still open. I trail after him, wanting to slam the door after him. As we make it to the front entrance, he turns in one unexpected move. He pins me against the wall, pressing his body against mine and his lips against mine. Surprised, I melt against him, allowing his tongue to slip into my mouth.

Damn, he's good.

'Little something to remember me by.' He wipes his mouth as he comes up for air. 'You'll need it.'

'What the hell is that supposed to mean?'

Aaron just grins. 'Bye, Natasha.'

He wrenches open the door to the film project and disappears into the street beyond. On the back foot but not understanding why, I appear on the threshold and holler after him.

'Fuck you, Aaron!'

He doesn't turn or give any indication he's heard me. Frustrated and angry, I watch him stalk back up the road towards Camden's high street. He disappears round the corner.

I rush back into the project, towards my desk. I unlock it and yank the entire drawer off its runners in my haste. Papers fall to the grubby carpet and I follow them, on my knees. I sift through them all until I find what I am looking for.

The letter to Dorothy from Dennis Nilsen.

I'd been hiding it from Maria, but I'd also wanted it as insurance in case Aaron took up interest in the homeless attacks again. Though it still has some pieces missing, it's more or less whole, now held together by copious amounts of tape. I know Aaron would love to have this in his possession to break down on that bloody podcast of his.

Well, screw him.

I don't have to worry about Aaron and his stupid, self-important investigations now. Any dalliance we had is history. Though he may never know it, I've done him a favour. He is out of the danger of Jack's deadly attentions, which means I can do whatever I want with the Nilsen letter.

Carrying it over to the aluminium sink next to my coffee machine, I grab one of Maria's lighters that she's left next to an overfull ashtray. I spark it up and touch the flame to the corner of the letter. I watch it curl and blacken, the plastic of the tape bubbling and melting. As it's consumed, I'm forced to let go and it collapses in the sink in large flakes of ash.

I turn on the tap and wash it down the plughole.

CHAPTER THIRTY-FOUR

I can hear screams coming from the living room, though they don't concern me. Jack knows better than to bring his work up here. He knows I don't like mess, plus he's meticulous. An artist, really. Da Vinci would have been burned at the stake during his time for digging up bodies to study them for his extraordinary, ground-breaking studies in human anatomy. It's not much of a leap to suppose Da Vinci might have killed his subjects too. Considering the gifts such an artisan gave the world, would that really have been so bad?

I have not delivered Jack a victim recently, anyway. The last one was almost a week ago and that victim is now interred under the basement floor with the others. I'd worried about managing the floorspace situation down there; we couldn't concrete the whole thing over, just to dig it up again when Jack inevitably killed again. That would be inefficient.

So I'd gone to Peckham cemetery for inspiration. After a day amongst the various monuments, I'd come back invigorated. I'd directed Jack to dig narrow, shallow graves in the earthen basement floor for each of his victims then pour concrete directly on top of them, sealing them inside like a sarcophagus. Along with Steve, there's five of Jack's kills in total down there, neatly lined up — with plenty of room for more.

Jack is never seen with his prey, ever.

That is my job.

Men and woman drinking in clubs and leaving together raise no suspicions; it's normal. With no police record and no prints or DNA on file, I can disappear into the shadows after spiriting them away.

Like the good researcher and archivist I am, I've paid attention to everything Maria taught me. I am methodical and distrustful of the Cloud (though unlike Maria's concerns about potential data loss, mine was my data being *found*).

I keep immaculate records in pen and paper only, which I keep in a locked box. I've painstakingly cross-referenced social media, rumours and local gossip to find only the worst of humanity to deliver to my son.

When I'd told Boz about my 'dungeon', his eyes had lit up. He couldn't wait to see it. I'd had no trouble tempting him back to my home, or into the basement. As he'd run an appreciative eye over all the equipment and moved in for a kiss, I'd stabbed him in the neck with a hypodermic of tranquiliser. I'd stood over his slumped body, musing how the archives was not my first 'proper' job after all; my experience helping Dean bag up his drugs for sale had come in handy.

My mind eased about Aaron at last, I'd hoped giving Jack the dungeon would give me some peace of mind, or at least make me feel a little more in control. I'm still waiting for that to kick in. Still, at least the blind terror of Steve and Dean's deaths is gone now, not to mention the endless nights of cruising around Camden looking for Jack in my car.

I guess we can all redraw the perimeters of what we find palatable, especially when we have good reason.

I must be practical, too. I've found Jack men who give nothing to the world but pain. No one will miss them. Even if they do, I have ensured there's no connection between them and us. I've delivered Jack loan sharks and wife-beaters; paedophiles and perverts.

I am willing to live with Boz's demise and others like him if it means my son can release his pent-up aggression. It could even be argued I am making the world a safer place. Boys will be boys.

You know it makes sense.

I stalk through the hallway into the living room. Jack is lying on the sofa, shoes on and feet up on my damn cushions. As I'd surmised, some horror movie is streaming on the television. I grimace in irritation as a chainsaw rips through a screaming victim on screen. My son has the volume up too loud, as per usual.

'Hey!' Jack objects as I grab the remote and make the movie blink off. 'I was watching that!'

I push his feet off my sofa and sink onto the cushions next to him, that weariness claiming my limbs. I'm perturbed to find him watching horror films, rather than doing his coursework. Jack has little time for fiction normally. If he's watching crap like this, it can mean only one thing.

'You look antsy.'

Jack's knee bobs up and down, a nervous tic. 'I'm fine.'

'Liar.'

Since our arrangement began, I've noted Jack's behaviour has changed, become cyclical. As part of my records, I started tracking it and noticed a pattern. I've never taken drugs, but Dean did. At first, he'd get this beatific smile on his face, slumping down on our bed, limbs floppy, good for nothing.

Then, the comedown: this was the worst time for me and Jack. Dean would blunder about our home, looking for any excuse to unleash hell on us for any transgression, real or imagined. I'd try and keep Jack safe, but it wasn't always possible. That's how Jack had ended up with a dislocated thumb; how he'd ended up pitched down the stairs, too.

Like father like son.

Directly after a kill, Jack seems to be on a high as well. After a few days of this, he comes down, but unlike Dean doesn't crash. My son is still relaxed and happy, even pleasant to be around. In these periods, he can't do enough for me: bringing me cups of tea, tidying the living room and loading the dishwasher.

This is my favourite time.

As time moves forwards, that inhuman need, that blood-lust, will grow. Jack will become agitated again, a coiled spring. He will be snappy, even a little frightening.

The only release is, of course, another kill.

There's just one problem: Jack is restless already, barely a week after his previous victim. The 'off' periods are usually longer.

'I need you to go on another hunt.' Jack averts his gaze, like a shamed little boy, caught with his hand in the cookie jar.

Fear strikes me, quickly followed by the sting of irritation at being taken for granted. Like most kids, Jack underestimates what I do for him.

It is not just a question of me going out, finding a random guy and dragging him back here for him. The days of finding a spare criminal in a bar like I had with Boz are long gone. To avoid suspicion falling anywhere near us, I now do detailed reconnaissance on intended victims, noting down their routines and surveilling them. Thanks to Maria's tutelage, I am a great researcher, but I am not a miracle worker.

'It's been days since your last kill,' I hiss. 'That'll have to last you a bit longer yet.'

Jack's eyes bug out at the thought. 'Mum, I *need* it.'

'I said no.'

'Mum, please!'

He jumps up from the sofa, tearing at his hair with his fists. His movements are jagged with anxiety. I'm alarmed as tears spring up and pour down Jack's face. I don't recall seeing him cry since he was a little boy.

'Sssh, sssssh.'

I stand up, taking Jack in my arms. He folds into my embrace, his body sagging against me. I have to take a step back to hold his weight; he's much bigger than me now, he almost knocks me back on to the sofa.

Like the night he came home with the dislocated thumb, I enjoy the feeling of him needing me. I stroke his hair to soothe him, just like I did when he was a baby. I sigh; without my intervention, Jack will lose control and go on the rampage. That could only end badly, for both of us . . . and for innocent bystanders, like Steve and Zane.

That cannot happen again.

I have to be Jack's mother and give him what he needs.

It's better for everyone.

Perhaps there's a way of ensuring my surveillance does not take as long. As loath as I am to trawl the likes of social media for a victim, needs must. We have also been pretty lucky so far; fortune favours the brave — and I've more than proven I've got what it takes. I will do anything for my boy. More mothers should be like me.

'Leave it with me,' I say.

CHAPTER THIRTY-FIVE

Darling Dorothy,

How I wish I could turn the clock back and never have met you. Those blue, bewitching eyes; the eyes of a devil. Your poison dropped in my ear; I was powerless against your charms. Do you know what you did to me? How you corrupted me?

The signs were all there but I barely saw them, until it was too late. By then I was in too deep: I was transfixed by you, I would do anything for you. I was beholden to you.

I needed your love and approval so badly; I would do anything to gain it.

Anything.

You knew this. You smiled with those red lips, but you had the keys to my psyche; you were my jailer. You knew that dark part of me; it is in you too.

But you never wanted to get your hands bloody; you had me for that. So you had me perform for you, like I was your pet.

Without you, there is no me.
Dennis

CHAPTER THIRTY-SIX

'What the hell is this, Natasha?'

I blink as Maria marches into my field of vision. My brain struggles to catch up. I don't understand why Maria is glaring at me; antagonism radiates off her in waves. I've seen her like this with other people before, but never me.

Maria tuts and presses her phone into my hand. I understand she wants me to check something out online. I press a finger to the screen, waking it up so I might see what the problem is.

It's a tab from Aaron's website. I pale as I glimpse the photograph she indicates. It's a note, made up of paper shreds. Confusion surges through me because I'd only destroyed what's in front of me yesterday.

It's the Dennis Nilsen letter I'd helped Aaron piece together.

The full text is transcribed below the picture of Nilsen and Dorothy, their bodies far too close together. I already know what it says. In it, Dennis Nilsen rails against Dorothy and implies he is a killer *because* of her.

Stalling for time, I scan the short blog post that accompanies the letter. It is as bad as I fear. Aaron speculates on the nature of Dorothy and Nilsen's relationship. He also gives the name of the archives. He directs everyone back to his podcast, for the full details.

On that webpage, I see his podcast has been downloaded over 200,000 times. I press the bottom of the text article and see it's been shared a further 27,000 times. Further links show the story has been picked up by a variety of other high-profile sites, too.

'It's gone viral,' Maria hisses. 'Why would you do this to Dorothy . . . To me? This is my *life's work*, Natasha!'

Maria's distress does not register with me. My own shock and denial at what I am seeing still shimmers through my brain. I'd never allowed Aaron to take the paper shreds away, plus I'd made him leave his phone and bag with me every time we'd gone looking. This can mean only one thing.

Aaron must have smuggled another phone in.

He's been sitting on it, waiting for his moment. Too late, I understand the subtext of his words: 'What's next for us?'.

He'd been offering me an ultimatum.

If I had told him we could be together, he would have trashed the photo and not put it on his podcast. I thought I'd got out of hell's kitchen, only to discover I'd walked through a door into a storeroom full of yet more shit.

'I-I can explain,' I stutter.

Maria shakes her head in disgust. 'It's too late for that.'

She tells me we're done. She says I should collect my things and go home, forever. She never wants to see or speak to me again.

I accept her word and don't fight her. The closure of the archives is only days away. There's no point in me remaining, but to leave under a cloud feels unbearable. I'm perturbed at how shameful it feels, to have to skulk out of there.

As I clear my desk and take my belongings out in a cardboard box to the car, hot tears prickle my eyelids and run down my rouged cheeks. I'd promised Maria I would follow her rules about letting insiders into the archive; that I would help keep Dorothy's good name and work intact. Now the old woman's precious collection and her philanthropy would be tainted by her association with Nilsen, forever.

Maria's been my — *only?* — friend and I've let her down.

Sliding behind the wheel, I regard my red eyes in the rear-view mirror. This must be Aaron's revenge, for breaking it off with him. Bastard.

He can't be as good a person as I thought he was . . . And after I'd tried so hard to keep him safe from Jack! I should have just taken what I wanted and let Jack have his fun with him.

Before I start the car, I call up my messenger app on my phone. Aaron's face is back on screen. He's unblocked me, after blocking me yesterday, as I guessed he might. He can't resist my reaction.

I type a quick message.

What the fuck, A??

Aaron's reply is swift. As I'd surmised, he's been waiting for my text.

Now you know how I feel.

Before I can respond, his avatar disappears. He has blocked me again. I scream in frustration, throwing my mobile in the footwell of the passenger seat.

Hot fury surges through me like lava. As it hits a crescendo inside my brain, I smash my forehead against the steering wheel, hard.

The blow connects and sends a bolt of pain into my neck, stunning me for a second. As pain blooms at the top vertebrae of my spine, my thoughts clear. Dennis' words from the letter return to my reeling brain:

You corrupted me
I was beholden to you.
I was your pet.

Aaron had told me back at that swanky awards bash he'd thought I was 'dangerous' and that I was 'corrupting' him. He'd acted as if he was besotted with me.

My stomach drops as I connect the dots. Aaron is not just getting his own back by publishing the Nilsen letter.

He's sending me a message.

Could Aaron know, or at least suspect, about Jack and my involvement with it all?

I flip through my memories as I turn the key in the ignition, following the back roads the short distance home. I can't think of anything I've done that might have clued-in Aaron about mine and Jack's dark secret. I'd always prided myself on thinking ahead, of nailing down those incidental details others don't, or can't, think of. I've never allowed Jack to send messages to my phone about our arrangement or even allowed him to chat in veiled language about the men and places I've identified for him. I never Google anything possibly incriminating.

As an archivist, I know all about paper trails. I never take my records anywhere, leaving them in a locked, fireproof box under my bed. The key is on a chain on my keyring, which stays with me wherever I go. I never even leave it out on the sideboard at home.

Not even Jack has seen inside the fireproof box. Only me. I don't think he even knows of its existence.

The car comes to a standstill outside my house. Without collecting my box of belongings or even locking my car, I race up to the front door. I don't stop as it slams back into the hall wall. I run through to the living room. As ever, Jack is sprawled out on the sofa asleep, face pale and drawn.

'Jack, wake up!'

He startles awake as I kneel and grab his shirt collar, my face close to his. I give him no time to recover.

'You seen Aaron lately?'

My boy wrenches himself out of my grasp. He sits up, his movements sluggish and pained. The dark shadows under his eyes makes him look like an addict. He is in withdrawal, but his drug of choice is murder.

'Who the hell is Aaron?'

'That podcaster . . . remember? You met him in the archives with me a couple of times. The good-looking one.'

This prompts his memory. 'Yeah, what about him?'

'Have you seen him, or spoken to him? Maybe online. Think!'

My son rolls his eyes. 'No, Mum. I haven't seen or spoken to him. Why, have you?'

'No, of course not.'

My sham denial seems obvious to me, but Jack is too preoccupied with the somatic pain in his limbs. He massages one hand and then the other, before cracking the bones in his shoulders. He has it bad. The only cure: a full toolbox and a victim, writhing and screaming in the basement.

I collapse in the armchair, my face in my hands. I'd been afraid of this. I'd noted Aaron had that almost supernatural way of reading people, of seeing deep into their psyches, way back when I'd first met him. The warning signs had been there, especially that first night we'd kissed at that nightclub.

Why had I let my lonely heart rule my head?

I'd flirted with the danger, instead of staying clear and hoping Aaron's interest would dissipate. He can't know the full details about Jack — I have to believe that, at least — but his message to me via Nilsen's letter seems too astute to let go.

I sweep back a lock of Jack's unruly hair from his clammy forehead. Despite my fears and frustration, he is a good boy, really. He's not defied me and gone out hunting himself. He's in such agony; it breaks my heart. I soothe him, kissing my cool lips to his hot forehead.

Jack's recent kill means I've had barely enough time to find and research another suitable victim for him, which takes a lot of time. But perhaps there is an obvious way out of this that will suit both of us.

'How'd you like to kill Aaron, darling?'

That steely, vibrant glint is back in Jack's eyes. 'You'll get him for me?'

My stomach goes into free fall. I'd liked Aaron and had gone out of my way to ensure he was safe from my son's homicidal tendencies. Whatever has happened between us, I still don't think he deserves to wake up in the basement with Jack. But I can't allow Aaron to expose us. I must be pragmatic and make the harsh decisions. It's what I do.

'Of course.' I smile. 'What are mums for?'

CHAPTER THIRTY-SEVEN

Maria letting me go from the archives early means I can get started on my new plan immediately. After tucking my son up in bed as if he's ill with flu, I tell him I will get Aaron right now for him. Jack drifts off with a smile on his face, the first time I've seen his strained features and jagged limbs relax in ages.

I scroll first through my apps and sites. Aaron has blocked me on every single one, as I expect. I fire off an email, but it bounces back.

I suck in a breath over my teeth. My anger at Aaron surfaces again. Resentment makes my veins pop up on my forearms: so what if I can't get him to come to the house after all? I don't need Aaron to deliver himself to Jack in the basement like a takeaway pizza.

I know where he lives.

In preparation, I open the bathroom cabinet and pull out my kit. Two or three hypodermic syringes still in their wrappers; a vial of liquid ketamine. I take them back to my bedroom and place it all in my handbag. I like ketamine because it doesn't necessarily knock the men out, just makes them pliable. I can even introduce a complete disconnect between body and brain if I want to. The drug dealer I'd bought it from had called it a 'K-Hole'.

His name had been Rupert, which seems like the weird-est name for a drug dealer I've ever heard of. I guess his parents hadn't been thinking ahead to the time their beloved child would take up such a profession; just like I never imagined Jack would become a serial killer.

I'd found Rupert in a wine bar out near Chelsea. The whole place had been dripping with cash and coked-up foot-ballers and their WAGs, as well as lawyers and hedge fund managers. I'd thought I'd stick out a mile, but as ever I'd blended right in, as if I belonged. Rupert had flitted towards me like a moth, and I was the flame.

Rupert was useful for a while, delivering me all the drugs I wanted to subdue Jack's prey. All he'd wanted in return was a few hand jobs; I'm not above that. Then he started asking questions. He is under the floor of the basement now, with the rest of Jack's victims. His entire ketamine stash should keep us going a while. We'll run out eventually, but that's okay. London is full of drug dealers. I'll work it out.

I always do.

Another wave of sorrow and disappointment surges through me. I'd thought Aaron was different to other men. I'd felt he was pure, without agenda. How wrong could I be? All the time he was acting concerned or helping me, he was gathering evidence against me for that damn podcast of his. I should never have gone near him.

Luckily, men are easy to distract.

Most of the time I don't even need to use drugs to get them where I want them. Boz had accompanied me of his own free will to the basement that first time. So had another of Jack's victims, a creep called Kevin I'd 'run into' in a back-street old soak's pub.

From weeks of surveilling both online whispers and real-life routines, I'd discovered Kevin liked to terrorise his wife and children every evening after work and every weekend, just like Dean had terrorised us.

Unlike Dean, Kevin was not dodgy on the surface. He'd been a primary school headteacher and presented as a 'nice guy' and 'pillar of the community' when he was anything but. I saw his wife wince in pain as she picked up their toddler. Kevin's eldest son would give him a wide berth, out of range of his wide, cruel hands as they walked down the street together. I saw Kevin's teenage daughter's haunted eyes; the way she would cringe away from him when he kissed her, those same vile hands never far from her hips or bottom.

Aaron might not be an outright creep like those other guys, but he's been keeping secrets of his own. Whilst by rights that shouldn't be enough to sign his death warrant, I'd given him every chance to do the right thing. He'd been the one who'd pushed for us to be together, then acted out like a typical toxic male when I'd said no. I've had enough of men making demands of me.

No, Aaron has only himself to blame.

I've justified Jack's homicidal urges all in my mind. Even though I'm repulsed by my only child's actions, I've been careful to remind myself there are people who don't deserve to live. Such men give the world and all around them nothing but pain. Hell, I've even told myself the homeless people Jack had terrorised are better off dead. What did they have to look forward to but more fear? Theirs had been mercy killings.

I'd told myself I could make up for those lost souls and for Steve. I can right the balance in the universe, by ensuring Jack never killed innocent men like them again.

The shutters in my brain come down. Aaron might not be like Jack's basement prey, but he's not like Steve, either. I know I idealise Steve, but he'd been a true gentle giant.

In contrast, Aaron is streetwise enough to know who he's messing with. He'd understood what I am even before I had; he'd made that clear from the beginning.

I can't allow Aaron to be a loose end. I need to ensure his threat is neutralised, whether I like it or not. I don't like it, for the record.

But it's the only way to ensure Jack is safe.

CHAPTER THIRTY-EIGHT

The streetlamps have turned on in the time it's taken me to get ready and drive over to Aaron's. I get out of my car, undoing the top button of my dress so my cleavage is visible and inviting before knocking on the front door of Aaron's shared house.

What feels like ten minutes later, someone finally answers. I stifle a groan as I catch sight of who it is: *not* Aaron, but one of his many housemates. She's got green hair and the sound of her Scottish burr jumps ahead of her.

'Hello, can I help you?'

The young woman smiles at me, but I'm in no mood for pleasantries.

'Aaron in?'

Her eyes bug out at my rudeness. 'No. He didn't tell you?'

'Tell me what?'

'He moved out.'

This unexpected news is like a physical blow to the stomach. I lean on the doorframe as fear whips through me, stealing my breath with it. It's clear Aaron has moved out to avoid me, but what does this mean? Perhaps I have broken his heart and he can't bear to see me . . . Or maybe he suspects I could be a real threat to his life, so he's protecting himself?

No, it can't be the last one. I've been so careful.

'He left a few hours ago.'

The housemate's voice is smug, her arms folded over that large bosom. She has guessed — correctly — Aaron and I were involved. I don't care. Whatever Aaron is playing at, one problem remains.

I promised Jack a kill, tonight.

He's been patient thus far, but what could happen if I were to turn up, empty-handed? I envisage myself strapped in that dentist's chair in the basement, my son leering over me instead. He's never killed a woman, or expressed an interest in doing so . . . But if I can't give him what he needs, it is not such a big jump.

What am I good for if I can't deliver?

I *can* offer Jack the only things he wants though: pain, blood, bone and screaming.

SHIT!

I grab the housemate by her shirt collar. 'Where to? WHERE TO!?'

Her demeanour changes in an instant, her face crumpling with fear. I slam her against the door and her weight makes the frame shudder. She's bigger than me; she could fight me off in an instant. This doesn't appear to occur to her though. Tears spring up instead, like the plus-size woman-child she is. How old is she? Easily thirty. Girls like this could never survive what I've had to deal with in my life. Ridiculous specimen.

'I don't know. He just gave us his keys and left,' she whimpers.

Where the hell could he be? London is massive. He could be anywhere and has a big head start.

But it *is* a Saturday night.

As an idea blooms, I let go of her and turn on my heel. The young woman shouts after me, her voice choked with emotion.

'Psycho bitch!'

Tell me something I don't know.

I slide behind the wheel of my car out on the street. Another housemate has joined the housemate in the doorway. I can't tell their gender. *She or He or It or Whatever* has arms around her. They both flick me *Vs* as I speed off from the kerb.

I know exactly where Aaron could be.

It's only a short drive away, so it's not long before my heels clack on Soho's dirty paving slabs. I approach my target like I'm psyching myself up for a race. I roll my neck on my shoulders and stretch my arms, before cracking my knuckles.

I press the bell on the door of that club I went to for the awards bash. This is the place I last saw Aaron out in public. It's hard to believe the archives was being honoured that night and just days from now it will be gone altogether.

'Password.'

I groan as that bouncer who greeted me and Maria peers through the slot at me. His expression is completely inscrutable. I can't tell what he's thinking. I know by instinct feminine wiles won't work on him. He will have seen and heard it all. I decide to go with honesty and see how far that gets me.

'I don't have it,' I admit. 'Is Aaron Gooding here . . . The true crime podcaster?'

The door closes in my face.

I sigh, resting my face against the cool glass of the shop window next door. Well, it had been worth a go. I try and still my flailing thoughts so I can consider my options.

I could wait here, see if I can catch Aaron leaving. But there's no guarantee he is even in the club tonight. There's no guarantee he is even still living in London.

Perhaps going after him is too dangerous? Maybe it's safer to assume that whatever suspicions Aaron has about me, or Jack, or both of us, are just that . . . suspicions. He can't prove anything.

Can he?

Maybe I am overthinking; Aaron could be clueless. Publishing Nilsen's letter could be standard revenge to get me in trouble at the archives. I had impressed the need on him to be discreet. The rest of my fears about him sending me 'messages' could just be the fevered workings of a guilty conscience.

I return to my more pressing problem.

I must deliver Jack prey. Tonight.

If I can't bring my son Aaron, I need to bring him someone . . . Anyone will do, at this point. But I've had no time to do reconnaissance, which makes it ultra-risky.

I'm thankful the story around Steve's supposed suicide has still held, but it won't be long before the police connect the disappearances of the others. So far there's only been enquiries and appeals for information. Could they become murder investigations, even without bodies? I know it's possible. I can't risk scouting in bars like Blue Balls, or even Camden this evening. They're far too close to home.

Every one of my nerve-endings screams against it, but I know I have to go hunting blind tonight. As an archivist, I loathe the idea of not doing my customary research and background checks. I also hate picking up a man who doesn't deserve to die at the hands of my son.

But if I don't deliver Jack prey tonight, I know it will be my head on the block. Literally. I must find him a man, any man. I can't afford to feel guilty; I don't have a choice.

It's him or me.

CHAPTER THIRTY-NINE

Luck is not on my side. I drive beyond the borough of Camden, but the first dive bar I come across won't even let me in. Thoughts racing and panic skewing my brain, I end up double-backing on myself.

I find myself out towards Regent's Park. I have the mad idea I can find myself a random male jogger, making his way up the concrete paths between the ornate ponds and trees. Being nearly ten o'clock on a Saturday night, I discover the place is deserted but for some doggers up near the bridge by the university.

I visit a couple of nearby pubs near Baker Street tube, but strike out in those, too. All of them are either touristy or filled with office types who've been there since late afternoon. Crescendos of laughter split the air. Tipsy and full-blown drunk men and women congregate in large groups, ordering food and flirting.

I wander, dejected, back to my car. As I slip back behind the wheel, I fantasise about leaving London — and Jack — in my wake. With a sinking feeling, I realise I have no idea where I could escape to. I don't have enough space on my credit cards to just disappear. I thought I'd finally got out of my bind by getting rid of Aaron, but I'm in over my head more than ever.

I am still trapped.

The solution for my predicament comes to me when I am driving past the Travelodge near Marylebone station. I haven't ever picked up a man in a hotel bar before.

That could work.

I avoid the glitzy and corporate chains. They are rife with cameras on the inside as well as outside. Far too risky.

Instead, I find a large but gloomy establishment out towards Primrose Hill. I walk through smeared glass doors, into a dark reception. There's no one there, plus the concierge is not at his post either. I pick my way across a sticky carpet into the bar.

A variety of traveller clientele, all-male and middle-aged, nurse their whiskies and boredom. My presence sends a ripple through the room as if they haven't seen life of the female type in aeons. Maybe they haven't.

I order a lime and soda from the bored barman and take a seat nearby. I only wait five minutes, but it feels like a year.

'Mind if I join you?'

Finally.

A man in his mid-forties hovers over me. He has silver hair and a kind face. He's also wearing a cheap, creased suit and enough bling to sink a small rowing boat. If I looked up the phrase 'salesman' in the dictionary, his picture could illustrate the definition.

I flash him a brilliant-white smile. 'Of course.'

He tells me his name is Mike and he is from Southampton. He's up in the capital for some conference on alarm systems. I see no ring on his finger. When he buys us another round of drinks, I spot no family pictures in his wallet.

As I listen to him drone on, I catch myself wondering why scouring hotels hasn't occurred to me before. Shame obliterates this errant thought. I remind myself I haven't gone to hotels looking for prey for Jack because I am not supposed to be finding *random* men, but men who *deserve* to die. That's what my research was for.

Half an hour later and Mike has invited me to his room. I tell him yes, but first that I need to go outside to smoke a cigarette. I don't smoke, but he doesn't know that.

From his mild-mannered chatter, Mike seems a half-decent guy. There's a part of me that hopes he leaves me his key at reception and waits for me upstairs. It's nearly midnight and that fatalistic urge in me has surfaced again. I decide that if Mike does not accompany me outside, I should return to Jack and take whatever's coming to me. If he does take his frustrations out on me, maybe he won't kill me. I am his mother, after all.

Mike comes outside with me.

To my relief, I don't have to coax him towards the back of the hotel, where the bins are kept. His body language is spring-loaded, anticipatory. I figure it's because he wants to kiss me and is working up his nerve. Once again, I feel sorry for Mike. He's given me zero reason to believe he is like Boz, or Kevin, or Rupert.

'Let's stop wasting time, shall we?'

I don't quite unpick what he says. I am distracted, checking out our surroundings. I cast an eye around for cameras. I see one, above a fire exit, but it's facing the other way.

Perfect.

I rummage inside my handbag, as if looking for a lighter and cigarettes. Really my hand closes in readiness around the syringe full of ketamine. I smile at Mike, my face a picture of innocence.

'Sorry, what?'

Mike is on me, in an instant.

There's a feral snarl on his thin lips as he pushes me back against the wall of the hotel. The mild-mannered salesman is gone. I can feel the dark intentions in his body as he presses himself against me.

'You're a right prick-tease, aren't you?'

Despite the obvious immediate danger, my heart lifts. In Mike's eyes, that steely glint I've seen often in my son's. The weight of guilt and worry I could be taking a decent man to his death tonight evaporates into the night air.

Ah, there you are.

He grabs me by the neck with one hand; one of my breasts with his other. He gives me a smirk, making it clear he expects access to my body. He doesn't care whether I give it willingly, or if he must take it. As far as men like Mike are concerned, it's theirs already. Such logic makes perfect sense to him: he has bought me drinks all night. I 'owe' him.

Mike is a predator, just like me.

My hand is still in my bag, gripping the syringe. He tenses as I bring it out, predicting my next move. He thinks I will try to grab his hands and prise them off me. Instead, I jab outwards with the syringe. The needle stabs the flesh in his side. I press the plunger down in one smooth movement.

Shock registers on Mike's face momentarily, then raw fury twists his countenance in a demonic sneer.

'You bitch!'

He balls up a fist, bringing it down on the side of my head. I am shorter than him, plus he's strong. His blow fells me to the ground. Stunned and seeing stars, I lie on my back, unable to move or get up. I hear Mike chuckle from somewhere above me.

'You're gonna pay for that . . . whatever *that* was. Crazy whore.'

He appears back into my field of vision as he leans over me. I feel his hands on my legs as he grasps me by my calves and drags me across the filthy concrete towards him.

As my senses return to me, I kick out with my high heels, catching him in the jaw. He hollers in pain as the blow connects, letting go of my legs.

I manage to push myself up on to my elbows and scrabble up on to my knees. I grab the syringe up off the alleyway floor and brandish it, like it's a dagger. It's literally pointless, the needle is bent and empty. Mike looks up from his hands and knees, his lip split, a stream of blood down his chin. He laughs at my ineffectual weapon.

'No one is gonna save you.'

Mike makes another grab for me, but lurches sideways. He stops, shaking his head. The intense drugged fog descends in his brain as I watch. He can't dispel it. That steely glint in his eyes like Jack's disappears. His pupils seem to mist over.

Mike's body betrays him next. He slumps forward and his head dips like it's too heavy for his neck. Drool pours from his mouth as the K-Hole envelops him.

Triumph floods through me as much as adrenaline. I stagger to my feet, walking around the neutralised threat at my feet. I lean in close, knowing Mike will still be able to hear me, even deep under the effects of the drug.

'I save *myself*,' I hiss.

CHAPTER FORTY

As I drive back home to Jack, Mike emits a low gurgling noise in the back seat. His whole body is slumped against the window, eyes closed.

I'd worried I would have to drag him back to my car, but incredibly the salesman and would-be rapist had risen to his feet. He'd been so disassociated I was able to herd him down the alleyway like a goose. I'd opened the door and he'd sat down, allowing me to reach over him and click his seatbelt on.

Safety first, even if you are on your final journey to my son's basement kill room.

I catch sight of the blue lights too late. I groan as I see a squad car up ahead near the bridge on the road that leads towards Camden Town station. The car ahead of me slows down and a police officer in a high-vis jacket approaches the window, ducking down to speak to the driver inside. I should have known that nothing comes easy.

My options are limited. I don't want the police to see Mike in the back of my car, but I don't have a lot of choice. I bark at my phone on the dashboard to call Jack. I'm grateful when he answers right away. Whatever the police incident is, it's nothing to do with my son. I had been fairly sure it wouldn't be; he knows I am bringing Mike back to him. I'd called him from the car when I'd buckled Mike in.

'You got my shirt then?'

The lethargy and anguish my son had exhibited earlier was gone. His excitement crackled down the line.

'Yeah, almost back from the er, launderette.'

I almost chortled at the ludicrous nature of what we're saying. None of this would be necessary if it wasn't for the fact all smartphones are pocket spies, along with Alexa and all her (its?) competitors. Lazy people have invited billionaire super-villains to record everything we do. How hard is it to turn on your own music, for God's sake? Bloody Skynet.

'Meet me out front.'

'Will do.'

Being a Saturday night, there's a good throng of pedestrians on the pavements. I can see more police moving them along, away from the crossroads. There's only a couple of vehicles behind me.

It'll be obvious if I do a three-point turn and get out of here. I don't want to pique the police's interest and make them call in my car registration plate. I decide to brazen it out. I move the car forward at a slow pace.

At the press of a button, my window comes down. I fix a smile on my face as the police officer appears next to me. She's just a kid, her hair in actual pigtails wound in circles next to her head like Princess Leia. She gives me a gappy-toothed grin.

'Evening, madam.'

'Evening,' I echo, careful to keep my tone light, 'anything I can help with?'

'There's an incident nearby.' The officer rolls her shoulders. 'We're asking that everyone takes a left at the crossroads for now.'

This is not a problem for me, I have to take that turn anyway.

'What kind of incident?'

The police officer smiles in apologetic fashion, her manner making it clear she won't be drawn any further. She tilts her head as she catches sight of Mike in the back. He's lolling forwards now, arrested only by his seatbelt. His jaw works up and down, like he's trying to get sound out. Nothing but a limp splutter falls from his lips.

'Your fella okay?'

I don't even look behind me. Ovaries of steel.

'Oh, him? He's fine.' I roll my eyes, as if the policewoman is my co-conspirator. 'But he's in for it, when he sobers up.'

The officer titters, like she can relate. 'Men, eh.'

She stands back, giving the roof of my car an amiable tap to say I can move on. I jam a foot on the pedal, pressing the window button as I do so. The glass closes just as a strangled animal howl emits from Mike, sending a shiver down my spine. He falls back in his chair with the effort. I look at him via the rear-view mirror.

'Nice try.'

I'd be willing to bet real money he'll be coming round within the next twenty minutes. Unlucky for Mike, I'm about three minutes from my house.

I flick the indicator left at the crossroads.

CHAPTER FORTY-ONE

'Did he do this?'

Jack grabs hold of my chin, his face close to mine. The blow from Mike's fist in the alleyway have caused a cluster of bruises that run from my temple to under my cheekbone. They still hurt like hell, yet don't look as bad as they feel.

I'd expected a black eye, but it hasn't appeared. I'm surprised; a lifetime of watching Hollywood movies had made me believe eyes puff up and go purple at the slightest strike. Jack's ocular fracture when he was five had looked almost as appalling as poor Steve's skewered, bloody orb the night Jack had descended into homicide, taking me with him.

'Any requests?'

I blink, surprised. I don't remember Jack ever asking me for instructions on how to dispatch his victims before. That said, I've never had my son's prey try to make me *their* prey before, either.

'Just make him pay, son.'

As Jack nods, a kaleidoscope of vengeance unfurls in my brain: I see sharp tools and blood spattering stainless-steel basins in my mind's eye. The medley of images blurs and then becomes crystal clear. I smile, my inspiration sending the spores of warm, dark satisfaction through my chest as an idea comes to me.

'You know what to do with rapists like him.' I mime a knife cut, but instead of across the throat, I lower my hand so it's in line with Jack's groin. 'Hit him where it'll hurt him most.'

Jack does not wince, or even seem to react. He nods, his expression impassive as ever.

'You're the boss.'

Shock means I'm still on time delay, so Jack's words don't register until the basement door closes behind him. Irritation rankles through me next: *I'm* the boss? The assertion is risible; if that were true, I would never have taken us down this homicidal road. My hand had been forced by Jack's actions, not my own. The urge to pull Jack out, make him explain himself seizes me. I almost wrench open the basement door and go down after him.

My feet come to a standstill by the closed door. My hand does not grab the latch. Unlike Jack, I don't want to hear Mike's hollers of anguish and pain. I never go in the basement when Jack is working. I try not to even know when his prey is dead. Jack knows the deal: I might catch his prey for him, but dispatch — including clean up — is up to him.

It wouldn't do any good, anyway. I've read enough parenting books and websites to realise teenagers never want to take responsibility for their own actions. Jack will have told himself I am in charge, even 'making' him kill, because it suits him.

It's probably why Dennis Nilsen blamed Dorothy Atkinson in that letter of his, too. Psychopaths have all kinds of twisted justifications for what they do. It's part of what makes them tick. The word 'psychopath' used to make me twitch, but there's no doubt in my mind now my son is one. From that steely glint in his eye to his predatory smile, through to how his gaze dulls as he deals with more practical matters, like the fresh-dug graves in the basement.

Yet all these things pale in comparison to Jack's attempts at mirroring.

raw. He'd boasted about how the aggressor had ended up worse off. Perhaps I can bait Aaron out of hiding? It's a long shot, but he has a massive ego, so I decide it is worth a try.

@PreyingMentis: Maybe I am @Cr1meScr1be . . . Wanna meet up in meatspace and find out? PM me for details.

Crossing my fingers mentally, I press SEND.

Less than five minutes later, the number 1 icon of my PM folder flashes. I click on it, daring to hope it's Aaron. My heart sings when I discover it is.

I open the message. It reads:

@Cr1meScr1be: You're on.

CHAPTER FORTY-TWO

A flurry of online messages later, it is agreed: Aaron will meet me at a car park round the back of a sandwich place off the high street that following evening. We trade insults one last time and I log off. I don't want to be there all night. I need to sleep.

The next day, I wake late and pad downstairs in my pyjamas. In the living room, a family gameshow plays on the television. Jack now lays on the sofa watching it and hugging a cushion. Contestants must clamber over walls and through rivers of slime for cash. The things people will do for money. Perhaps it's desperation.

I can relate to that, at least.

My communications with Aaron last night had become increasingly confrontational, which both amuses and vexes me. I'd already known how easy it is to bait some men. Jack and I had done it unintentionally with Dean, over and over. Just talking or walking around seemed to set him off. He'd forced us to walk on eggshells every minute of every day.

Even so, I'm disappointed in Aaron all over again. I had hoped he would be above brutish behaviour. Yet here he is, willing once more to settle such a trivial matter with his fists. I close my eyes and see Aaron behind my lids, smiling at me in the archives; kissing me in the club; looming over me in his attic bedroom.

I'd really liked him, but he was just like all the rest.

I blink and return to my home. I figure it's important I don't go looking for Aaron myself. I can't risk him turning it around on me, making me doubt myself. Someone ruthless and immune to Aaron's charms needs to bring him in.

Luckily, I know just the man for the job.

'I need you to go and net Aaron.'

In our living room, Jack gives no indication he has even seen me. He's glued to the television screen, like he's made of stone.

'I've written down where and when the meet is. Here you go.'

He makes no effort to take the bit of paper. I sigh.

'Jack?'

I know my son has heard, but he still ignores me. I stand in front of the television, obscuring his view. Jack finally looks up at me and growls in irritation.

'Why do I have to go?'

I hesitate before replying. Though it suits me to have Jack kill Aaron, it seems foolhardy to reveal my secret relationship with the podcaster. Jack's rage is unpredictable. I don't want my son thinking I broke my word about not getting involved with any more men. I mean I obviously did, but *only* to protect Jack. He won't understand that though, teenagers are very black and white. Worse, he might even think I was working *against* him.

'Because Aaron will recognise me.'

'He met me too.'

The lie feels heavy on my tongue. I watch my only child's brow furrow, as if he detects something is amiss. I grasp for something — anything — to throw him off the trail.

'Only in passing. He came into the archives a lot, maybe he liked me.'

It works, but not in the way I intend; Jack raises a dismissive hand at me.

'That's a good thing, isn't it? Do whatever it is you do to get the horny fucker back here.'

Volcanic anger surfaces, obliterating any concern I had moments earlier at covering my dalliance with Aaron.

'Just do as you're told, will you?'

Jack sits up, giving me a mock salute. '*Ja, mein Führer.*'

My body reacts.

I don't think it through. In a blink I am across the room next to my son, raising my hand. My open palm connects with Jack's cheek with a sharp *thwack*.

Unprepared, Jack's head snaps to the side, his jaw hanging open in shock.

Silence.

His own hand pressed to his reddened cheek, Jack gapes at me, stupefied.

Instant shame floods through me as I comprehend what I've done.

How could I do that to him, after everything Dean put us through?

'Oh God, I'm sorry, I . . .'

My words dwindle away as I watch venom flood through my son's features. The sharp teeth of terror bite hard: Jack is bigger than me now. He could grab me by my elbow or hair and force me downstairs to the basement.

My heartbeat ricochets around my ribcage as we freeze where we are, his dark resentment uncoiling between us.

Jack lets his hand drop from his face and stands up. He makes no move to make a grab for me. I take an exaggerated step backwards just in case, putting the coffee table between us. His expression melts back into that cool impassivity, though the fury still shines in his eyes as our gaze meets.

'You don't get to do that again. *Ever.*'

He snarls the last word, enunciating each syllable with the same amount of stress. I nod, relief replacing the adrenaline in my veins.

'I promise.'

My son turns his back on me and stalks out into the hall. I follow and watch him retrieve his jacket from the peg. He looks in the large mirror, checks out his hair. He could be any normal young person preparing for a night on the town.

'Where are you going?'

He sighs. 'Where do you think? To find Aaron. Like you wanted.'

'Wait, wait . . .'

I run into the downstairs toilet, grabbing a syringe and vial for him in the cabinet. I keep them in every room. I'd taken Rupert's keys and relieved him of his entire stash in his flat while Jack worked on him down in our basement. I appear in the hallway.

'You'll need this.'

Jack regards me with undisguised contempt. Though not as tall as Aaron, he towers over me, the wiry strength in his hands and shoulders obvious. He can handle himself if events turn ugly.

'I won't need that kind of help.'

'What if you kill him by accident, getting him here?' I point out. 'You have a long history of that.'

Jack's eyes narrow. 'Would it be a problem if I did?'

Shit.

Almost caught out. I don't want Jack to realise I want my own revenge on Aaron, too.

'No-no,' I splutter. 'Just would be a shame for you, that's all. I know you like to take your time.'

My son rolls his eyes and grabs the drugs from me, shoving them in his pocket. He glares at me as if to say: *Happy now?*

He turns and grabs the Yale lock on the front door, leaving me alone in the hall.

CHAPTER FORTY-THREE

I startle awake as the door catch snaps back in place. Fresh night air floods back into the hallway, bringing the smell of cigarette smoke with it. A shadow moves towards the light and flicks the switch, flooding the hall with light.

Blinking furiously as I shake off sleep, I realise I'd drifted off sitting on the stairs waiting for Jack, like all those years ago. This time, he does not cradle one hand in the other, his thumb dislocated. My relief does not last long.

'Where the hell is Aaron?' I demand.

Jack digs his hands in his pockets. He shrugs, belligerent.

'What's that mean . . . Did you see him, or didn't you?'

'Didn't see him.'

I can't believe it. I'd been certain Aaron's ego and need to be right would send him to the car park we had agreed to meet at that evening. The possibility of failure, of him not even turning up, had not even occurred to me.

Now what?

I grip the newel post and rise with difficulty, my back protesting at sleeping sitting up. My feet edge downwards, one step at a time, like I am an old woman. Thoughts clamour through my brain like reflections in a hall of mirrors.

Did Aaron stay away because he knew it was me behind the @*PreyingMentis* handle and if so, how? Or did Aaron see Jack waiting in the car park . . . But if he had, did he give him a wide berth because he recognised him as my son? If he did, that still doesn't explain if he knows about us. Or maybe he just had a change of heart and never turned up at all.

'What's the big deal, anyway?' Jack watches me wince as I move towards him. 'I dispatched Mike this week. We don't need Aaron.'

I'm on perilous ground again. Jack can't find out about me and Aaron. I can already feel my grip on the situation unravelling. Stalling, I stop by Jack and give him an exaggerated sniff of his clothes and hair.

'Why do you smell of smoke?'

It works. Jack shrinks away from me.

'The people I was with were smoking.'

I grab his fingers and raise them to my nostrils. He permits me. The smell of smoke is no stronger, nor is his skin yellow. He is not lying to me. The significance of his words finally registers with me.

'Who were you with?'

'Just people.' Jack's tone is exasperated. 'I asked around, to see if Aaron had been about tonight. Or any other night lately.'

Pride flowers in my chest at my boy's clever thinking.

'And has he?'

'Yes.'

Aaron hasn't left the borough. That's something, at least. I follow Jack into the kitchen. He gravitates towards the refrigerator and pulls a carton of juice from the door, taking a long slug straight from it. I can't be bothered to bawl him out; I am too impatient to hear the results of Jack's investigation.

'Well?'

Jack stops drinking, wiping his mouth with his sleeve. 'He hangs out in several places apparently. The only one I recognised is the Sleepwalking Flamingo.'

The name is familiar to me, too. Steve's face bursts into my mind for some reason, then guilt quickly follows. Of course: it is that hipster pub that's replaced Steve's coffee joint, 1939. I give brief thought to how Jack knows the Sleepwalking Flamingo but dismiss it. He's a grown man now, he's probably gone drinking there himself.

He's never brought a boyfriend home, but I know he must have them. I've smelled unfamiliar cologne on his shirts putting them in the washing machine; spotted bits of paper with telephone numbers scrawled on when I've turned out his pockets. Typical hypocritical teenager: he doesn't have to abide by the same rules he's imposed on me.

It doesn't matter, anyway. I might have to keep extra tabs on Jack given his proclivities for murder, but he still deserves some privacy.

'You're going back?' I hear the question in my tone, as if it's up to Jack to decide. I reframe it so he can be sure he is. 'You're going back.'

Jack flashes me a malevolent look as he slams the fridge door shut again.

'Yes, *Mother*. I'm already aware I have no choice in the matter.'

'What the hell is that supposed to mean?'

I grip my fists next to my sides. I don't want to risk striking him again like I had earlier, but this is too much. Jack's taunts and resentment are unfair. Why is he acting like I'm the enemy? I've been the one who's kept my son safe *and* delivered him what he needs.

Everything I've done, I've done for him! I am a good mother.

Ungrateful, spoiled brat.

'Never mind.'

Jack's belligerence seems to evaporate. He averts his gaze, backing down. I'm not ready to let it go, though. I cross my arms, like this is a normal argument with a rebellious teenage child.

'No, you clearly have a problem with me, let's get it out in the open.'

Jack stares at the floor, head bowed.

'Got nothing to say for yourself?'

I circle him like I had Mike when he was on his knees in the alleyway behind that rundown hotel. I recognise that despite my fears, the balance of power is still with me. Yes, Jack could knock me down on the tiles and bash my head in where I lie, but he is still my son.

I push against his shoulder with my outstretched hand. It's not a strike, but he reacts as if it is.

'Don't,' he growls.

'What are you going to do?' I taunt. 'Kill me?'

A tiny voice in the back of my brain squeaks, *Don't provoke him.*

Yet still that reckless fury flows within me, making me flirt with the danger. It's like I am watching myself from above. I can't believe what I'm doing. I've been afraid of my son, of what he's capable of, yet right now I'm inviting his possible aggression.

Did I want him to lash out, murder me?

Perhaps I do. Then all of this will be over.

I tap a fist against his collarbone, harder this time. My knuckles rap bone and he winces in pain.

'Come on then,' I sneer. 'Do it! Put us both out of our misery!'

'Stop it,' Jack whispers. 'Please, Mum.'

My stomach lurches as I see a tear roll down his cheek. Unlike the previous time, he is not wailing or panicked, just sad. He seems broken down, weary with it. Jack's gaze is on the floor, his wrists turned out in a submissive gesture towards me. I stand back as the implications of this hit me.

A young man at the end of his rope.

'Please don't hit me,' Jack murmurs.

I hold out my arms to him. 'Oh, darling. Come here.'

Jack peeks up at me, his body language relaxing as he sees me welcoming him towards me. I wrap him in my embrace and feel the relief coursing through him as he leans down, burying his face in my hair.

My own dark emotions dissipate. Anxiety and anger melt away as another feeling replaces them: wonder. For the first time, I realise something important. Jack can't manage without me. He is desperate for my approval.

He will do whatever I want, *not* the other way around.

I really am in charge.

CHAPTER FORTY-FOUR

Aaron seems to have the luck of the devil. Every time I send Jack out to trail him at covert distances, the podcaster is surrounded by friends and other people.

I don't believe Jack at first, certain there must be moments where Aaron is alone. Jack brings me mobile phone footage of Aaron in bars and clubs. It's true, he is never on his own. As days turn to weeks of Jack trailing him at a distance, I regret sending Aaron the threatening IMs, challenging him to a fight. It had seemed like a good idea at the time, but I'd been angry.

Now it appears as if the podcaster has people watching his back. This inescapable fact also lends credence to my concern Aaron knows about Jack, or at least suspects him as The Camden Killer. It's not such a leap to suppose he also suspects I am the woman seen drinking with Boz that he mentioned in his podcast.

Shit.

May rolls in with blue skies and a shower of pink and white blossom. My last pay cheque from the archives cashed and paid out on utilities and food, I check my bank balance daily. I watch my funds deplete as Dad's nest-egg money runs out.

I hear nothing more from Aaron. I dare to hope it was all grandstanding on his part and he's moved on. Combing the jobs sites, I make application after application, but fail to get an interview for even the paltriest of jobs.

I find myself stuck between two worlds. The menial jobs tell me I am over-qualified; the professional ones tell me I am not experienced enough. It feels like a horrible metaphor for the crossroads I find myself at as my fortieth birthday approaches. Not so long ago, people would marry in their teens and become parents straight after. Nowadays, a person's thirties are supposed to mark those brand new beginnings instead. Yet here I am, the widowed mother of a grown-up son. I feel like an old, forgotten relic from outside my time.

Jack wakes me on my birthday with breakfast in bed. He presents me with a tray with a carnation on it, as well as a cafetiere of coffee and a bagel with Nutella spread thickly on it, my second favourite breakfast. He flashes me a sheepish smile and tells me he'd attempted to make me my ultimate favourite: a poached egg on avocado on toast. He'd left it too long and set the egg pan on fire downstairs.

I'm touched. I'd not mentioned the date was coming up and I don't recall him ever marking the occasion before. As I take a tentative sip of my coffee — it tastes rather bitter — he presents me with a card. Opening it, I discover he has bought me a gift: a day in a spa and overnight stay at a nearby hotel, via one of those voucher discount sites. I am delighted he has thought of me.

'Thank you so much, darling.' I lean forwards and plant a kiss on his forehead.

'I thought you could go today?' Jack smiles. 'I can drop you off. Jim said I could borrow the car. It's all arranged.'

I can't believe my luck. The obvious issue of his killing aside, I really do have the best son any mother could wish for.

'Wonderful!'

An hour or two later, I'm standing outside the hotel Jack has chosen for me. I wave my son off all smiles. The place looks nice enough: the building is on a Georgian terrace, on a small square looking straight onto an oak tree and another row of residential houses opposite. I can hear the buzz of Soho and a primary school a few blocks away.

Like the Atkinson Project, it's a very different story inside. The reception is dark and dank, with black mould on the walls in full view. A bored-looking woman with pencilled-in eyebrows and a viciously scraped-back ponytail stands behind the scarred Formica reception desk.

I waste a polite smile on her as she checks out her nails. As she taps my details in the computer and assigns me a room, I notice a spiral staircase leading down into the basement from the hallway. A makeshift sign reads SPA in felt tip. It's just a piece of cardboard, from a cereal box if I am not mistaken. The thought of a stranger touching my bare feet or kneading my flesh in this fleapit is too much to bear.

Nope. NopeNopeNopeNope.

I react on instinct. I don't think it through, just turn on my heel and stalk back out. The bored receptionist does not bother to call after me.

Despite the London pollution, the early summer air feels welcoming as I make it back outside; in that hotel I could see and taste the old dirt in the air. Putting some distance between myself and the decrepit old building, I find myself in Soho, somewhere near Poland Street. I look up and down the crowded narrow street, spotting tourists and office workers milling about.

I spot a French café and sit down outside on a little aluminium table and chairs. A young, chic woman appears to take my order. She's the opposite of the hotel receptionist, smiling and engaged. I know immediately I have done the right thing.

Yet I can't just go home; my rejection of his present would crush Jack.

What to do?

As my coffee is delivered to me with one of those little biscuits I love, I realise I could go window shopping in Westminster, to some old bookshops. I love to walk on wooden floors and smell the musty pages in the air. I could peer at first editions behind glass, dreaming of the day I might have an entire library of them all to myself.

Then I could go to Leicester Square and see if I can spot any famous actors passing through on their way to rehearsals for the shows (the last time I'd gone, years ago, I'd seen Jason Donovan). Then to round off the day: cake. Because, obviously. Though I'm supposed to stay overnight, I can go home later, pretend to Jack I missed him too much.

Sorted.

My decision made, the hours rocket by. Growing up as a motherless girl with a self-employed father who worked all hours, I'd become accustomed to pleasing myself. I wander through the tourist spots, ending up having a delicious lunch in Chinatown. I check out the bookshops I scout out first on my phone, then read some of my purchases in the sunshine on a little bench for an hour. I people-watch in Covent Garden, then buy a single rose on a whim from a street vendor near Leicester Square.

I really do have a wonderful time.

I return to Camden on the train, walking home from the station rather than bother Jack. I pick up one of those DIY Indian takeaways from the Tesco Metro for us on the way back. He loves those. The plastic bag bangs against my leg as I amble back to the house, feeling more content and at peace than I have in years. Jack is sure to notice my lightness of mood, but that's good. He will put it down to the massage he'd paid for in that shitty hotel.

I give a cheery wave to my neighbour Celia as I pass. The old woman stops where she is on the path, brow furrowed, as if she can't place me. Then she raises a single hand in acknowledgement, grabbing her wheely bin from the kerb to drag it back inside.

Still smiling and carefree, I let myself in to the house. The evening sunlight passes through the prism of the glass panels in the door, creating rainbow colours on the faded hall carpet. As it catches my eye I follow the colours, moving past the kitchen, towards the space that runs under the stairs.

My good mood vanishes in an instant as I see something propped up against the wall next to the closed basement door.

A traveller's rucksack filled to the brim, a camping roll beside it.

Could Jack have gone hunting without me today? I strain to hear any screams from the cellar, but I already know the soundproofing works. Fearing the worst but not wanting to go downstairs, I crouch down beside the oversized bag. I pull open the top flap, undoing the many toggles beneath. I rifle through it, finding nothing surprising: men's jeans and trackie bottoms, rolled-up T-shirts, folding cutlery, a couple of stainless-steel camping pots and other containers. I've seen none of the items before, but I know exactly whose they are, even before I hear his trainers descending from upstairs. I stay where I am, still crouched beside his belongings.

Whistling, he swings round the newel post at the bottom of the stairs, landing in the hallway. He clocks me right away and freezes, eyes wide, caught in the act, his arms full of toiletries from the upstairs bathroom. He drops them on the floor.

Jack.

CHAPTER FORTY-FIVE

'It's not how it looks,' Jack says.

'And how does it look?'

My son just stands there, moving foot to foot, unable to meet my eye or give me a straight answer. I brace myself on the wall, rising with difficulty from my crouched position. I feel the tingle of pins and needles as the blood rushes back into my calves and feet.

Denial and confusion swirl in my brain as I attempt to process the situation. Hurt crashes through me next; he'd planned all this? Jack hadn't paid for that disastrous birthday gift out of the goodness of his heart, to celebrate my birthday. He'd wanted me out of the house, so he could leave without me trying to pull him back.

How could he!

'So, where are you going?'

I attempt to keep my tone neutral, non-accusatory. I've read enough parenting manuals to know the worst thing you can do is meet teenagers' belligerence with yet more belligerence. If I am to have any chance of turning this situation around, I need to keep us both away from panicked ultimatums.

Jack just shrugs. My hands flex next to my sides. The urge to fly across the hallway and slap his face again is all-encompassing. I can't believe the violence welling in me. Had it always been there?

No. This is Jack. He's done this to me.

I've given my only son everything. I've sacrificed so much! My job, my loves, my *whole life*. I am alone because I've literally gone above and beyond for this child, yet this is how he repays me?

Ungrateful little BRAT.

I bite my tongue to stop the toxic words from spilling out. I take a deep, cleansing breath instead.

'What does that shrug mean? You don't know where you're going, or you don't want to tell me?'

'A bit of both,' Jack mutters, eyes still on the hall floor.

'But you *are* leaving home?'

The silence that follows feels unrelenting, though it can't be more than a second or two. A tiny little corner of my heart wishes I am mistaken; that there *is* a victim trussed-up in the basement downstairs and the bag is his, not my son's.

This ember of hope is extinguished when Jack finally nods his confirmation.

'Why?'

My voice cracks, drawing Jack's scornful gaze back to my face at last.

'Everyone leaves home eventually, Mum.'

'Not *everyone* is a fucking serial killer!'

My retort rips out of me, though my voice is thankfully not loud. I am used to having to keep a lid on my feelings, just like Dad taught me.

Even so, Jack takes an exaggerated step backwards. The truth hangs heavy in the air like poisonous fumes between us. I've never used the word 'serial killer' around Jack. We have never spoken in detail about what we've been doing. We've tiptoed around our homicidal activities, using euphemisms like 'work', 'prey', 'catch' and 'dispatch'.

'Did you think you could just give all this up, be "normal"?' I throw my hands up in air quotes like Maria. 'It's too late for that, Jack!'

'You see, this is why I never said anything. I knew you wouldn't get it.'

That avenue of conversation shut down, we return to staring at each other.

Impasse. Loggerheads. Deadlock.

I feel the frustration working its way up through my body. I don't want to be the first one to speak again, but I know I can't hold it inside for long.

Sure enough, seconds later the words explode out of me, questions pouring from my lips like burning oil.

'What did you think would happen when I returned to find you gone? Did you think I would just accept it? That I wouldn't come looking for you, or worry about you? How long did you think it would be before you would need to go hunting again? How were you planning to do that, without my help and research? Or without somewhere safe to do it, like the basement? How long do you think it would be before you got caught!'

Jack just offers that maddening shrug again.

I raise my eyes skywards as I count to ten. I pace from right to left in the narrow hall, only managing two or three steps before I have to turn. The adrenaline surges through me, forcing me into motion. I know that if I don't move, I will grab my boy by the throat.

That won't lead anywhere good.

Jack opens his mouth to reply at last, then appears to think better of it and closes it again. I proffer a sarcastic little wave at him.

'Please, say whatever you were going to say.'

'No. You'll turn it round on me, just like you always do. It's always about you.'

An incredulous bark of laughter escapes me. Dean had said this too. The word-weapons men throw at women to hurt us! Society says women are supposed to give all the time, exhaust herself making everyone else happy.

The moment any woman wants something back for herself? *She's* the problem.

248

Well, fuck that.

Another burst of weariness overcomes me, forcing me to stop and lean against the basement door. We stand like that for a minute or more. It's so quiet in the house I can hear the *tick-tock* of the clock in the kitchen and the thud of my own heartbeat in my ears.

'Everything I've done, it's *for you*. Don't you get that?'

A mocking snicker erupts from Jack. Fury erupts within me. In the blink of an eye, I am across the hall, my hand raised again.

Like before, Jack still shrinks away from me, eyes wide. Unlike like the last time, my blow does not connect. I manage to stop myself.

This emboldens Jack, who raises himself to his full height. He towers over me. He places one hand on my shoulder, to hold me at arm's length from him. I can feel the strength in him, moving from his arm as his finger pads clench my flesh.

I tense up as once more I appreciate his physical advantage. He could push me down to the floor and kick me to death if he wants to. It would not take much. I'm literally half his size.

He doesn't.

My son lets go and digs his hands in his pockets. He tilts his head, appraising me. I don't like the shift in power between us, one little bit.

'I'm leaving home tomorrow.' Jack's voice is calm and clear. 'I'm going on a trip, around the world. Far away from you. You can't stop me.'

I make one final attempt. 'Okay, fine. But at least wait a few weeks more? Until your exams are done.'

'So you can work on me, break me down?' Jack shakes his head. 'No chance. The tickets are bought. I'm going tomorrow, no matter what.'

Helplessness floods through my body. I feel like slumping to the floor, defeated. I've felt like this before when I was with Dean. I'd called it my 'play dead' mode. He'd crushed my spirit, pummelling it into submission along with my body. I've not felt like this in years. The fact my own son has brought me back to that terrible feeling fills me with a dark wrath.

I touch my cheeks and discover my fingers are wet: I am crying. I take a shaky breath and push it all down, back into that velvet box, just like my father taught me.

'I understand.' I smile. 'Forgive me. It's just a shock. I wish you had discussed this with me first, but I guess you had your reasons. I can see you would need your own space.'

Jack's eyes narrow in suspicion. He thinks I am bluffing. He flinches as I move towards him, but I am on my way to the downstairs toilet. I pat him on the arm as I pass, indicating my face, the tear marks tracking down my cheeks.

'I just need a tissue, that's all.'

I grab what I need and reappear in the hallway, dabbing my eyes with some toilet roll. I sigh as I see Jack still skulking there, unsure what to do.

'Come here.'

I open my arms to my son for a hug. He hesitates, then gives me an uneasy smile and leans down towards me. He puts his arms around me, resting his chin on my shoulder. I breathe in the masculine scent of him: my big, tall, grown-up boy.

'I love you, son.'

He starts in surprise as I sink the syringe into his side, just like I had with Mike. But Jack doesn't strike me like the would-be rapist had. He blinks at me, confused.

'What have you . . . ?'

He sways from one foot to the other, lurching towards the kitchen door. He overcompensates, throwing out a hand, trying to steady himself on the door frame. It doesn't work; his elbow bends like rubber. He falls to one knee, then the other. His voice is thick, like it's a struggle to form the words on his tongue.

'*Mum . . .*'

His face creases with betrayal, then disbelief as the drugs take hold. I watch, intrigued. I'd given him the same dose as

Mike. They seem a similar height, but I reason it's probably because Jack is considerably thinner. When I'd helped Dean package drugs for his dodgy empire all those years ago, he'd mentioned how a person's weight can affect how they react.

Oops.

I feel no triumph like I had with Mike in that grotty alleyway. Tears stream down my cheeks again.

'Don't fight it.' I join him on my knees, stroking his fringe out of his eyes. 'Go to sleep. There's a good boy.'

Jack sinks under.

CHAPTER FORTY-SIX

What do you do when your child defies you?

There's only one place for Jack.

The basement.

Moving Jack is not as easy as it had been with Mike.

Struggling to get Jack *into* the basement is not the only unpleasant surprise. When I finally get him down the steps, the bare overhead bulb illuminates the large subterranean room has been stripped.

All the painstaking, expensive renovations I'd made for his birthday are gone. It has been returned to the dank, dour cellar it was before. I feel like Jack had looked when I'd injected him upstairs: disbelieving and vacant.

Where is the dentist's chair? Or the large rolls of single use plastic, the aluminium trays and steel surgical instruments? I'd spent thousands on its recent makeover and kitting it out with equipment for him, yet only a single tool chest remains.

Betrayal blooms in my chest as I search his pockets for weapons. I find only his phone, which I place on top of the tool chest, out of his reach.

I try and think back to when I'd last been in the basement. I recall bringing Boz on his last dance for Jack's birthday; Kevin too. It's true I've been avoiding the kill room, so maybe I'd not brought Rupert the drug dealer down here? Jack had been the one who'd brought Mike down here. That I do remember.

I've really taken my eye off the ball.

Whilst I let my thoughts of revenge on Aaron consume me, Jack had been planning his escape, right under my nose. He probably sold all the stuff I bought him to pay for his damn aeroplane ticket.

Shit.

I let Jack slump by the back wall and rifle through the tool chest for what I need. I'm relieved to discover my son has at least spared some of his equipment from his cull. My son secured, I drag a kitchen chair down the steep steps.

I sit and wait out of reach, a safe distance away from my son's semi-conscious body. About forty minutes later Jack groans. He attempts to bring his right hand to his head like a drunk with a hangover. He discovers he can't. As his senses return, he comprehends why.

His wrist is handcuffed to the water pipe that runs the back wall of the basement.

My son's mouth twists in a feral snarl as he barks expletives at me, crashing the handcuffs against the water pipe. I tense up as I hear the cuffs clank and scrape, metal against metal. I have no idea if the water pipe will hold. If Jack manages to wrench it from the wall, he will be able to slide the handcuffs straight off. From the volcanic anger and seething hatred in his eyes, I do not want to be present if he breaks free.

After a couple of minutes of this Jack sags in defeat, leaning his head against the crumbling wall of the basement. He's pale and exhausted; the effects of the drugs still course through his system. His hand is suspended above him, his arm bent at the elbow. The pose reminds me of those one-armed reins parents use to keep toddlers by their sides when walking around town. For some reason, this strikes me as funny and I can't stop a burgeoning smile curving my lip. My son mistakes this as triumph.

'Fuck you,' Jack hisses.

I massage my temples; the weight of stress and sorrow well within me. There are so many books, blogs, articles and manuals about raising children, but no one ever really tells you what a thankless task parenting is. Everyone gives a high-light reel about their little darlings online, saying how proud they are of them, sharing school pictures, class certificates and exam grades.

The truth is, no matter what you do for kids, it's never enough, or it's wrong. Children always think their perceived way is the 'right' way; they never think about whatever they want or need costs their parents. The more you do for your kids, the more you need them . . . yet perversely, the less they need you.

Parenting is the ultimate in unrequited love.

Yet we're not allowed to talk about any of this, especially if you're a mother. Every time you have a problem with one of your kids, others line up to remind you to be grateful you ever had a kid at all.

There are millions who can't, remember!

The concern trolls won't let you so much as complain about kids forgetting their packed lunch, never mind any-thing serious. There must be parents who have had thoughts about having kids, years after the fact, when it's too late for an abortion? I can't be the only parent who's woken in the middle of the night, wondering if every sacrifice I've made for my child has been worth it. How different could my life have been had I not had Jack . . . Would I have had the chance to be me?

'What am I going to do with you, hey?' I sigh.

Jack shoots me an insolent glare. 'Why don't you kill me?'

'Maybe I should.'

'You don't have the guts,' Jack declares. 'Anyway, I'd be missed.'

'Who by? You were already sacking off school and there's a plane ticket with your name on.' I shrug. 'Who's to say you haven't left on that trip you were planning?'

I'm just messing with him, but I can't deny the thrill. There's a delicious moment as he comprehends he is at my mercy and my whim. For real.

Finally.

'This is typical of you,' Jack mutters. 'You've never let me be.'

I flinch like he's struck me. 'I'm not one of those mothers who has a problem with her kids growing up, Jack. Is that what you think this is?'

'You've handcuffed me in the fucking basement!'

He rattles his cuffs for emphasis. I lean forward in my chair, head in my hands. I can't believe I am having to explain this to him again. I enunciate slowly and deliberately, so he can follow and process what I'm saying.

'Yes, because you're unable to control yourself! If you leave now, you'll only kill somebody else . . . But you won't have me, checking and researching for you. You'll end up landing us both in the shit. You *need me* to keep you in check.'

'Unbelievable.' Jack emits a growl of frustration, leaning his head against the bare brick wall. 'What the hell kind of mother are you?'

'A good one,' I retort. 'I've sacrificed everything for you! *Everything.* And this is the thanks I get?'

An incredulous chuckle escapes Jack. 'You really believe that, don't you?'

'Why wouldn't I? It's the truth.'

'You wouldn't know the truth if it punched you in the face!'

In Jack's fury, he surges forward, forgetting in the moment he's handcuffed to the water pipe. His movement is arrested abruptly, his right hand twisting behind him. The cuffs bite deep into his flesh. He sucks in a pained breath as he massages his wrist and shoulder joints with his left hand. He tuts at me as he clocks me watching.

'I bet you're loving this.'

I'm puzzled and hurt by this accusation. 'How can you say that?'

'Because you've loved *all* of this!' Jack waves his left hand around the basement.

I stand up and advance on him, though I'm careful to leave space between us. I don't want him to grab me by the arm or sweep out a leg under my ankles.

'What the hell is that supposed to mean? You killed your father.'

'Yeah I did —' Jack's lip wobbles — 'but why would *an eight-year-old* do that?'

'Because you're a psychopath!' I snarl. 'You always have been. I see that now. You killed Steve. You attacked those homeless men. You're a bad seed.'

'Or maybe I'm Frankenstein's Monster.'

I can't believe my ears. 'No, you *begged* me for more prey. What was I supposed to do, turn you into the police? But you weren't going to stop either. I had *no choice* in any of this!'

My son's scrutiny burns me from across the room. 'You created me. You created all of this. I am what I am *because of you.*'

Pacing now, agitation works its way through my muscles. I can't have this. It's not true. Jack can lie to himself if he wants. If this ridiculous, twisted justification is what he needs to be able to go through with his 'work' in the basement, so be it. But to stand here and tell his own mother, who's sacrificed everything for him, that it's *my fault* he is like this?

No way in hell is he going to get away with that.

'I only kill because of you,' Jack says in a small voice.

'Stop it.'

'It's true. You made me this way. You—'

'Stop it, Jack.'

'You control everything. You pretend you're so hard done by, but the reality is you always have been the one in the driving seat. Dad was bad enough, but you? You're something else. You turn everything around, make me doubt myself constantly. Even stuff I see with my own eyes, you will tell me it's a lie, that it never happened . . . Or it *did* happen, but the way I remember it is wrong.

'Up is down, down is up, right/left . . . you name it. You're a control freak, you have to have everything your own way. You cast yourself as the victim, poor you, everything happens *to you* . . . when really? You're the puppet master. Nothing is allowed to threaten your warped worldview. If it does, you rewrite history, twist it into what works for you. I never had a chance, growing up with you for a mother.'

'*ENOUGH!*'

Another loaded silence falls between us. Jack stares at me shiny-eyed, mouth still twisted by scorn. I can't bear that my only child is looking at me as if he hates me.

'You don't mean any of this.'

I know he does. I understand, in this instant, that Jack would love to do to me now what he did to his father over half his lifetime ago. He *would* kill me if he could; it's what I've always feared. The disappointment and fury at the injustice of the realisation feels like a knife to the chest. I struggle to recover my voice.

'Look, Jack . . .'

I'm interrupted by something vibrating. It sounds like a horde of angry bees. I can't understand what's going on for a moment, then my beleaguered brain connects the dots: it's Jack's phone on top of the tool chest. I snatch up the handset.

On the screen, a notification from a spycam app flashes: *DOOR.*

Jack must have rigged it up so he can hear the doorbell down in the soundproofed basement. The time catches my attention: almost midnight. No one ever calls on us at night.

Who the hell can that be?

Leaving Jack behind, I take the basement steps two or three at a time. I make my way back up to the hallway, remembering to close the cellar door behind me.

The doorbell still chimes: one, two three times, jaunty and carefree. A dark shadow casts its way on to the hall floor, the porch bulb like a spotlight.

I wrench the door open. It takes me a moment or two to reboot as I take in who it is.

'*You,*' I manage to splutter.

'Hello, Natalie.' He grins, tipping me a wink so I know it's a joke.

I'd been looking for him. Now he's here, in the middle of the night when my errant child is handcuffed in the basement. I've finally got my wish.

Aaron is on my doorstep.

CHAPTER FORTY-SEVEN

My first instinct is to send Aaron away, back into the night.

'Now's not a good time.'

Aaron shifts from foot to foot, hands in his pockets.

'C'mon, Tasha. Let's not play games?'

I hesitate. Aaron's timing could not be worse. I don't know why he's suddenly reappeared. I still can't decide if he had been trying to send me a message with the Nilsen letter, or not. I also can't deny the flush of pleasure at seeing him again. That reckless yet ruthless part of me surfaces again.

I need to find out.

Flashing Aaron a seductive smile, I am careful to keep my tone light and undemanding. The dance begins.

'What can I do for you? It *is* the middle of the night.'

I lean against the doorframe, knowing that will afford him a good view down the V-neck T-shirt I'm wearing. I'm a little put out when his gaze does not flit straight there.

He looks straight over my shoulder like he's checking for other people in the house, behind me. I tamp down my irritation. He is probably worried about Jack still being awake and seeing us together. I had made a big deal of keeping them both separate, after all.

Well, Aaron doesn't need to worry about Jack right now.

He appears reassured. Perhaps he thought I would bawl him out? It has been a while, plus we hadn't parted under the best of circumstances. Aaron proffers that smirk of his and lets his eyes wander over my body.

'I missed you.'

I'm not surprised as the urge to grab him and press my lips to his surges through me. I'd always felt that strong, electric current of attraction between us, right from the first day he'd appeared in the archives. I *am* surprised to comprehend I have missed Aaron too.

I push it back down, as always.

Lock it away, hen.

'You got me fired with that Nilsen letter stunt.'

He at least has the grace to look ashamed. He averts his gaze from mine.

'Sorry about that.'

'Well, the archives was closing anyway.' My tone is begrudging. 'I went to your old house. Where've you been?'

Aaron sniffs. 'Around.'

'You been avoiding me or something?'

'Now why would you think that?'

Shit.

I don't want Aaron to detect my real motive for asking. I can't have him guess it was me baiting him online, or that I'd sent Jack out looking for him. I back off immediately. Poker-faced, I eyeball him and shrug, like I couldn't care less either way.

'Just wondered. What do you want?'

Aaron sighs. 'Call it loose ends. I'm moving away, for good. I don't want to leave it like this between us for all eternity.'

Bingo.

I stand to one side.

'You better come in, then.'

Aaron grins and wipes his feet on the welcome mat. He moves ahead of me, down the hall and towards the kitchen, sitting down at the breakfast bar like he's been here a million times before. I go to the cupboard under the sink where I keep the liquor.

'Drink?'

'Please.'

My back is to him. I don't ask him what he wants. I already know: four fingers of bourbon, like a cowboy. He'd been drinking it the night of that awards bash; I'd finished his off when that creep on the dancefloor had tried it on with me. I present it to him, before retreating towards the sink. I lean against the counter, arms folded and watching him.

'You not having one?'

'I don't like bourbon.'

Aaron's eyebrows shoot up as he slugs the bourbon back. 'Could've fooled me.'

'I'm full of surprises.' I watch him place the empty glass down on the table. 'So, what couldn't wait 'til morning?'

Aaron smirks. 'Tasha, don't be like that.'

I bite my lip to stop myself smirking back. I feign innocence, still playing the game.

'Like what?'

Aaron rolls his eyes as if to say, *Oh go on then.*

He stands up from his chair and clears the space between us in a few paces. He pushes me up against the sink, pressing himself against me. I let him, turning my face up towards his. He strokes my long hair back from my face with his left hand, his right finding my waist.

'You are so beautiful,' he murmurs. 'I'm sorry.'

I snort. 'For what?'

'This.'

In one unexpected, fluid movement, Aaron grabs my arm and twists me away from him. I cry out in panic and surprise as he forces my right hand up towards my shoulder blade. I know the restraint: a half nelson, a move I've only ever seen on television and in movies.

I flinch and holler, expecting it to hurt. It doesn't, but it does push me forwards against my will, immobilising me.

My left flails, useless; I can't reach him. There's no way I can break free without Aaron releasing his grip.

'You weren't supposed to be here, Tasha,' Aaron sighs. 'Where's Jack?'

It all feels horribly inevitable as the truth dawns on me.

'Jack *did* find you out in town!'

'Yup. He told me everything.'

Alarmed, I renew my struggles. 'Everything?'

'Yes. How you control him, won't even let him leave home. He knew you would never let him go. I said I would help him.'

Tears prick at my eyelids as anger and hurt lodges in my throat. I'd thought the discovery Jack was trying to sneak away from me was the worst of it. How could my own son lie to Aaron like this? More betrayal on top of betrayal.

'What's in it for you?'

'Not gonna lie, at first it was revenge. You really pissed me off, Tasha, breaking it off like that after taking what you wanted.' Aaron leans in. 'But then I started thinking about all your excuses, saying you couldn't be with me "because of Jack". I thought it was weird at the time but put it down to being overprotective. But you're not, are you?'

I groan. So Aaron was playing me or Jack — or both of us — all this time.

'If you thought I was so weird, why fuck me, then?'

'What can I say? I'm weak.' Aaron mistakes my quiet for shock and confusion. 'Why do you think I bloody moved house? You're a control freak. There was no way you were going to leave me be. I could sense the crazy in you, from the very moment we met.'

Aaron must have been keeping tabs on Jack's dark activities from afar, via me. I'd never distracted him at all. *I'd* been the one to put my son in danger. Loneliness and horniness on my part has condemned both me and Jack to prison.

Fear lances through me as I see Aaron's game for what it is: he wants to expose Jack as the killer in the borough, make it an exclusive on Crime Scribe. It's so obvious.

I must do something.

'What about your new bestie?' I snarl. 'Does Jack know about you and me?'

Aaron's silence answers my question this time.

'He'll kill you when he finds out. You must know that.'

Aaron just laughs. 'You're deluded. Now, where's Jack?'

I can't understand why Aaron's acting coy. If he knows Jack is the Camden Killer, he must know about the basement. It doesn't take a genius to work out Jack is down there.

'Where the hell do you think!'

Aaron's grip slackens on the wrist pushed up behind my back. I seize my chance and surge forwards, the momentum helping me to break free.

I stumble and fall to my hands and knees, knocking a chair to the kitchen tiles. As it hits the floor I am outside of my body for a second. I see Dean, eyes bulging as he pulls the knife from his own chest, the arc of blood hitting the refrigerator again.

I blink and banish the vision, scrabbling to my feet, chest heaving. I turn to see Aaron swaying. He staggers backwards a couple of steps.

'How did you . . . ?'

He braces himself against the sink to stop himself falling. It doesn't work; his knees buckle underneath him.

The drugs I slipped into Aaron's bourbon are finally taking effect.

Rupert the dealer's stash is all over the house. Adrenaline makes me feel light-headed. I right the chair and sit before I collapse myself. My talent for forward-planning gets me *out* of the hole and Aaron *into* one.

Aaron can't finish his sentence. My voice is cold as I do it for him.

'How did I know?'

I watch as he folds forwards onto his palms.

'You knew the kitchen was at the back of the house. All the other houses on this street, it's at the front. You've been here before.'

At my feet, Aaron still fights the effects of the drugs; he's a stubborn one. It's no good. His hands and elbows give way.

'Like I told you when we first met, it's always the little things.'

He falls onto his chest, banging his forehead against the tiles. I lean over him.

'Thought you were smarter than me, didn't you?'

Aaron passes out.

CHAPTER FORTY-EIGHT

I pour an ice cream tub of tap water straight over Aaron's head. He startles awake, gasping, eyes bulging in horror at his predicament as he takes in where he is.

'What the hell have you done, Tasha?'

I ignore him. My shoulders sing with pain; I've pulled a muscle in my left side. My body had kicked into hyperdrive to get Aaron into the basement. I'd dragged him down there, step by agonising step. My brain gave me a running commentary the whole time.

What are you doing?

There's no way out of this.

You need to give yourself up.

It's the only sensible thing to do.

When he'd seen Aaron's unconscious form dragged into his view, Jack had added to the cacophony inside my head. He'd yelled at me to let his friend go. He'd even said he'd come with me, to the police. He said we could end it all, today.

The nightmare would finally be over.

But Jack doesn't get it. He won't survive prison and I certainly won't. Everything I've done, I've done for him. If I give up today and admit defeat, it's like I've erased the last ten years of my life and my role as his mother. I will be redundant. I won't allow that.

Jack is mine.

Aaron blinks and attempts to raise his hand, only to discover it's cuffed to the water pipe. He is distracted by the sight of Jack, cuffed next to him.

'What the actual fuck?' Aaron extends his free arm towards Jack, though he can't reach. 'You okay . . . she didn't hurt you, did she?'

'I'm fine,' Jack confirms, his voice dull.

Aaron's gaze falls on me across the basement. I've retreated to a safe distance by the steps, out of their reach. He smashes his fist against the water pipe with a metallic *clunk*.

'I fucking knew it!'

I can't help myself. 'Knew what?'

'It was you, all along,' Aaron says. 'The Camden Killer.'

Shaking my head, I make the noise of a buzzer in a quiz show game.

'Oh, so close! But you're wrong.'

I turn away from Aaron and fix Jack in my sights.

'He's not helping you get away from me out of the goodness of his heart, you know. He's stitching you up. Both of us!'

Jack's mouth drops open in shock. 'No. No, he wouldn't.'

'Too right I wouldn't,' Aaron says. 'This is about you, Natasha.'

I roll my eyes towards the basement ceiling. Jack might be naïve, but I'm not.

'You left me with no choice.'

'All of us always have a choice,' Aaron growls, 'even when you're a crazy bitch!'

I don't like how he's not frightened of me.

'Insulting the only person who knows you're both down here is not a wise move. You know that, right?'

To my chagrin, Aaron still ignores me. He rattles his cuffs. He twists back and around, kicking at the pipe with his trainers. Following his lead, Jack joins him.

I'd been wary about tying both of them to the pipe for this reason. I'm still worried they might be able to pull it from the wall, especially if they work together. But there had been nothing for it but to put Aaron down here in the basement as well. Thanks to Jack clearing the kill room out, the pipe had been the only option left.

To my relief and gratitude, the pipe holds. Both of them give up kicking it, panting from the effort.

'You met him that first night I sent you out?'

Jack shoots daggers at me, belligerence painted all over his face.

'Yes.'

I flex my hands by my sides. I'd always thought Jack a poor liar, yet he'd been planning his escape and I'd been clueless. What my spoiled, ungrateful son doesn't understand is he'd pleaded for help from the one person who's capable of getting us both sent down for life. Busting a real-life serial killer is exactly the type of exposure Aaron's been courting for his podcast for years. How could he resist?

Jack's delivered us both to him gift-wrapped.

'How could you, Jack?'

Aaron rests his elbows on his knees.

'Look, you don't exactly have the moral high ground here. You've cuffed us both to a fucking water pipe! Talk about an overreaction. You have no claim on me, Tasha.'

Jack's eyes narrow as he reads between the lines of Aaron's statement. He can't quite believe it yet. Triumph blooms in my chest as Jack spits words out in a feral snarl.

'What are you saying?'

Aaron meets Jack's eye. 'It was nothing.'

'That's not what you said back then,' I scoff.

Jack whirls back to me.

'I can't believe this . . . *You* —' he points at Aaron — '. . . and *him*?'

That savage, steely glint comes over my son again. Aaron backs up away from him. He thinks it's just possessiveness emanating from Jack, rather than real danger. I smile. Aaron raises one hand in surrender but ends up looking like he's doing the boy scout pledge.

'Whoa, whoa! Just calm down, all right? This was ages ago! You don't need to be jealous, Jack.'

Now it's my turn. Like Wimbledon, my head swivels from Aaron, then to Jack. My son pales, his ferocious expression disappearing. In an instant, I catch up on the subtext in Aaron's words. I'm caught on the back foot.

'Hang on a second. Are you saying you . . . *and Jack*? You're not just friends?'

Aaron shrugs. 'No. We've been seeing each other for weeks. That's why I agreed to help him leave you . . . 'cuz I know what a bitch you can be from bitter experience!'

'But we slept together . . .' My poor brain is reeling. 'I thought you were straight?'

'I thought you were gay,' Jack mumbles to Aaron at the same time.

Aaron shakes his head. 'I'm bisexual, for Christ's sake. And we were never exclusive, Tasha. Jack's a consenting adult. I didn't do anything wrong!'

A hysterical laugh bursts out of me. A myriad of forgotten moments resurfaces and race through my thoughts: first up, Aaron telling me I'm dangerous. He'd said I was corrupting him at that night club; that he doesn't normally 'do' women like me. He didn't just mean older women, maybe he meant women generally. Perhaps he usually prefers men. I don't know how this stuff works.

'He doesn't love you, you know,' I tell Aaron, 'he doesn't love anyone. Jack's just an opportunist. He likes what you represent: freedom from his supposedly tyrannical mother. As soon as you're not useful, he'll toss you away. Just like he did me.'

I can't believe I could have missed Jack and Aaron hooking up, as well as the clearing out of the basement. There's no denying the past few months have been hectic, but then I already know I was too preoccupied with thoughts of revenge against Aaron for getting me fired. I must have been really lost inside myself to miss all this going on. Damn it.

'Sounds to me like someone else in this room.' Aaron's brow furrows. 'Even if Jack and I weren't involved, I still would've helped him get away from you. You're a murderer!'

Oh yes, that.

I'm intrigued why Aaron thinks I am The Camden Killer. It makes sense now that Aaron would not have called the police yet; he wanted to ensure Jack was 'safe' from me first. But why did he think it was all me? As this thought occurs, another connection fires in my brain: a self-confessed knight in shining armour like Aaron will always be just one step away from misogyny. If he's not infantilising women, he'll blame them. Men like Aaron never have a clue about the tough choices mothers like me must make.

'I'm not a murderer, for crying out loud. Why would you even think that?'

Aaron sighs. 'Your boyfriend going missing, presumed dead.'

Now he has my full attention. 'So? Steve killed himself. The police found his car at Beachy Head. The case is closed.'

'Oh, I know' — Aaron's expression is earnest — 'you covered it up well.'

He's bang on the money, but I can't let him know that. 'You're sick.'

'Am I? I thought it was odd you were so receptive towards me flirting with you, just weeks after your boy-friend's supposed suicide—'

'That was a *test*?' I cut in.

Aaron shrugs. 'I had a hunch. Anyway, I went to the funeral.'

'I didn't see you there.'

As I mumble this, I realise it's a lie. I *had* perceived a man in a suit, his back to me walking away when I'd come back to greet Steve's sister Rosie after the service. There had been something familiar about him, but I'd let myself get distracted. Fuck.

It had been Aaron and I'd missed it.

'Maybe not, but I saw your weird freakout in the church. Running out, like you felt guilty or something. I told myself it could be because you hadn't seen the signs he was depressed, so I did some more digging.

'Only I thought your name was Natalie, didn't I? Googling "Natalie Rose" got me nothing of interest about you. Then—'

'I told you my real name.' I groan as I connect the dots.

'Right. At that awards bash.' Aaron smiles. 'You were so grateful when I rescued you from that guy on the dance floor. Best two hundred and fifty quid I ever spent. Good old Phil, that old whore will do anything for money.'

'That was a *set-up*?' I can't believe it.

'Of course. And you walked straight into it. I must say, you weren't much of an adversary, Tasha. I guess you got complacent, always being the one in charge.'

I want to slap his face. I don't.

'So anyway, I Googled "Natasha Rose" and what do you know . . . there you are. Steve wasn't the first partner you lost, was he? Dean Rose was the first, ten years ago. I thought, what are the odds of losing not one, but two fellas in ten years? The first, murdered by drug dealers. The second, to suicide. Talk about unlucky.'

I brazen it out. 'This doesn't explain anything. I went through all of this with the police. People *do* have shitty luck.'

'True, so I decided to stay close to you and you made it remarkably easy.' Aaron flashed me a lascivious smile. 'Thanks for that.'

Next to him, Jack grimaces and shudders in disgust. Aaron is too proud of his own detective skills to notice.

'All I had to do was wait and watch,' he declares. 'Before long, people started paying attention to the homeless attacks in the borough. No one saw who it was, but I knew. It was you, Natasha. Dressed in a black hoody, a pipe in your hand. Only ever seen from a distance by witnesses, but it was obvious when I came into the archives that time after I'd had that fight. Your concern for me was so false.'

'That wasn't why I was asking. I—'

He cuts in, content to talk over me like the good mansplainer he is.

'Then there were reports of men full-on disappearing. What did they all have in common? Not much, as it goes, except for one thing. Before they'd gone missing, they'd all been seen drinking with a woman in her late thirties to early forties. Petite, brunette, buxom, looks good for her age. Who does that remind you of?'

My nostrils flare. 'Again: that proves nothing.'

'Right,' Aaron says, 'which is why I published the Nilsen letter.'

I'm confused. I'd thought he'd published the Nilsen letter in a fit of pique, because I'd broken it off with him? Yet he hadn't been upset with me, or even wanted to be with me for real. That too had been a carefully calculated ruse on his part, to bring me out into the open.

He'd set me up from the very beginning.

The letter might have brought him to the archives in the first place, but Aaron had sniffed a much bigger story.

Me.

First he had made himself a honey trap, then made himself bait. As I make this connection, it must show on my face because Aaron chuckles.

'Right, I even knew you were PreyingMentis. I waited for you at the agreed time and place, but you sent Jack instead. Big mistake. He wanted out, told me all about your coercive control. I agreed to help him.'

'Well, aren't you the bleeding heart?' I scoff.

Aaron lets my scorn wash over him. 'I'll admit it, at first my intentions were less than pure. I did want the scoop for my podcast. But listening to Jack, what you'd done to him — to his own father! — made me reconsider.'

My eyes widen. 'He told you I killed Dean?'

If I'd thought the hurt of my only child's betrayal was over, this lie makes it burn like acid all over again. All this, to cover up the monster my son has become only to be framed as being behind it all? Outrageous. Unreasonable. Unthinkable.

'It's all over, Tasha. You might as well let us both go.'

I raise my eyes to the cracked basement ceiling. 'If I'm the murderer you say I am, why would I do that?'

'Because you wouldn't kill me. Not in front of your own son. You won't kill him. Then you'd have no one to control.'

Now it makes sense why Aaron hasn't been scared of me, even cuffed in the basement. Aaron's logic is sound, but not for the reason he thinks. I speed through my available options. It would be a mistake to release them. They're both bigger than me and can overcome me easily. I don't want to end up cuffed to the water pipe myself.

The sensible thing to do would be to throw them both keys to the cuffs, then get the hell out of there before they set themselves free. I could drive around until they go. Aaron might think briefly about going to the police, but he hasn't yet in his search for internet notoriety. Even if Aaron is insistent, Jack would surely dissuade him? He would not want the police combing through the basement. He'd convince Aaron the best course of action would be to leave, if only to save his own skin.

Let the thankless little sod slope off with his boyfriend to wherever they'd been planning.

Once the coast is clear, I could return to the house, pack a bag. I could catch a plane myself to somewhere without an extradition treaty to the United Kingdom. I could sell the house from afar via one of those all-inclusive estate agent websites. All this could happen before Jack inevitably gets sick of Aaron too and kills him, bringing the heat down on himself. Meanwhile, I'll be untouchable even if my darling son tries to drop me in the shit.

I'm a genius.

Before I can make a grab for the keys to the handcuffs, Jack shifts next to Aaron. He eyeballs him, the resentment clear on his face.

'So, who's better in the sack, Aaron: me or Mum?'

Oooh, damn. Things just got interesting.

Aaron's posture sags, like he doesn't want to answer. I scrutinise our mutual lover, my hands on my hips. I can't deny there's a certain part of me who'd love to know as well. Presumably Jack's only just got started in matters of the flesh, so I feel pretty confident I could have the edge based on experience. Do bisexuals have preferences, or are they fifty-fifty? Some of them must be more gay than straight and others vice versa, right?

At least, I can tell myself that if Aaron picks Jack.

'Jack, for God's sake,' he says. 'You sought me out, remember?'

I smirk as I recall how I'd sent out Jack to kill Aaron. It vanishes from my lips as it strikes me how Jack had no intention of ever murdering the podcaster. Maybe he had carried a secret torch for him from that first day they'd met at the archives. Or perhaps Aaron was only ever just a means to an end to cast me by the wayside, like I'd said.

'Tell me,' Jack spits, 'pick your side?'

Aaron sighs. 'I don't know what you think being bisexual means, but it's not as simple as that.'

To be honest that had been exactly what I'd thought. But never mind. My son's downcast eyes stir that cruel side of me back into action. I want to hurt them both.

'C'mon A, you don't have to commit to women or men forever. Just tell us who you prefer.' I grin. 'Me or Jack?'

Jack fixes me with a hurt glare as I say this. 'Yeah, who is it to be?'

'Again, *you* sought *me* out,' Aaron reminds Jack. 'I did not two-time you with her. I would never do that. Yes, I probably should have told you I'd slept with your mother, but it's early days. I would have, eventually. I just didn't want to freak you out and scare you off.'

He reaches for Jack's chin with his free hand, but my son jerks his face away. Aaron lets it drop, shoulders slumped.

'I love you, Jack,' he mutters to the floor.

Silence falls as we all digest this. The sting of Aaron's words, so soon after Jack's own character assassination of me, feels brutal. I sit back down in the chair, my thoughts and stomach churning.

'Did you love her?' Jack enquires in a small voice.

Aaron turns to him. 'Of course not, Jack. Tonight proves what a psycho your mum is, like I've always said. She drugged and locked us down here! You still have a chance. *We* still have a chance.'

I watch, horrified, as Jack takes the hand Aaron offers. My ex-lover smiles as they entangle their fingers. He puts his lips to the back of my son's hand.

Rage crashes through my brain, coursing through my body like fire. I can feel the bulge of the veins in my neck and forearms as wrath overcomes me. It sweeps me up in its dark embrace.

It literally doesn't matter what I do for this boy.

I've kept his murderous secret since Jack was eight years old at huge cost to myself, but he will always cast me as the villain. I've made myself feel better by telling myself he doesn't understand the sacrifices I've made for him; that people can't offer what's not in them to give.

This has gone far enough.

Jack will never so much as give me the thanks or respect I deserve. I have wasted too much time on this cuckoo in my nest. It's time now to purge my responsibility towards my son, cast him out. There's just one thing I must do first.

Punish him.

'Jack is the Camden Killer,' I say.

CHAPTER FORTY-NINE

Aaron blinks as he attempts to process my words, but he can't do it. He'd made up his mind who was responsible: me. Well, sod him and sod my errant son, too.

'Say what now?'

Mouth dropped open, Aaron just stares at me. He looks like his brain has left too many tabs open.

'You heard.' My gaze wanders from Aaron's to my son's.

'Mum, don't,' Jack pleads.

A titter escapes Aaron. The momentary shift in power I'd enjoyed a nanosecond earlier evaporates. I watch and listen as his snigger becomes full-on laughter. It wracks his shoulders, the release obvious. He sighs, a bitter smile etched on his face.

'You would literally say anything, wouldn't you?'

Petulant ire floods back through my body. It takes me all my concentration to not stamp my foot like a six-year-old having a tantrum.

'It's true!' I hiss. 'This, the basement you're in right now? It's a kill room. Jack murdered four men down here.'

Aaron casts his gaze around the stripped-down space. Devoid of Jack's equipment and tools, only the faint tang of bleach remains in the subterranean room, all but obliterated by the much stronger odour of damp. Aaron's disbelief makes me stomp towards the single remaining tool chest.

'How do you explain all these, then?'

I pull out the trays. Inside there are no common garage tools, like wrenches or spanners. Only a variety of fetish items: paddles, ball gags, clamps, blindfolds. Jack had used them all on his victims for reasons other than sex. It had been easier to source them, plus the companies more discreet. I indicate the handcuffs around both men's wrists.

'So this place used to be a dungeon. And?' Aaron shrugs. 'Liking BDSM doesn't make people serial killers. It doesn't even make them violent. The Life is all about enthusiastic consent, the subs have the control. You of all people should know that.'

The subtext of this comment dawns on Jack. He winces.

'That's an image I can't *un*see, thanks.'

I'm gratified to see Jack pull his hand from Aaron's.

'This dungeon was probably yours anyway,' Aaron snarls. 'Maybe you got into BDSM and took it too far and killed someone, because you're an abusive cunt. Then you got a taste for it. Now you're busted, you've decided to blame Jack? Sounds about right.'

I let his ad hominem attack wash over me.

'Jack was the one who attacked those homeless guys, too.'

'Stop lying, Tasha—'

'Remember Jack's would-be "stepdad", Steve?' I do more quotation marks for emphasis. 'That was Jack. He even killed his own father, he—'

'*STOP IT!*'

I purse my lips. Fine, if Aaron doesn't believe me, I will have to show him. I turn on my heel and point my phone's torch into the darkness, at the new patches of concrete on the earthen floor. Each one emerges under the weak light, marking where Jack's victims have been lain to rest.

'Here's Steve. He was a good guy. The rest, a shower of bastards. Boz, some paper gangster and loan shark, feeding off people's desperation . . .' I moved to the next concrete grave. 'Here lies Kevin, wife-beater, abusive father and paedo. Here, Rupert, drug dealer, hooking innocents on his toxic trash. Mike, my would-be rapist, who knows how often he was successful the other times?'

None of my words have the impact I desire. Aaron just shakes his head, that infuriating bitter smile on his lips.

'This doesn't prove you didn't kill them, Tash.'

'Jack killed them all, Aaron.'

'So *you* say.'

The podcaster raises his eyes towards the ceiling, dashing my hopes he believes me. My sights meet with my son's across the basement.

'Tell him.'

Jack sits up straight, eyeballing me. Belligerence bristles off him in waves.

'I have no idea what you're talking about.'

Stalemate.

Aaron inhales. He's careful to keep his tone neutral, I notice.

'Just let us go, Tasha. It's still not too late.'

It is too late.

There's only one way I want this situation to go now: Aaron gone and Jack punished. I have worked too hard. Aaron had been my moment of weakness. I can't let him waltz in now, turn everything upside down and snatch everything from my grasp. As this last, desperate realisation lands, it brings another with it.

'Stay there.'

More incredulous, mocking laughter from Aaron.

'Where the hell are we going to go!'

I ignore him and race back up the cellar steps. In my haste, I half-run, half-slide across the tiles to the bottom of the stairs to the first floor. I pull myself up by the banister, clearing the stairs two or three at a time.

I leg it across the landing and back towards my bedroom, crashing through the door. I drop to my knees and pull that fireproof box from under my bed.

In the box, all my carefully archived records. My notes on each of them when I'd surveilled them. I'd also detailed my methods in getting them to our house and the basement. I'd reflected on what had gone well and what had not gone well, so I might make decisions on what to do or not do next time. I'd also tracked Jack's moods so I might make educated guesses on when he might need prey, though that had not worked as well as I'd hoped.

I fish in my pocket for the keyring that's in my pocket as usual. I fit the box's key in the lock and turn it, pulling up the lid. I see immediately something is wrong: I pull out the sheafs, my eyes bulging in horror. All my meticulous notes are gone; the papers are blank.

'Motherfucker!' I shriek.

Jack has stolen all my records.

CHAPTER FIFTY

'How the hell did you know?'

I almost trip and fall on my arse down those death-trap steps back into the basement. I fling out my arms, regaining my balance, landing on the stone and concrete floor in front of my son and his boyfriend. Aaron and Jack are still sitting on the floor, their wrists suspended above their heads. Jack grins, his face full of triumph.

'Know what?'

Aaron clocks my unhinged fury and takes his own cue from Jack. He smirks, as if he is enjoying my lack of control too. The real danger he is in still has not dawned on him. He doesn't know what Jack is capable of. He still thinks I won't kill him in front of Jack.

The arrogance of men.

'About my records!'

I stride forwards, throwing the blank papers at him. They flutter with unsatisfying grace around him and Aaron. My son doesn't even flinch.

'Where the hell are the real ones?'

Jack leans back against the water pipe, all studied nonchalance.

'Like I said, I have no idea what you're talking about. But *if* I took your records, seems a good idea to keep them where you'd have no chance of finding them?'

I make the connection. 'As an insurance policy.'

Jack shrugs. 'If you say so. Again, I've got no clue what you're on about.'

'What are these supposed records of?' Aaron enquires.

'Jack's kills.'

'Oh, right.' Aaron's maddening smirk makes me want to punch him in the face. 'The ones *you* did, you mean?'

'No.' My own expression is dogged. 'I kept records of each one. Photographs, descriptions and summaries. I had to be certain Jack was only killing bad men.'

Aaron zeroes in on this. 'You said he attacked homeless men, too.'

'Some of them might have been bad.' I don't let him suck me in. 'We don't know they weren't. Anyway, none of them died . . . did they?'

'No,' Aaron confirms, 'but so I'm clear: you were playing judge and jury and Jack was executioner?'

'Yes, that's it exactly!' I am delighted he's finally getting it at last. 'I would pick the victim and catch him for Jack, he would dispatch them.'

'Let me get this straight,' Aaron muses. 'You were facilitating him?'

'No!' I can't believe what I am hearing. 'It wasn't like I wanted to do it. I had no choice in the matter.'

'He force you, did he?'

Aaron makes a pointed glance from me to Jack. My son might be taller than me, but next to Aaron he looks thin and wan. Even I can admit he doesn't look like a depraved killer.

'You don't know the whole story, how this all started,' I insist. 'I. Had. No. Choice . . . If you had kids, you'd understand.'

'Oh, here we go,' Jack says. 'Apparently everything is "for" me, I should be grateful, blah blah blah.'

I shoot him a laser-like glare, silencing him. Aaron appears to mull all this over, then rolls his eyes.

'It's official, Tasha: you have lost your mind.'

'It's the truth!' I grasp for more evidence that might convince him. 'Again, to remind you: *Jack* is the serial killer!'

My son regards me via a perfect poker face. 'So *you* say . . . and apparently I began my murder career at just eight years old, with my own father. Seems pretty unlikely, no?'

'That's right,' Aaron agrees. 'Yet another homophobic parent who can't handle her son being gay.'

'And going out with her ex-boyfriend.'

This addition makes Aaron's gaze meet Jack's. The subtext is not lost on Aaron; he looks relieved Jack has not split with him. They smile at each other. It turns my stomach.

'She attacks them, drugs them, then locks them in the basement,' Aaron finishes.

I clench my fists, digging my fingernails into my palms. This helps me focus.

'To be honest, I've covered weirder true stories on Crime Scribe, Tasha.' Aaron laughs. 'Tell me: the whole time your teenage son was marauding the streets apparently killing people, what were *you* doing?'

I raise an eyebrow; I can't resist after his theorising. 'You.'

'Touché.' Aaron's gaze meets Jack's, who looks disgusted again. 'Sorry.'

Lethargy overcomes me again. I slump down in the chair by the cellar steps, still unsure what to do. Aaron won't believe Jack is the Camden Killer. Jack must have guessed I would try and burn him if any of this came to light; his contingency measures have been one step ahead of me this whole time.

He's done a great job of covering his tracks, clearing out the basement and hiding my records. He's used society's misogyny and homophobia against me too, making out I am just another possessive crazy bitch mother, which Aaron has bought wholesale. If I wasn't the recipient of such wretched skulduggery, I'd be impressed.

Now what?

I'm running out of time. I can't just leave them both chained to the water pipe forever. If only I had turned Aaron away at the damn door. Except that wouldn't have worked either, now I think of it. He and Jack are involved, he would only have come back to look for him later. Keeping them both prisoner for any length of time requires far too much work: tending to their needs for food, drink and toileting makes me exhausted just thinking about it. I also don't want to keep my own child locked in the basement.

What kind of mother does that?

That buzzing noise from Jack's phone catches my attention again. I snatch it up off the top of the tool chest. To my immense relief, it's not the front door again, just an Amazon notification: Jack's hair gel has shipped. The thought of having to deal with Celia or Jim right now is too much to handle. I don't have another pair of handcuffs, for starters.

Something shifts in my peripheral vision. It's a tiny movement, but it still draws my eye. I note Jack's body language has changed. He leans forward, visibly tense, his gaze fixed on the mobile in my hand.

It takes me a nanosecond to work out why: he wants me to put the phone back down again. As he spots me clocking him, he relaxes back against the water pipe, but the damage is done. I regard the phone in my hand and I notice something.

This isn't the mobile I bought Jack a couple of years ago. It's a much fancier model, one I couldn't afford even though Jack mithered me for months for it. I do recognise it though, courtesy of the picture of him and his precious niece and nephew he's saved as wallpaper. I'd recognise the man bun and beard anywhere.

'This is Steve's phone.' I hold it up at Jack. 'You had it all along!'

'Is that true?' Aaron mutters to Jack.

Jack averts his gaze from both of us, refusing to confirm or deny it. As he does this, another series of images sears its way through me.

Jack, on the sofa, flicking through pictures.

Engrossed watching videos, his ear buds in.

Jack, taking a picture of me — with this same phone! — at Steve's funeral.

What a monster.

He'd had this phone in his possession since the night he'd murdered Steve. Right under my nose, hiding in plain sight. This realisation does not bring me down for long. I smile as another follows. The proof I need to show Aaron The Camden Killer's real identity is in my hand.

There's incriminating material on the phone.

I swipe across the screen: it asks for a passcode.

'Damn it,' I sigh.

'That's mine, put it down!'

Jack's voice is full of faux outrage. My announcement the phone is Steve's must have got to Aaron, though.

'What does it matter, Jack, if you have nothing to hide?' he counters.

I ignore both of them. Jack eyeballs me with that steely glare of his, but he doesn't scare me when he's all tied up. In fact, he seems almost comical. It takes all of my willpower not to stick my tongue out at him.

Rotating my wrist, I tap in a variety of possible passcodes. Jack's birthday. My birthday. Aaron's sodding birthday.

Nope.

Our house number, plus street. The date he killed his father; each date of all the other murders in his short life. All of them are a no-go.

Shit.

It's possible my son has an entirely random number pro-grammed to open his phone. I'm willing to bet real money he needs a reminder like most of us. He can't even remember to take his dish to the sink.

Taking a deep breath, I settle back in the folding aluminium chair. I close my eyes and tune out Aaron and Jack's racket of renewed complaints and accusations.

What else is important to Jack to create an easy-to-remember passcode?

A picture of my father bursts through my consciousness. He's seated in that raggedy chair of his; the one he died in, the one I couldn't bear to part with even when I'd redecorated the living room and it didn't match anymore. He's wearing that ubiquitous Arsenal shirt of his and rolling umpteenth cigarettes for later since I'd make him smoke in the garden.

His eyes are glued to the television screen. Next to him is a much-younger Jack, his body language antsy, but not like when he needs prey. His expression is joyful as he stares in the same direction as his grandfather. Excitement surges through his body as he inclines forward, his bum barely on the edge of the sofa cushions.

I feel myself squint, even though my eyes are closed and it's just a memory. The image jumps forwards, bringing the television screen closer and enhancing it, like cops magically do to CCTV footage in police procedural shows.

The screen is green as a young man in red dribbles a ball across a grass pitch towards the goal. The football player shoots and scores. Both Dad and Jack leap up with a roar. The pair of them continue to jump, arms around each other. On the television screen, the football player and his teammates react with similar jubilant triumph, throwing their arms round one another.

I can see this goal-scorer as clearly in my mind as if I were watching it on television myself. I know this man . . . or at least, know *of* him. My father had gone on and on about him being the best player the Gunners ever had. He'd been his favourite player. By extension, he'd been Jack's too. Everything his grandfather did, said or thought, he would imitate.

My eyes open. 'Thierry Henry.'

Jack pales next to Aaron but attempts to bluff it out. 'What?'

'Came to the club in *ninety-nine*, became number-one player of all time at Arsenal . . . That's what your grandad always said, isn't that right, Jack?'

'Mum, c'mon, please . . .'

I tap in 99. I must have heard my father recite this litany over and over every season, every year.

Aaron looks bemused, but his expression falls as he sees Jack's mood change. My son looks jittery, like a dog cowering in expectation of a raised hand.

'Henry had two hundred and twenty-eight goals scored during his career.'

I press 228 next.

The screen opens up for me. I turn the handset around and show Jack.

'Now I've got you.' I smile.

CHAPTER FIFTY-ONE

I swipe through Jack's texts, apps and inboxes. He's wiped all of Steve's gallery and numbers. I am relieved to see there's no pictures of my boyfriend's dead body stored. Jack must have swiped his missing handset while I wrestled Steve's poor body into plastic, or maybe when I'd driven his car to Beachy Head.

Sure enough, various loved-up missives from Aaron turn up on screen. There's a sharp pain in my throat as I swallow. I can't deny the pang of betrayal when I see that Aaron has sent my son the same kind of texts he always sent me: hearts and flower emojis; morning hellos and goodnight XXXs; pictures with his shirt off. I'd deleted all of mine and barely responded, telling Aaron I'm a technophobe, but Jack has kept his. I scan through their text chains and emails quickly, then close the app.

My finger hovers over the gallery, next. I'm not keen on seeing Jack's camera roll for obvious reasons but needs must. There must be something incriminating in there that relates to Jack's kills. I open it up and am rewarded with a video jumping to life immediately. It must have been open already, which means Jack has been watching it himself.

I recognise the dark, dank surroundings of the basement in the video. It's pretty empty, so must be recent; the dentist chair has been gone a while, then. Both triumph and disappointment flood through me. Here is the evidence I need, yet Jack has gone against what I taught him and kept a souvenir like this.

Silly boy.

The picture in the video shudders side to side, like the person holding it might be laughing. There's no sound, but I can't face unpressing the MUTE button yet. It's Jack, of course: I recognise his jeans and shoes as they dip into frame.

He stands over a pallid, shivering figure on the floor. There's a man in just his underwear hog-tied on the floor, his shirtless back a mess of carved skin and red raw flesh.

This is what Jack wanted my carrot peeler for: it's Mike.

I press PAUSE on the video and approach both of them, still a safe distance away. Jack knows what I'm going to do. There's tears tracking down his face. He shakes his head, side to side, like that will repel me somehow.

I can tell Jack's reaction has Aaron both spooked and curious. His love for Jack means he *doesn't* want to know what the hell is on the phone. Yet I can also see the conflict in him: he has to know, too.

Turning the phone around for Aaron, I press PLAY again, this time with sound.

The basement is filled with desperate bargaining, angry threats and then fraught pleading, all from Mike. Aaron can't tear his eyes away. His gaze grows ever wider, his mouth dropping open in silent horror.

I don't need to watch the video to imagine what is going on; I can hear the metal clink of tools, the crinkle of plastic wrap, the pained squeals and gargles of terror bursting forth from Jack's victim. It's why I'd made sure the basement was soundproofed.

On the video my son says nothing, just letting loose the odd snigger. He makes no attempt to engage with my would-be rapist. He does not taunt him, nor does he reply to Mike's many distressed cries of: 'Who are you? Why are you doing this!' When I hear the high shriek of a circular saw start up, this seems enough to make Aaron recover his voice.

'Okay . . . okay! I believe it!'

Aaron averts his eyes from the video, cringing away from it in an exaggerated manner. As I turn it off, the podcaster retches violently, crouching on his knees and just the one hand, the other still cuffed to the water pipe. He brings up only bile, but he can't stop. He retches over and over, hysterical with it.

Jack attempts to place a comforting hand on Aaron's back, but he reacts like my son's touch burns.

'Get off me, man!'

He backs up, rattling his cuff down the water pipe towards the opposite corner, as far away from Jack as he can possibly be. Jack stares at him, sad-faced and wretched.

'She primed me for this.'

'Your own mother *made* you do this?' Aaron shakes his head. 'No. No way, I saw the video. You were alone. You were enjoying that!'

Jack takes this on board and mulls it over for a moment. He raises his free hand to his face, tracing the cheekbone underneath his left eye.

'Ever notice one side of my face is slightly lopsided? Ocular fracture, from when I was four.' Jack looks at me the whole time I'm saying this. 'I fell down the stairs. In fact, it's more accurate to say I was *thrown* down the stairs.'

'It's true, his father was abusive.' I confirm for Aaron.

'Well, that was the official story: Daddy did it. And like you've talked about on your podcast, Aaron, lots of serial killers had head trauma as small children, right?'

Jack looks from his paramour to me, smiling as he sees my unease grow.

'But in recent years, I've begun to wonder . . . What if it was *you*, Mum?'

'Why the hell would you think that?'

'Because it makes sense. You've lied to yourself as well as me, all these years. What if it wasn't Dad who was the abuser? What if it was you, but you turned it all around in your fucked-up mind? Justification for your own psychopathy. Like mother, like son.'

'You killed your father!' I holler. 'What kind of eight-year-old does that?'

Jack grins as his own question from last night jumping from my lips now.

'An eight-year-old directed to, by his mother . . . just like you did when you gave me this kill room and instructed me on who to kill.'

I feel myself on the back foot again. I don't like it. Can Jack really turn it back on me, even when Aaron has seen the video evidence with his own eyes? Surely not. I watch as Jack fixes Aaron with his sincere gaze.

'Head trauma, abusive background, facilitator mother with high expectations . . . You see, Aaron, I didn't have a choice.'

'We always have a choice,' Aaron whispers, his words from earlier returning like a boomerang. 'Kids grow up in the shit all the time. Beaten every day, emotionally abused, raped. Neglected, starved, thrown out on the street. They decide to break the cycle, heal the damage—' Aaron stops short; he can't bring himself to finish. 'How is it possible I missed all this? Who *are* you people? What are you!'

I'm keen to move on. 'Look, it's probably morning by now. Jack, we need to get this sorted and tie up this loose end.'

The subtext is not lost on Aaron. 'You're going to kill me . . . Look. I won't say anything, I swear!'

'I won't kill you,' Jack promises.

'Yes you will, Jack Rose. Aaron's whole business is true crime, there's no way we can let him walk out of here alive,' I lecture my son. 'Plus it will be a gesture of good faith to me, after all this bloody palaver. Frankly it's the least you can do to make it up to me.'

I turn to Aaron and shrug. 'I'm sorry, it's not personal. Actually, it kind of is. But I want you to know it's also a practical decision. I will make sure Jack makes it quick.'

'We should let him go. We deserve to go to jail!' Jack speaks slowly, addressing me like I am the child. 'I told you, I won't kill Aaron. I love him.'

'I can't be with a serial killer,' Aaron mutters.

Jack nods. 'I know. You're a good person.'

I snort. 'No, he's not. He saw a grieving woman and smelled a story. He's as big an opportunist as you are.'

My son continues as if I never spoke. 'I was willing to give it all up for you, take a stand against Mum finally. You saved me.'

I can't stand the icky sentiment in the air, or the fact the focus is off me.

'Fine! Then I'll kill him.'

Both lads round on me, remembering I'm there.

'You haven't got the guts,' Jack sneers, 'that's why you always had me do it.'

I cross my arms. 'I can accept it might look that way, but no. I'm perfectly capable.'

Jack rolls his eyes, dismissing me. Teenagers always think they've invented things, don't they? He thinks that this is all a big game of chicken, that all they need do is wait me out and I will let them both go eventually. They'll slope off into the sunset together and I will have nothing. I'm tired of being underestimated all my life.

'It wouldn't be the first time I killed someone.'

My son regards me, open-mouthed. 'Who?'

'Your grandfather.'

CHAPTER FIFTY-TWO

I can still recall that rainy Wednesday afternoon in crisp detail. I receive my father's phone call at work. He babbles at me about needing to talk about Jack.

He doesn't seem himself, but I think he might have had a tipple too many watching his planned footie game at the pub. I hadn't been at the archives long back then and didn't want to ask Maria if I could dash home. I'd asked Dad if it could wait.

He'd told me I had to come right now.

Distress was tangible in the air as I let myself into the house. I can smell cigarette smoke; that means it's serious. Since I'd returned home all those years earlier, Dad had agreed not to smoke in the house because of Jack. He was a good grandfather, so for him to forget, something monumental must have happened.

As I trudge unwillingly to the kitchen at the back of the house, I attempt to dredge up some possible scenarios of what it could all mean.

Perhaps Jack had taken something of his grandfather's without asking and broken it? No, my father would not believe that would warrant calling me home from work.

Maybe Jack had been excluded from school and Dad had gone to fetch him, as he was an emergency contact? That was too serious for my father to not call me, but he'd get me to go with him to the school, so it couldn't be that.

I already knew what it was, anyway.

'Dad?'

The door to the kitchen opens to reveal my father seated at the kitchen table, head in his hands. Next to him, an overflowing ashtray.

'Tash, thank God.'

On the table: a dog lead. I recognise it right away: it had been Otto's, my father's big, three-legged, shaggy mongrel. He'd had to be put down after waking in the night, shaking and vomiting. Dad had been heartbroken.

'What's going on?' I attempt a smile. 'You had me thinking this was an emergency.'

'I just . . . I just don't know what to do.' Dad abandons his half-smoked cigarette in the ashtray and picks up the dog lead, holding it with both fists. 'The boiler was acting up, so I had to go into Jack's room to fix it. I found this in the cupboard with it.'

'So? He loved Otto too.'

'I also found these.'

Dad pushes a shoebox towards me I hadn't noticed on the table. Curious, I open it. Dad watches me, stroking his right hand up and down his left arm.

Inside the box, there appears to be a variety of kid junk. I sort through it, pulling out items, one by one. The first, a jar of tiny plastic tags with numbers on, like the kind you find twisted around bread wrappers. It takes me a moment to realise it's the kind pigeon racers fix around their birds' ankles. There must twenty or thirty in there.

There's a couple of cat collars, too. I pick them up: MISSY is inscribed on the first pet name disc, our dead cat. It's dirty, like Jack has dug it out of the earth.

With further dread, I pick up the second: sure enough: MARBLES. Evidence our supposedly disappeared cat did not vanish after all.

Dad joins the dots for me anyway. 'Jack killed them all.'

292

Feeling faint, I kick a chair out from under the table and sit down on it heavily.

'Okay, well this is obviously horrible. But they are just animals.'

'*Only* animals?' Dad catches himself like he always does before he starts shouting. He takes a deep breath. 'Even if that were true, he's been doing it a long time. This is not some "boys will be boys" crap. This is serious. Tash, these are *trophies*.'

Cold, shocked silence settles over us as we sit opposite each other at the table.

I don't know what Dad wants me to say, or what he wants me to do. He doesn't know the full story. The truth was, Jack had been on this path since he was eight years old. Longer, if the modern school of thought about serial killers, abusive backgrounds and head trauma were to be believed.

'Jack's a good boy really,' I find myself murmuring, 'this is just a phase.'

I jump as my dad brings his fist down on the table.

'Stop lying!' he yells, spittle on his moustache. 'For God's sake, Tash, take some responsibility!'

My brain reels under this onslaught. I can't recall Dad ever shouting at me before. I remembered my mother had though, before she got ill. Dad would always try and take the brunt of her outbursts and odd behaviour. He'd always entreat her to get help. She would for a while, but within a few weeks she'd declare the latest medication was 'useless' and 'not working'. Then we would be back on the merry-go-round of her ceaseless, mercurial behaviour.

Whatever Mum had was not treatable anyway. She'd crash around the house, hollering at us, throwing pots and plates and shoes; she'd slap me or Dad across the face for various transgressions, real or imagined. Once she'd burst into my bedroom and grabbed me by my nine-year-old ankles and pulled me out of bed so I cracked my head on the bedroom floor, cackling with glee as I begged to be left alone.

I'd skulk into rooms, wondering how she was going to react today: all smiles and smothering hugs? Or like she hates me and wishes I were dead? It was exhausting. When she'd got cancer and been confined to bed, I'd finally been left alone . . . and I'd liked it.

With Mummy gone, Daddy and I were free.

'I tried so hard,' Dad continues, eyes full of tears. 'I know your mother damaged you, warped you, I'll always be sorry for that. Perhaps I should have taken you away, but then your mother had cancer and I felt like I couldn't leave. Then she died and I thought we would be okay. Then *he* came along.'

'Jack?'

'No, Dean!' Dad snaps, then sighs. 'I should have seen it coming, I realise that now. I was working all hours and left you alone too much. Stands to reason the moment you went off to uni that you would go off looking for another father figure.'

I feel the sting as my father's words hit home. 'History's repeating itself, is that what you're saying?'

'No. Maybe. I don't know what I'm saying!' My father throws his hands up in the air in despair. 'All I know is my grandson is a very damaged boy, spiritually and literally. How can he not be? Thrown down the stairs when he's little more than a baby. Watching his parents tear chunk outs of each other . . .'

'It was Dean, he was the one—'

'Stop it, Tash! I know you've taught yourself to believe that. But there's too much of your mother in you. The only difference is, unlike me, Dean fought back.'

I say nothing. Dad is too close to the truth.

'Jack told me how you'd attack his father, actively try and bring about him losing his temper. Dean was a no-good scrote and he should never have hit you or the boy. He should have left like I should have. But *you* were the one who put that little lad in harm's way, every time. You *still do*.'

The truth lodges in my throat like that knife had in Dean's chest. I try to splutter a reply, tell Dad he is wrong, but I can't conjure the words into being.

Everything Dad said was true: I *had* done everything in my power to aggravate Dean. When we fought, something delicious powered up inside me. It was like Dean could see me, as if I finally mattered. My juvenile mind had told me this was what 'real' couples do.

Doesn't everyone say love hurts? Or that 'the path of true love never runs smooth', there's 'a thin line between love and hate' and all that other bullshit. I was drip-fed this via the relationship modelled for me in my own home growing up. I saw my sweet, gentle father taken to his knees by a cruel woman who loved to inflict pain, both spiritual and literal. Even when she was gone books, movies and TV shows told me mine and Dean's was real passion instead of the dysfunction it really was.

'What's been created from that toxic mess, Tash?'

Dad swallows a sob. He cradles his left arm in his right as he delivers his most devastating blow.

'There were no loan sharks, were there . . . You killed Dean, didn't you?'

There it was, the moment I'd feared for years: Dad asking questions I didn't want to answer. After Dean's murder, Dad had taken us into his home, provided for us, supported us. He'd never once pried too deeply into the events of that Sunday night eight years earlier.

I'd thought it was because he'd believed me, accepted my word.

Now I understood it was really because he suspected I was the one who'd killed Dean and didn't want to hear the truth. Hot tears pricked my eyelids as I worked through this second revelation, on top of his proclamation I was just like my mother.

'No. It wasn't me,' I mutter.

It wouldn't have mattered if I'd shouted it. The truth was not loud enough to dissuade my father from his assumption. Not that I could blame him. It made much more sense I would stab my abusive husband than the eight-year-old Jack.

Child killers have occurred since the beginning of time in every society, but adults never want to think about this unpleasant phenomenon too deeply. If we did, we would be forced to confront our role in creating such mini-murderers. It's easier to pretend such kids are born 'evil' or better still, that they don't exist.

Why face such an unpalatable reality when you don't have to? Opt out and move on. Out of sight, out of mind.

Yet adults were all children once. Though personality has to count for something, it's undeniable we're all the products of our environment.

But just how much?

We're back to nature/nurture. The real, unanswerable question my father posed to me just minutes earlier. He thought Dean's death was connected to his own failure in keeping me safe when I was a girl. He was right, but not in the way he imagined. It never is: real life is messy, which is why it's a constant flow of contradictions and nasty surprises.

Dad shakes his head, like he is disappointed in me. 'I just don't know what I can say or do. How can we fix this, Tash?'

'There's nothing to fix,' I say through clenched teeth. 'Jack has been having some problems, okay. I accept that, I will look into counsellors for him. But I didn't kill Dean. It happened exactly the way I said it did.'

'Tash, you and I both know that's a lie.'

Ice-cold fear seizes me. What was worse, my father thinking I had killed Dean, or realising his own grandson had? I didn't know what to do. Would Dad turn me in? Could I persuade him to keep the secret, for Jack? I understood I was out of options.

'You should—'

Dad stops in the middle of his sentence. He blinks furiously, as if the room is spinning for him. I watch him loosen his collar. His face is beetroot-red, beats of sweat springing up on his forehead. Within seconds, his breaths become laboured.

'Are you okay?'

I move towards the sink and fill a glass of water for him. As I present it to him, he does not take it from me. He leans forward, unable to speak, his face contorted with pain. As he grips his left arm that has been dangling useless by his side, I finally catch up.

Dad's having a heart attack.

Panic surges through me, obliterating my sensible thought patterns.

What do I do, what do I do?

I reboot and go through the motions we're all taught in childhood, pulling my phone out of my bag to call 999. Before I tap the buttons, I remember my father has an angina spray he usually keeps in his breast pocket. That first, *then* 999.

I take hold of him. 'It's okay, it's okay . . .'

It was not okay. I didn't know if the pointless reassurance is for me, or for him. I pat down his shirt and jeans pockets. Nothing.

Shit.

I stand back up and whirl my gaze round the kitchen, trying to spot his spray.

There, standing next to the kettle.

Racing across the kitchen, I almost trip over chairs and my own feet, bashing my hip straight into the counter in my hurry. As soon as I pick up the rounded, small bottle in my hand, something clicks in my head. I feel like I soar outside of my body for a second, right up to the ceiling. A single thought punches its way into my brain.

All this can go away.

My father makes a strangulated groan at the table, drawing my attention. I turn back towards him. I stay where I am, next to the kettle, the spray bottle in my hand.

Our eyes meet.

I appreciate Dad is not quite ready to comprehend why I am delaying. Perhaps he thinks I am in shock. No matter what I did, Dad had always given me the benefit of the doubt until the evidence smashed him in the face.

To help him along, I replace the angina spray back beside the kettle. He tries to breathe through the pain and process my betrayal at the same time. He can't.

I watch Dad attempt to stand. His legs won't support him; he falls to his knees. I move forwards, catching him under his skinny armpits before he falls forwards on to his chest. He tangles his stubby fingers in my long hair, opening his mouth in a desperate plea, though no words come. Just a low, animalistic, dying moan.

I don't react. Our faces are just centimetres away. I can smell the sour tang of death on him before he's even gone. I watch as the light fades from his eyes. His body slumps in my grasp.

I know his loss will hurt later, but in the moment my more pragmatic side surfaces: Jack will be safe now, so will I. I shut his eyelids and rest my forehead against his.

'Bye, Dad,' I whisper.

CHAPTER FIFTY-THREE

'I put him in his chair, hid *your* trophies back where they were and then went back to work.'

I'm met with shocked silence in the basement as I finish my story. This rankles me; I'd wanted some gratitude from Jack, at least. I had made the ultimate sacrifice. I'd loved my father and watching him die had been traumatic. I'd done it all to keep my son's secret.

Because I am a good mother.

The best.

'I did it for you, Jack.'

Another disbelieving bark of laughter erupts from Jack.

'I was the one who found him! When I came back from school. Remember that?'

I do. As I'd stood over my father's body, I'd agonised over what to do for the best. I couldn't be in the vicinity of another dead man, especially when Dad had died comparatively young. I didn't want paramedics or police officers to notice anything 'odd' about me and share their theories with one another. That could only lead to Dean's case ending up under the microscope again and that wouldn't be good for Jack.

It was unfortunate my son had to go through discovering his grandfather's body, but like the good mother I am,

I'd made sure he was accommodated for. I'd sent him to Cheryl and ensured he got bereavement counselling, as well as antidepressants. I'd even dared to hope it might even help with his 'other' issues. I had only been thinking of him. The injustice of Jack's sneering contempt works its way under my skin.

'What would you have had me do?'

'Oh I dunno, how about *not* kill my grandfather?' Jack's sarcasm flows out of him, bitter and sharp. 'All of this was avoidable, Mum. All you had to do was what you were supposed to do, what any *normal* person would do!'

'You should have given him his spray,' Aaron murmurs.

I ignore him, addressing only Jack. 'But he was on to us?'

'No, he was on to *you*,' Jack hisses. 'He wouldn't have turned you in, you must have known that really. He would have tried to help you, to help me. The real problem was Grandad finally stood up to you and you couldn't hack it. You opened the door to all this shit.'

I feel the weight of the truth in his words. Too late, it occurs to me that finding his grandfather dead could have caused Jack's psychopathy to accelerate. Could Dad's benign influence have been keeping Jack in check? Yes, there was still the troubling fact of the pets' demises. Yet cruelty to animals, however repugnant, is not guaranteed to lead to the serial murder of human beings. If it was, there would be a lot more serial killers walking the streets.

Dear God, by letting Dad die and having Jack find him like that, could I have inadvertently created the catalyst for all this?

If I had, Steve never needed to die, nor any of the others.

I had lead Aaron right to us.

I had put events in motion from the offset.

I shut both thoughts down before they can take root. I can't go down that avenue.

I just can't.

'It doesn't matter anyway, it's done now —' I extend one hand towards Aaron — 'and we have to deal with him.'

'Wait, wait, wait!'

Aaron's voice is unsteady. He understands now I am a real threat. Desperate and scared, he tries to pluck a solution out of the ether.

'Tell you what. Just let us both go. Me and Jack will leave, together. You never have to see either of us again. I won't breathe a word, forget about the podcast! I promise, Tasha.'

That sensation of having concrete in my bones is back. Everything seems insurmountable.

'You must think I was born yesterday.' I tilt my head and regard him. 'You can't be with someone like Jack, not now you know what he is. And Jack . . .' I move towards my boy. 'How long before you tire of him? You'd tell yourself you'd never hurt him. But one day, you will. You wouldn't be able to help yourself.'

'I love him.' Jack is unwilling to give even an inch.

'You don't know the meaning of the word. You've said that to me your whole life.' I indicate the near-empty basement. 'Now look what you've done! You've stripped it all from me, taken all I have to give, just like you did this room. It's not your fault, it's just your nature.'

Jack curls his lip at me. 'I get it from you.'

I sigh. 'Maybe. But it's kinder this way.'

'Oh no you don't,' Aaron declares.

I'm surprised by his renewed moxie. For a man about to die today, his voice is calm and his body language dignified. He sits up as straight as he can, forcing me to meet his eye.

'If you're going to kill me, you can at least admit it's not for *my* fucking benefit. It's for yours! All of this, it's been for you: the cat and mouse games; the righteous revenge on no-good men; your son the avenging angel, doling out the punishments *you* direct. Admit it, there's been a part of you that's enjoyed this, isn't there?'

'No. Of course not.' I can hear how unconvincing I sound.

Aaron proffers a sad little smile. 'Myra Hindley, Rose West, Carol Bundy. I've read about so many women like you. They get called accomplices or accessories, but what if they were *directors*? Everyone says, "Oh, it must be the man who led them astray." It can't be anything else, surely . . . Women are nurturers, good and innocent at heart. Society and even feminists infantilise them. They think that being born female is a special virtue that can only be corrupted by the evils of testosterone.'

I chuckle. 'I never had you down for a sexist, Aaron.'

'I'm saying the exact opposite, you psycho!'

He takes a breath, composing himself again.

'I'm trying to say psychopathy is nothing to do with gender. It never has been. But we've all let it flourish in between the cracks of society. As we've all been distracted by arguing the toss about men coming from Mars and women from Venus and all that other crap, people like you and him have been able to do whatever you want, behind closed doors!'

I raise an eyebrow at his rant. 'You finished?'

Aaron raises a hand in dismissal at me, shying away from Jack as he attempts to draw himself closer. With renewed vigour, I turn on my heel back towards the steps. Jack's voice falls on my back as I go back upstairs.

'What are you doing . . . Where you going now?'

As I leave, I hear Jack repeat his promise that he won't kill Aaron. The podcaster bats his assurance away, telling my son it doesn't matter whether I kill him or Jack does. Aaron now realises he is not leaving the basement alive.

He's got that right.

I make it to the top of the stairs and let myself out, remembering to close and lock the door behind me this time. Morning sunlight filters through the front door. I stop for a moment and enjoy its rays on my face. It feels like I've been underground for days, not overnight.

There's post on the mat, so I pick it up and take it through to the kitchen. I leaf through it and make myself a coffee, considering my options.

I don't have many. If Jack won't help me kill Aaron, I'll just have to give him a massive overdose of ketamine. It

302

shouldn't take much, especially given the dose I administered to him last night in my kitchen must still be in his system.

Once Aaron is dead, I can give Jack an ultimatum: he falls back in line, or he gets the hell out. Since he will have just watched his boyfriend die at my hands, he will realise I am serious. I feel confident he will choose the former and everything can go back to normal.

If Jack does still choose to leave, I can't believe he will turn himself in at the police. But if he does leave, the moment he goes I will be out of here. The police can try and track me down, but by the time they've issued an arrest order and got a warrant to search the house, I will be on a plane.

My coffee drunk, I rummage under the sink for more drugs. There's not much left in there, so I fetch another vial from the downstairs bathroom. I fill the syringe right to the top. I hope Aaron will be one of those stoic victims and won't fight me too much. If nothing else, I don't want him to knock the syringe from my hand and smash it on the concrete basement floor. Here's hoping he is sensible, and it doesn't play out that way. I don't want to have to use a knife on him.

Humming to myself, I turn the key in the basement door, opening it outwards as usual. There's a flutter of movement in my peripheral vision as I step over the threshold. My brain connects what the movement was, as a hand from below grabs me by my ankle.

Jack.

I try to kick out, but his grip is too strong. I freeze where I am. There's a piquancy of sweat and terror in the air: mine and his.

He's two or three steps down from me, where he'd lain in wait for me. I drop the syringe and it smashes in the darkness somewhere. I don't care. My eyes slide to the bottom of the stairs, to Aaron across the room. The water pipe is still intact, Aaron is not free. Even though the evidence is flesh and blood right in front of me, I can't compute.

How the hell did Jack get out of his handcuffs?

'Jack, don't!' I shriek.

Too late. He yanks my foot out ahead of me. This movement twists my body and I pitch forwards, towards the edge of the steep steps and into the room below.

I windmill my arms to try and regain my balance, but it's no good. There's no guiderail to grab. I snatch at the air in vain. My fingers scrape against the brick ceiling and walls, but they fail to stop my forced descent as I go past the point of no return.

I go over. I claw at the chasm of nothing underneath me, turning by accident so I'm facing the wrong way. I am falling backwards. I can't do anything about it. Our eyes meet and I see his are shiny with tears. So why do this?

Jack, I love you, son.

As the back of my head smacks the concrete, a myriad of pictures as sharp and clear as diamonds smash through my mind in tandem with the hard ground.

Dean, pulling that knife from his chest again, the bloody arc decorating the refrigerator and wall. Arterial spray patterning my face.

The toddler Jack, falling down the stairs because I *had* pushed him, just like Jack had accused me. He'd been difficult all day, I hadn't meant to, blah blah blah . . .

I don't even know what is true anymore.

One thing is obvious though; Aaron had been right.

History really does repeat itself if you let it.

I can feel myself starting to fade. My son, pale and listless, stands over me. There's no triumph on his face. He just looks exhausted and relieved.

I can't lift my head, or my limbs. I know by instinct the connection between my brain and body has been severed. Blood must be pooling around my smashed skull like a macabre halo, yet I cannot feel it. There is no pain. I know I am dying, that there's no way back from such a catastrophic injury. As my eyes roll back involuntarily, I catch sight of the last image they will ever see on this earth.

Jack cradles his left hand in his right.

His thumb is not dislocated now, because he's popped it back in, just like I'd shown him in the kitchen.

So *that's* how he'd realised he could escape the handcuffs and lie in wait for me. Though a part of my fading brain is angry I've been bested, I can't deny the warm feeling that offers the last dying embers of pride as my consciousness disappears.

My final thought sparks and dies with me.

My clever boy.

CHAPTER FIFTY-FOUR

'You finished?' she'd said, looming over Aaron in the basement.

That's Mum all over, Jack thought.

That was when Jack knew he had no other choice. Mum pretended she wanted to hear opinions, to give others a voice, but really she was just marking time until she could speak or whatever else it was *she* wanted. Her ego was just too big to accommodate anyone else's needs or wishes.

It had always been about her.

His piece said, Aaron raised a hand in dismissal at her. Jack tried to slide closer to him, reassure him, reach for his hand — but Aaron cringed away from him. Tash chuckled softly and turned away, practically skipping up the cellar steps. Jack called after her.

'What are you doing . . . Where you going now?'

No answer. As her legs vanished up the steps, Jack turned his attentions back to Aaron.

'I won't kill you. I swear.'

Aaron sighed, leaning his head against the exposed brick wall.

'It doesn't matter whether you kill me or she does. We both know I'm not leaving this basement alive.'

Jack could hear the truth in Aaron's words as tangibly as the scrape of the key in the basement door. As his mother slammed the door again and locked it, resolve bloomed in Jack's gut and spread through his body. He'd wanted to avoid confrontation; it was why he'd done all he could to get her out of the house, so he could slip away unnoticed until it was too late. He'd wanted the 'happy ever after' with Aaron; he felt he deserved it, having spent a lifetime with the mother from hell.

Enough was enough.

Jack recalled only feeling like this once before: that first night, when he'd killed his father.

He'd woken in the night to raised voices. Again. It was the background noise of his entire childhood: screams of fury, the throwing of plates and furniture, the endless acts of violence, both verbal and physical.

Most often it would start with his mother's demands and accusations; she would start it off with a carefully laid manipulation or ambush his oblivious father would always walk headlong into. Occasionally she would go straight to the point and start proceedings by splashing him with hot water, or a surprise slap across the face.

Every time Mum would accuse his father of infidelity or of looking at other women. For his part, his father would do nothing to soothe her fears. He would laugh and even boast of various conquests; real or imagined, it didn't matter. The claims were designed to inflict pain, just as she tried to inflict on him.

It would not be long before it would degenerate into blows. Jack's father was twice the size of his mother, but that did not mean she couldn't hold her own. Once she picked up the iron and brought it down on Dad's head, knocking him to the kitchen tiles, stunned and muttering incomprehensibly. She was less careful than he was; whilst Dad would hit Mum around the kidneys or back, she took great delight in marking his face. It forced him to have to lie to those enquiring about his latest black eye, which amused her.

But worse than the arguments or the blows was what came next. Jack would wait with bated breath as both would go silent. He knew what that meant: they'd lock eyes, chests heaving with exertion. Their need for violence spent, they'd grab at each other, pulling off clothes, tearing and biting. His father would push his mother onto the kitchen table, pushing up her skirt as she goaded him, telling him he wasn't a real man who could satisfy her. She'd laugh as he thrust into her, locking her legs around his back.

Jack couldn't listen to it. Not again.

That was why he'd crept from his bed that night. He'd appeared in the hallway just as his father had slammed his mother's head against the kitchen doorframe. Almost senseless, blood pouring from a head wound, his mother had scrabbled up on her hands and knees. She hollered something nonsensical as she fell again, face first, onto the hall tiles. His father grabbed her around the waist, picking her up off the floor as if she was a toddler. He pulled her hair aside, hissing in her ear.

'You done yet?' he'd demanded.

Mum hadn't answered. Instead she'd reared up, slamming the back of her skull into his face. Dad cried out, dropping her again. Mum careered into the kitchen, Jack at her heels.

'Mummy . . . Mummy!'

She didn't hear him. She didn't even see him. This was the story of Jack's life: his parents were so hell-bent on making the other's life a misery, they had no idea they'd already succeeded in making Jack's daily existence a litany of awfulness. She laughed, still yelling at Dad.

'You're fucking dead!' his father roared.

Had Jack thought he was serious? Maybe. He'd dreamt many times of waking to find both his parents dead in the kitchen. Unlike most children, these were not nightmares. When Jack awoke, there was always a smile of blessed relief on his lips.

In the manner of so many childhood memories, Jack's recollection skipped ahead. He didn't remember picking up the knife, or even where he got it from: the kitchen drawer maybe, or perhaps the counter.

It didn't matter, anyway.

'What have you done . . . *What have you done*?'

Mum's hoarse voice brought Jack back to earth. The fluorescent glare of the kitchen strip light seemed to burst through his vision, illuminating the truth in front of him.

The knife was buried deep in Dad's chest.

Jack's palms were bloody. He blotted them on his onesie, watching as his father's brain caught up with what had happened to him. He staggered backwards, pulling the knife out.

Big mistake.

An arc of red patterned the wall. Mum tried to catch Dad as he fell, but they both went down. She tried to put pressure on the wound. She screamed something at Jack, but he wasn't listening. All he could think about was how the nightmare was over. If there was only one of them, they couldn't go through this endless circle of vitriol . . . right? As he stared at the life leaving his father, all Jack felt was that sense of relief, just like he'd dreamt so many times.

It was all over. Finally.

Except it wasn't. Jack couldn't face up to himself, but something had come undone deep inside him long before his mother had brought that boyfriend — that *Steve* — home. He had been consumed by anxiety since his grandfather's passing, which was why he'd gone searching for victims. The only way he'd felt alive was when he had a pipe in his hand and a wretch of a man begging for mercy at his feet.

Mum had told him about Steve with stars in her eyes. Jack could tell Mum saw a future with Steve; that would mean him moving into their house, or them getting their own place. Jack would be expected to come too. How long would it be before her relationship descended into the same toxic mess she'd created with Dad?

Then Steve was gone and Mum had seemed to accept Jack's propensity for violence, even encouraged it. At first he'd felt so close to her: his desire for blood seemed to work in tandem with his mother's endless urge for revenge: against life, men, whatever. Then he'd realised it was all a lie: he was his mother's pet, a ferocious rottweiler she'd trained since his fucked-up childhood. It was all her fault.

Jack was what he was *because* of her.

It could have been different. If Grandad had still been alive, Jack could have stayed with him. Or perhaps he could have continued to try to contain Mum's impulses, endless mood swings, lies and manipulation as he had for a decade before she brought Steve home. But Grandad was dead before his time.

She had killed him.

Enough was enough.

'I'm gonna get us out of here.'

In the basement, Aaron's expression was far away, vacant. In his mind's eye, he was watching the highlights of his life cut short. He made no indication he'd heard as Jack grimaced and cried out in pain, pushing down hard on his left thumb joint.

Nausea swept through Jack as the joint yielded. He gasped the stale air in as he slipped his hand out of the handcuffs attached to the water pipe.

Aaron's focus snapped back towards him.

'You leaving me here?'

Jack didn't answer him. He heard the key turn in the basement door again. He raised his right index finger to his lips at Aaron. He nodded, wide-eyed, watching as Jack crept towards the cellar steps. At the top, his mother was humming like she was going to tend to her damn garden, not kill his boyfriend. What the hell was wrong with her? Whatever it was, it was untreatable.

As her feet appeared, Jack grabbed hold of her ankle. His mother shrieked in surprise. She tried to kick out, but Jack gritted his teeth and held on fast. She dropped the syringe of ketamine she'd gone to fetch in order to kill Aaron. It disappeared into the darkness. It didn't matter.

Nothing mattered . . . Except getting rid of her, once and for all.

'Jack, don't!' Mum hollered.

Jack yanked her foot out ahead of her. She tried to regain her balance, but it didn't work. Snatching at the air, she pitched forwards, turning as she fell. The back of her head smacked the concrete, her skull breaking open with the wet sound of an eggshell into a mixing bowl.

Jack wasn't sure how long he stood there, staring down at his mother's broken body. If Aaron spoke to him, he did not hear him. His mind was occupied with a non-stop litany of two words:

You're free.
You're free.
You're free.

Since that night in the kitchen when Jack killed his father, she had moulded him in the image of a perfect, vengeful son, just like Aaron had said. She had encouraged Jack just like she had his father, but this time she had all the control. She'd not been able to own up to this fact, not even to herself, but it was obvious for all to see, just like he'd accused her earlier: if Jack was a monster, then his mother was the mad scientist who'd created him.

But that was all over now. With his mother gone, Jack could be happy. He could live his life with Aaron, contained by his love. He could be normal . . . Something that was impossible when his mother still walked the earth.

Finally, Jack looked across the basement to Aaron. His lover stared at him, his expression blank with shock. Jack cast his gaze around the cellar for the keys to the handcuffs.

'Let's go,' he said.

EPILOGUE

Aaron watched the tall policeman and woman leave the room. He'd been in police stations before, but only ever as an arrestee. Unlike the darkened interview rooms then, he'd been shown into a room with a window and water stains on the carpet. In the corner was a clanking old water heater and a table full of papers. If he didn't know better, it might have been a teacher's lounge in a rundown school.

Through the internal window Aaron saw two uniformed officers deep in conversation with DI Judd and Sergeant Martens. Anxiety skittered through him all over again as he considered what had happened the night before, that morning. It seemed hard to believe, even for him. The police had found the car. He'd heard them.

Would they believe his story?

Jack had stood over Natasha's body in that basement for what seemed like aeons. Seeing Jack's murderous predilections in full technicolour visited on that poor bastard in the phone footage had struck the fear of God into Aaron. Even chained up, he had been gung-ho when he'd thought Natasha was behind the Camden killings, at least until she'd demonstrated she had the stomach for killing as well. Then

Jack had stepped in, slipping his hand out of the cuffs and lying in wait for his mother.

Even so, Aaron had been afraid to draw his attention again in case he was next.

'Let's go.'

Jack stepped over his mother's splayed, broken body. He retrieved the key for the handcuffs and crouched next to Aaron, releasing him. Aaron stared at his lover with wide eyes as Jack massaged his wrist, kissing the back of his hand.

'I'm so sorry about her.'

'That's okay,' Aaron found himself saying.

'I love you. You know that, right?'

Jack looked up at him with those baby blue eyes.

'Y-yes of course,' Aaron stammered. 'I love you too.'

The relief on Jack's face was palpable. He flashed him a huge grin and kissed Aaron on the lips. He leant his forehead against Aaron's, who forced himself not to cringe away.

'Let's get out of here,' Jack said.

Unsure what else to do, Aaron followed Jack out of the basement. They grabbed Jack's stuff from the hallway, then retrieved Aaron's own backpack which he'd stashed by the porch as he'd come in. They locked up the house and took Natasha's keys. Jack had to find them first, directing Aaron to search the kitchen while he checked the living room.

The keys found, they both slid into the front seats of her car on the street outside. Jack pushed the keys in the ignition and turned to Aaron, beaming.

It was now or never.

In that microsecond before he did it, Aaron remembered Natasha's disgust at him in the basement. What had she said about him, to Jack? Oh right . . .

He saw a grieving woman and smelled a story. He's as big an opportunist as you are.

It was true. Aaron had never really been interested in Natasha. She'd intrigued him, yes; there was something strangely fake about her, like she was acting in her own mind

313

movie. Sometimes she'd even look to the side, as if she was receiving instruction from people backstage when she forgot her lines.

Whatever it was, she'd appealed to the investigative journalist Aaron was sure he was. The fact she had a smoking hot body made the intrigue and potential story for his podcast all the more attractive to him. By the time he connected the dots on The Camden Killer story, Aaron was certain he had a career-making hit on his hands.

Jack had been a different beast. The vulnerability in him had made Aaron feel like a hero. He'd been certain Jack was an abused boy, caught in the middle of both his mother's coercion and her sick homicidal tendencies.

It's hard climbing the ladder; Aaron had been lonely for a good while. In Jack, he saw a second opportunity to get what he wanted: a partner, as well as the story.

For Aaron, it had been a win-win.

Aaron couldn't believe the sweet boy he knew was a sick serial killer who delighted in the pain and torture of his victims. He had been certain the true perpetrator was Natasha; she was certainly crazy enough. Aaron had planned to publish his podcast on the road with Jack, at a safe distance from her. He'd already seen the subsequent uproar and adulation online in his mind; he would be number one in the true crime podcast world. He and Jack could get rich and enjoy the inevitable Netflix deals and chat shows that would come next.

All that was shot to shit now.

The threat of Natasha dispelled, something worse was in its place: her dead body. No one was going to believe that her son and his boyfriend didn't just murder her for the hell of it.

'Where to?'

Jack's voice was light, filled with optimism. There was even a smile on his face, like they were simply deciding on a place for a walk and a picnic. Not going on the run. Aaron cleared his throat, playing for time.

'W-where have you always wanted to go?'

He couldn't fool him. Jack tilted his head, his eyes narrowing.

'Are you okay?'

Aaron fought the urge to laugh. He couldn't risk it. If Jack knew his true feelings, he might take Aaron straight back to his kill room.

'Of course. It's just . . . all a bit much, that's all.'

Jack sighed. 'I know. I'm sorry. But it's all over now, I promise.'

Leaning over the gear stick, Jack took Aaron's face in his hands. He pressed his lips against his. Aaron closed his eyes and let Jack kiss him, sorrow sweeping through him as they parted.

'Sorry, Jack,' Aaron said.

Confusion, then betrayal flashed across Jack's eyes, swiftly followed by pain. Gasping, he looked down at his own chest.

The knife Aaron had taken from Natasha's kitchen protruded from it.

With an anguished yell, Aaron pulled the blade free. Blood surged forth, spraying both of them and the windscreen. Jack screamed in pain and fear, but that didn't stop Aaron. He had to do it. He brought the knife down again.

Again.

And again.

As he did it, more images unravelled through his mind.

Natasha, dead at the bottom of the steps of her own basement, her brains leaking into the concrete.

That poor fucker on the phone footage, the flesh on his back scraped red and raw.

Jack kissing Aaron on the lips, resting his head against Aaron's shoulder.

Both of them arrested for multiple murders, Aaron claiming in vain he had nothing to do with it.

Aaron on a stage in a suit and tie, accepting an Oscar for best documentary.

Jack wasn't going to hurt him, Aaron knew that. But he also didn't want to be on the run forever, blamed for

Natasha's death and possibly for the men under the basement floor too. Better for others to believe he'd killed Jack because he'd made him his hostage.

Aaron had been building his podcast for years; something like this was bound to get him the fame and fortune he'd always craved. He could leave his humble roots behind and be the true crime guy who escaped not one, but two serial killers.

It was like being written a blank cheque. Aaron could not resist it.

But first one thing stood in his way: Jack.

The frenzy over, Aaron recovered his senses. The smell of gore in the air, adrenaline coursed through his veins. Nausea hit him as he saw what he'd reduced his lover to.

Regret surged through him next. Aaron grabbed Jack's hand as his eyes fluttered back in his head. He tried to say something, ask Aaron why, but blood bubbled up from his lips instead.

With a final wet hiss of air, Jack was gone. Sorrowful, Aaron placed his thumbs on the back of Jack's lids and closed his sightless eyes.

'I had no choice,' Aaron said.

THE END

THE JOFFE BOOKS STORY

We began in 2014 when Jasper agreed to publish his mum's much-rejected romance novel and it became a bestseller.

Since then we've grown into the largest independent publisher in the UK. We're extremely proud to publish some of the very best writers in the world, including Joy Ellis, Faith Martin, Caro Ramsay, Helen Forrester, Simon Brett and Robert Goddard. Everyone at Joffe Books loves reading and we never forget that it all begins with the magic of an author telling a story.

We are proud to publish talented first-time authors, as well as established writers whose books we love introducing to a new generation of readers.

We have been shortlisted for Independent Publisher of the Year at the British Book Awards three times, in 2020, 2021 and 2022, and for the Diversity and Inclusivity Award at the Independent Publishing Awards in 2022.

We built this company with your help, and we love to hear from you, so please email us about absolutely anything bookish at: feedback@joffebooks.com.

If you want to receive free books every Friday and hear about all our new releases, join our mailing list: www.joffebooks.com/contact.

And when you tell your friends about us, just remember: it's pronounced Joffe as in coffee or toffee!